POWER
PLAY

Books by Rachel Dylan

CAPITAL INTRIGUE

End Game

Backlash

Power Play

ATLANTA JUSTICE

Deadly Proof

Lone Witness

Breach of Trust

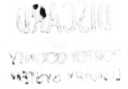

CAPITAL INTRIGUE · 3

POWER PLAY

RACHEL DYLAN

BETHANYHOUSE

a division of Baker Publishing Group
Minneapolis, Minnesota

© 2021 by Rachel Dylan

Published by Bethany House Publishers
11400 Hampshire Avenue South
Bloomington, Minnesota 55438
www.bethanyhouse.com

Bethany House Publishers is a division of
Baker Publishing Group, Grand Rapids, Michigan

Printed in the United States of America

Library of Congress Cataloging-in-Publication Data
Names: Dylan, Rachel, author.
Title: Power play / Rachel Dylan.
Description: Minneapolis, Minnesota : Bethany House, a division of Baker
    Publishing Group, [2021] | Series: Capital Intrigue ; 3
Identifiers: LCCN 2020053194 | ISBN 9780764234323 (trade paper) | ISBN
    9780764239236 (casebound) | ISBN 9781493431571 (ebook)
Classification: LCC PS3604.Y53 P69 2021 | DDC 813/.6--dc23
LC record available at https://lccn.loc.gov/2020053194

This is a work of fiction. Names, characters, incidents, and dialogues are products of the author's imagination and are not to be construed as real. Any resemblance to actual events or persons, living or dead, is entirely coincidental.

Cover design by Faceout Studio

Author is represented by the Nancy Yost Literary Agency.

21 22 23 24 25 26 27   7 6 5 4 3 2 1

To Mama.
Thank you for always being my biggest fan.
I'm so glad that I get to share these stories with you.
I love you so much.

CHAPTER ONE

It's going to be a long night. Vivian Steele checked her glossy pink lipstick one final time before exiting the ladies' room and entering into the shark tank—otherwise known as a diplomatic dinner in the Washington, DC, area. But this wasn't just any dinner. This was the premiere annual summer event hosted in a chic five-star hotel in northern Virginia, attended by a who's who of diplomats from around the world.

Vivian's boss had insisted she attend. She worked in the Office of the Legal Adviser at the State Department, and as a lawyer for State for six years, she'd seen and experienced a lot. But nothing made her palms sweat more than swanky DC power-player events. She felt completely out of her league as she glanced down at her knee-length black cocktail dress. Frills and bling were so not her. She'd gone for a more classic look and had no problem blending in with the crowd.

She let out a sigh of relief when she saw Layla Karam McCoy walking over to her. Her best friend hadn't stopped beaming since her wedding. Wearing a long, sparkling gown, Layla was the definition of elegance.

"What are you doing here? I didn't think they let spies into this event," Viv joked in a hushed tone.

Layla groaned. "I wish I weren't here, but I'm the Agency rep for the dinner. My boss bailed at the last minute and told me I had to suffer through this, especially since I have my State Department cover."

Viv moved in closer to her friend. "How many of these so-called diplomats here do you think are actually part of the intelligence community?"

Layla glanced around the room. "Probably ten percent. Maybe more."

Viv had quickly learned that intelligence agents often used diplomatic covers, and other countries worked similarly. Layla's cover was as a State Department analyst.

"Hey." Layla grabbed Viv's elbow. "Who is that hunk of muscle with the dark hair giving you the eye?"

"Who are you talking about?" Viv asked.

"Give it a second and then look at your two o'clock by the hors d'oeuvres table."

Viv waited a couple of beats, then glanced that direction. Layla hadn't been exaggerating. The guy in question stood well over six feet tall. He had dark wavy hair and was built. Very built. "I have no clue who that is."

Layla laughed. "Well, it seems to me that he wants to know who *you* are."

"It's just your imagination." Viv sighed. "Marriage has made you a complete softie and an active little cupid." Layla desperately wanted Viv to find someone, but the match-making had not been going well.

"I'm not going to stop trying." Layla smiled warmly.

Viv stole one more glance at the mystery man. "Well, as far as that guy goes, it seems like he's on high alert in general, not just about me. He has military written all over him."

Layla gave her hand a squeeze. "Yeah, but I *know* what I saw."

A chime sounded, indicating it was time to take their seats. Unfortunately, there was assigned seating, so Viv wasn't able to sit beside Layla.

"Let's connect after," Layla said. "Or if you need to see me during, just text, and I'll rescue you from your tablemates."

"Will do." Viv made her way to her table. Her friendship with Layla was one of the constants in her life that she was forever grateful for.

Viv did her duty and made small talk at her table, which included diplomatic representatives from a variety of countries—thankfully all of whom could speak English. Unlike Layla, Viv did not have a vast array of language skills—her only other language was Spanish, and she wasn't even fluent.

She was about to take another bite of her bland roasted chicken when a loud shriek sounded behind her. Instinctively, she jumped up out of her chair as chaos built around her, and her pulse picked up to a quick beat.

As screams continued to bellow throughout the room, she ran over to the table where the commotion was occurring and saw the Egyptian ambassador to the United States lying motionless on the floor. Her stomach dropped. She knew this ambassador—Ali Zidan was a strong US ally and friend.

A man was hovering over Ambassador Zidan, about to administer CPR, when Zidan's security entourage appeared and swarmed over him. Viv was no medical expert—she only had basic CPR training—but it looked to her that no amount of CPR was going to change the situation.

The Egyptian ambassador was dead.

An arm pulled her backward, and she tried to break free from the strong grip. She whipped around. "Let me go."

"You should back up, ma'am."

She looked up into the big brown eyes of the mystery man from before. "And you are?"

"Jacob Cruz, supervisory special agent of diplomatic security."

Ah. "Did you see what happened?"

He moved a step closer to her. "Wait a minute. It's my turn to ask who you are."

There was no reason to stonewall him. "I'm Vivian Steele. I'm an attorney with State."

He frowned. It must have been the word *attorney* that turned his expression sour. She'd seen it before. "Please step back, ma'am."

Viv noticed he hadn't answered her question about what he'd seen, but given the upheaval in the room, she let it go and did as she was told. She looked around and spotted Layla with her cell to her ear, no doubt phoning in to the CIA what had just happened.

The microphone screeched, and then the evening's emcee began speaking. "Everyone, if you could, please return to your seats in an orderly fashion. We have a medical emergency, and we need to be able to render assistance. If everyone would please return to their seats quickly and calmly. I repeat, please return to your seats so a medical emergency can be handled." The announcement was then repeated in a couple of other languages and appeared to calm some nerves, as most people were obeying the direction.

Viv watched the ambassador's body being taken out on a stretcher. She didn't specifically support the Bureau of Near

Eastern Affairs, but her legal work touched every region, so she knew Zidan's death was going to have a major ripple effect. He stood strongly against the anti-democratic forces in Egypt. His death would be a huge loss.

She checked her phone to make sure no one had texted or called. Her tablemates were abuzz about the ambassador, spouting theories. Some said he must have had a heart attack, while others noted that he was an avid chain smoker. Viv kept quiet. She didn't really have anything to add, and the last thing she wanted to do was speculate. A man had just died, but it wasn't long before those around her started drinking and eating again. *What a crazy world we live in.*

By the time dessert was served, Viv had a raging headache, but she knew she couldn't excuse herself just yet. She took a bite of the strawberry cheesecake and a sip of coffee and tried to figure out what her next move should be and how she could extricate herself from the after-dinner mingling. People had already started to abandon their desserts in favor of cocktails and were milling around, probably anxious to get away from their assigned tablemates after the past two hours.

She noticed Penelope King, the US ambassador to Belgium, standing close by, talking to the ambassador from Turkey. Penelope waved, and Viv started to walk in that direction. As she approached, she noticed that the color had drained out of Penelope's face.

"Ambassador King, are you feeling okay?"

"Viv . . ." Penelope took a step toward her and grabbed Viv's arms as she collapsed to the ground, almost pulling Viv down with her.

Viv squatted at the ambassador's side as Penelope started convulsing. "Help! Help!" she screamed as loudly as she could. A deep feeling of dread washed over her. What if the food was poisoned? What if they were all going to die?

"What's wrong with her?" the Turkish ambassador asked. "She was completely fine a minute ago."

"I don't know." Viv's voice shook as she tried to make sure Penelope still had a pulse.

The Turkish ambassador took a step back, and the next few minutes were a whirlwind as EMT personnel rushed in. Since Viv was right there, they asked what she had seen, and she recounted it to them before moving out of the way to let them work. She knew Penelope. Not extremely well, but seeing her lying there on the ground, pale and shaking, was shocking. Her body was clearly being ravaged by something. This was no heart attack. The ambassador was in her forties, an avid runner, and in great shape.

"You again."

Viv turned to see Jacob Cruz scowling at her.

"It's just like a lawyer to go chasing trouble."

She'd heard enough lawyer jokes and put-downs for a lifetime, and she didn't have it in her to hold back right now. "SSA Cruz, if I were you, I'd be a lot more worried about whether you have an entire room of diplomats at risk than about me being a lawyer. Aren't you in charge of security here?"

He raised an eyebrow. "Yes, and we'll be doing a full investigation. Including the fact that you were one of the last people near the ambassador before she fell ill."

"You can't think that I had anything to do with this!" She was so angry her voice cracked.

Jacob crossed his arms and glared at her.

She put her hands on her hips, feeling like she might explode. "I suggest you *stop* harassing me and *start* doing your job."

She feared what else she might say, so she walked away, not giving him time to respond. She needed to find Layla ASAP. Yes, the Egyptian ambassador probably had a heart attack, but now with Penelope's collapse, Viv had a lot of questions. This was something far more sinister. And she wasn't sure whether the terror was over or just beginning.

CHAPTER
TWO

Jacob had been up all night after the diplomatic dinner on Saturday, so he'd taken a catnap before this meeting, like those he'd learned to take as a SEAL during his ten-year military career.

He'd been the lead agent on security for the event and had obviously failed. His boss had reamed him out good, and he deserved every word of it. But how could he have protected against an attack like this? Assuming there was an attack. He'd played through the sequence of events over and over in his head. They'd run countless scenarios on security for the event, gaming out all types of threats, but nothing like what had happened. This one had truly come out of left field.

Jacob still thought there was a good chance the Egyptian ambassador actually did have a heart attack and that the only real target had been Penelope King, but they were going to have to do a lot more work to come to that conclusion officially.

That was why he'd been called in on Sunday afternoon for a meeting at the State Department. He wasn't sure who would be there. All he knew was that he had to be. No questions asked.

He hadn't been in the job but six months, and this wasn't exactly going to be a great résumé builder for him. He shouldn't even be in this job. He should still be out in the field, running ops with his SEAL team.

But that wasn't possible.

Jacob walked into a secure room at State known as the SCIF and was met by a sea of faces.

"Good, Jacob, you're here." His boss, Assistant Secretary for Diplomatic Security Sherman Oaks, nodded at him.

Jacob had thought he was close to being on time, but obviously being one minute late was really late for this crew. And this crew included some big players, including the newly minted director of the FBI, Lang Phillips. Phillips was known as a no-nonsense, tough-as-nails guy who'd risen through the ranks.

As Jacob surveyed the room, he recognized another face— this one belonging to the persistent but attractive lawyer from last night. Her hazel eyes narrowed when she saw him looking at her. She clearly hadn't forgotten him either.

"Thank y'all for coming." Lang Phillips stood up. He had a full head of silver hair and a deep southern drawl, as he hailed from Tennessee. "So everyone is on the same page here, I wanted to update you on the latest. Ambassador Ali Zidan was pronounced dead when he arrived at the hospital last night. We are operating under the assumption that Zidan suffered a heart attack, but we can't be sure, given the attack on our own ambassador."

Sherman Oaks cleared his throat. "And unfortunately,

just before I came in, I had a discussion with our Egyptian friends. They are refusing an autopsy of Zidan on religious grounds. It's not something we can push, given the religious implications. We may be in the dark as far as the exact COD for Ambassador Zidan."

Lang nodded. "Before we go any further, it makes sense to let everyone know that we have formed a special joint task force to investigate exactly what happened last night at the diplomatic dinner. Under my direction, we're bringing together resources from the FBI, State, and the intelligence community to deal with this crisis. Look around. You're in this room because you are the task force. We'll liaise with the CIA as appropriate. We should do introductions because not everyone knows one another."

Sherman cleared his throat. "For those who don't know me, I'm Sherman Oaks, assistant secretary for diplomatic security. Others from State should go ahead and introduce themselves."

Jacob waited to see who would speak up first.

A petite dark-haired woman began. "I'm Rania Assad from the Bureau of Near Eastern Affairs. I work the Egypt desk, so that's why I'm here."

The lawyer Jacob had met last night looked around before starting. He guessed she was about five foot six, and today her light brown hair, which she had worn down at the dinner, was pulled up in a severe lawyer-type bun. "I'm Vivian Steele. I'm a State attorney. I support the Office of the Legal Adviser."

Lang jumped in. "I know some of you may wonder why we have a lawyer on the task force, but Vivian's role will be critical. We've got a lot of balls in the air here, and we want to make sure we're covered from a legal perspective. Also,

Vivian happens to have been at the dinner and was first on the scene to help Ambassador King, so we think having her on the team will be invaluable."

The jury was still out on whether Vivian Steele would be friend or foe. Jacob's natural inclination was not to trust anyone, and Vivian had somehow found herself deeply intertwined in this mess.

A tall, dark-haired man with glasses took the floor. "I'm Cody Rico. I'm the rep for the Office of European Affairs."

Silence hung for a moment, and Jacob realized he was the last person affiliated with the State Department. "I'm SSA Jacob Cruz with the Diplomatic Security Service."

"Those are our State reps," Lang said. "Let's move on to the FBI."

A woman with long, curly red hair and bright green eyes spoke up. "I'm SSA Delaney O'Sullivan."

"And I'm Delaney's partner, Special Agent Weston Lee," the younger, blond-haired man said.

Jacob sized up the twentysomething agent. He wondered how they were all going to work together.

"All right," Lang said. "Listen up. Staying put in the building, running ops from State, will be Rania and Cody. Everyone should be filtering relevant info and intel back to them, and they will start our war room. For field teams, SSA O'Sullivan will be working with Agent Lee. Vivian, you'll work with SSA Cruz."

Jacob couldn't help but feel like he was getting the baby-sitting assignment here as punishment because he had been in charge of security for the dinner. He wanted to be where the action was, and he had a good idea that Vivian was more of a desk jockey—as she should be. Lawyers weren't trained to be field agents.

Lang leaned forward. "We need multiple sets of eyes on all of this, and we can't afford to make any more mistakes. We've got the Egyptians breathing down our necks to make sure we can give their government confidence there was no foul play. And we have one of our own fighting for her life in the hospital. Until this case is closed, this is your only and top priority. Understood?"

A murmur of affirmations spread throughout the room.

Lang stood. "All right. Break into your teams and get to work."

The group dispersed, but Jacob didn't immediately move, instead waiting for Vivian to come to him. He had no clue how he was going to handle this.

"Well, looks like you're stuck with me." Vivian sat down beside him.

"It does, doesn't it, Vivian."

"Please just call me Viv."

"I can do that." *Viv* seemed to suit her more anyway.

She turned to face him. "We need to set some ground rules."

Her take-charge attitude was amusing.

Her eyes widened. "Why are you smiling? Do you not realize how serious this situation is? The Egyptian ambassador is dead, and our ambassador is lying in the hospital and could die at any moment."

He didn't want her to get the wrong idea. "I wasn't smiling at the underlying situation. It's just funny that you think you can give me orders."

She shook her head. "We're a team. And we're not in the same chain of command, which means neither of us should be trying to pull rank." She paused. "Speaking of rank, you were military, weren't you?"

"Yes, ma'am."

Viv bit her bottom lip. "Special ops?"

Now he was really amused. "Yes, ma'am."

"Ranger? SEAL?"

"SEAL, ma'am."

"Can you speak more than two words?"

"Maybe." He could tell that he'd already found his way under her skin, and that was how he wanted it. He had to keep her off-kilter. Maybe she'd come to her senses and realize that fieldwork wasn't for her, and he could get a legit partner.

She crossed her arms. "What's your problem with me? I've met a lot of people who didn't like lawyers—even hated them—but you've got something extra special going on here, and we need to air it out if we're going to be productive. You don't even know me. Not even a little. What's the deal?"

He let out a breath. "I don't have anything against you personally. I'm just not used to teaming up with lawyers. That's not how I roll."

She laughed. "Well, it is now."

"To be honest, whenever lawyers got involved in operations, things never went well. That's just my experience."

She reached out and touched his shoulder, causing him to flinch. "I will give this my all. I know it's unorthodox, but this investigation is really important. I can't help that I was right there in the middle of all the action. I'll work as hard as I can to get to the bottom of this."

He moved away from her. "And I'll give it my all, too, but I can't have you slowing me down. You got that?" He expected her to bite back, but she didn't.

"Yes, sir."

He held back another laugh.

"Let's get down to business. We need to assume that Ambassador Zidan's death wasn't caused by a heart attack and that whatever killed him is also what hurt Penelope."

He raised an eyebrow. "Don't you mean Ambassador King?"

She tucked a stray hair that had fallen out of the bun behind her ear. "Yes, sorry. I knew her. I mean, I know her."

This was the first time he had seen her frazzled. "She might pull through."

Viv hung her head. "Yeah, it's possible, but I'm not getting my hopes up."

"How well do you know the ambassador?"

"We aren't super close, but I worked with her on a project a few years ago, and we became friendly. She's a mover and a shaker."

"What's your theory on what happened?" he asked.

"I think they were poisoned. And as long as Ambassador King is alive, her life is still in danger. I assume you've put extra security at the hospital."

"Of course. She's locked down tight." That was the first thing he'd done last night when she was en route to the hospital.

"Good. Because I fear this is far from over, and someone might come back to finish the job."

CHAPTER THREE

On Monday morning, Viv waited for Jacob at a coffee shop in Foggy Bottom so they could figure out their strategy. They'd talked yesterday, but it was more of a what-went-wrong analysis and how to move forward with security as opposed to the nuts and bolts of the investigation.

SSA Jacob Cruz was a lot more complicated than she had first imagined. Initially, she'd believed he was just annoyed by lawyers—a shoot-from-the-hip type who didn't like rules and felt like attorneys impeded his ability to get the job done. But she had a nagging feeling there was more to Jacob's story. She was always looking to help others. It was one of the reasons she'd become a lawyer, but she'd learned the hard way that not everyone wanted the help. And she feared Jacob could fall into that category.

Regardless, she would be relentless in her pursuit to aid in the investigation and to prove to Jacob that she was up for the job, because she loved nothing more than a good challenge.

"Hey." Jacob set a cup in front of her. "Sorry I'm late, but you looked empty-handed. It's just regular coffee—the old-fashioned way, with cream and sugar."

She smiled. "Thanks for the coffee, it's perfeçt. But being late seems to be a theme with you."

He lifted a hand. "Hey, I was only one minute late yesterday."

She took a sip of coffee before responding. "For that type of meeting with the bigwigs, you know you need to be early."

"Honestly, I didn't know Director Phillips was going to be there."

She found that hard to believe. "Your boss didn't tell you?"

He shrugged. "Nope. I barely talk to my boss. He's a hands-off kind of guy. In fact, he's not even going to be day-to-day on the task force. Director Phillips is the one running the show. That's why Oaks let Director Phillips take the lead yesterday. Between you and me, Oaks is pretty political, so he'd rather take a back seat in case this thing goes sideways."

"It's up to us to prevent that."

Jacob picked up his cup. "I've heard Phillips is fiercely loyal but will also hate you forever if you cross him."

That didn't sound good. "Then let's not cross him." She took a sip of coffee. "What's going to be our strategy?" She wanted to get his input before she told him what she wanted to do.

"The team has created a secure electronic workspace so we can share our efforts and make sure we aren't duplicating anything." He pulled his tablet out of his bag and placed it on the table.

Viv scanned the initial actions of the other team members. "We should visit the Egyptian embassy."

"You think the two of us are best suited for that? What about Rania? Isn't she the expert on Egypt?"

"You're right that Rania seems like the natural fit, but I'm the one who actually got invited."

He raised an eyebrow. "How?"

"I have a contact there."

"Do you speak Arabic?" he asked.

She laughed. "No. Do you?"

"Actually, I do know some from all of my deployments."

Another surprise from this man. "Good. Then this will work very well. I know the players, and you know the language. Although most of these guys speak pretty flawless English, so Arabic won't even be necessary."

He propped his elbows on the table. "And exactly how do you know the players?"

"I've worked with several of them over the past few years on various assignments. We're close to the Egyptians, and with everything going on in the region, our relationship with them is vital to US interests."

He leaned back. "Now you sound like some policy wonk instead of a lawyer."

She should set something straight. It might even make their working relationship better. "Remember, I'm not a trial attorney. I'm not in a courtroom arguing cases before a judge. I work to support the mission of the State Department. Policy is a good chunk of what I do. I have to be knowledgeable about the policies so I can advise on the law and the risks involved. My job is much different from your average attorney, and it's one of the things I love about it. My strengths don't lie in being in a courtroom. I'm better behind the scenes."

Jacob rubbed his chin. "Yeah, I guess I wasn't thinking about it like that."

"I should call the embassy and let them know we are accepting their invitation. They won't like us showing up unannounced, even if they extended the olive branch."

He shook his head. "It's better to just go. That way we'll get more from them."

That wasn't going to happen. "No way. I know these guys. If we just show up, they might not even let us in. The invitation wasn't open-ended. There's diplomatic protocol here."

Jacob rolled his eyes. "Protocol? Their ambassador is dead. Ours very well might be any minute. I'd say we should all be less concerned about diplomatic niceties."

This guy had a lot to learn about how things worked in her world. "How long have you been working in diplomatic security?"

He looked away. "Six months."

She laughed. "You clearly should've stayed in the field as a SEAL."

His dark eyes locked on to hers. "Believe me, there's no place I'd rather be, but that's not an option."

She wanted to ask him why, but now wasn't the time to pry, and she felt bad for making that statement, given his reaction. He was in this job by necessity, not by choice. "Let me make that call."

"Good."

And just like that, Jacob shut down again. How was she going to work with this guy?

❖

They hopped on the Metro, got off at Van Ness, and made the short walk to the Egyptian embassy. Jacob didn't want to admit it, but Viv seemed like a pro at the diplomacy stuff. He didn't understand how anyone could have the patience to deal with all the hoops. She'd been on the phone a good forty-five minutes talking to this person or that person before they'd gotten the approval to visit today. And she'd waited until everything had almost been agreed upon before mentioning that she'd be bringing him along. It was a smart move. He had to admit that her diplomatic savviness might come in handy. His approach was more straight to the point, which was one of the million reasons he could never work on the actual diplomatic side of things. Security was the best fit for him. Muscle and tactics were his strengths. And he lacked patience, which he was quickly learning was going to be a problem.

They checked in at the guard station and waited to be approved. Even though the Egyptian embassy was on US soil, they still had to get the express permission of the Egyptians to enter the embassy. And that was where Viv came in.

"Stop frowning," she whispered.

"I'm really not. This is just the way I look."

"C'mon. Make an effort here, okay?"

He tried his best to keep a neutral expression and promised Viv he would follow her lead.

They were greeted by a short, stocky man with a receding hairline. "Ms. Vivian, please come into the conference room where we can talk." He eyed Jacob with skepticism.

"Samir, thank you. This is Supervisory Special Agent Cruz with DSS."

Samir nodded at Jacob but didn't say anything else as he led them into the conference room.

"Ms. Vivian, we are all in great mourning over the untimely passing of our ambassador."

"We are truly sorry, Samir. You have the sincere condolences of everyone at the State Department. Ambassador Zidan was a friend and a great man."

Viv was laying it on thick, but Jacob assumed that was part of her larger strategy, and he was just along for the ride.

"You understand that we want to get to the bottom of this just as much as you do," Viv said.

25

Samir nodded. "I have some information to share with you. We've spoken to Ambassador Zidan's physician. He did have a preexisting heart condition."

"So you're operating under the assumption that he died of a heart attack?" Viv asked.

Samir looked down. "That is going to be the official position of the Egyptian government."

"But?" Viv raised an eyebrow.

Samir frowned. "Unofficially, we would like to confirm that is what happened. Given the situation with Ambassador King, there are some in my government who are nervous. Quite worried that this might be something larger. A coordinated attack of some kind."

"Rightfully so," Jacob said.

"Do you believe you know something, Agent Cruz?" Samir asked.

Of course Jacob didn't *know* anything, but he had a gut feeling they were only at the tip of the iceberg. Unfortunately, his gut wasn't going to get them very far. "Not yet, sir, but we intend to investigate and find out."

"How is your ambassador doing?" Samir asked.

Viv answered, taking back control of the conversation. "Unfortunately, she's still in critical condition. It's touch-and-go. They're still doing a lot of testing."

Samir shook his head. "I'm sorry to hear that." He took a breath. "I know I said that my government wants answers, but we also need to be discreet, and they have asked that I pass that message on to you. The situation in my country is a bit tenuous at the moment, and we don't want to spark panic."

Or more political turmoil, Jacob thought.

A stern glance from Viv let him know that she wanted

him to keep his mouth shut. And he did just that, but he didn't trust Samir. In fact, he wasn't certain he trusted anyone right now. Not even Vivian Steele. He wasn't sure what her deal was. Yeah, they had to work together, so he had to soldier through it, but that didn't mean he was going to trust her. Trusting the wrong person had a way of getting you killed.

Viv took a step closer to Samir. "I assure you that this is not only a top priority for the US government, but also that we completely understand the need to treat this situation delicately for all parties involved."

Samir gave Viv a warm smile. "Thank you, Ms. Vivian. I knew we could count on you."

Jacob wondered what the backstory was between these two. It didn't seem romantic, but there was something there. Some sort of shared history that he wasn't in the loop on, and that only made him more suspicious.

Viv glanced at him before turning her attention back to Samir. "And as for what you can do to help us, if you know of anyone who would have wanted to harm Ambassador Zidan, now would be the time to provide those names."

"I predicted as much." Samir pulled a thumb drive out of his suit jacket pocket. "Here is everything I could come up with. Make sure you treat this as highly sensitive. The political climate in my country is delicate. The president has many enemies who act like friends. The anti-democratic forces are growing in power by the day."

"I understand," Viv said.

"Thank you for coming. It's probably for the best that we keep this meeting short."

"You're worried about people in the embassy?" Jacob asked.

Samir's eyes narrowed. "I'm worried about everything."

"We'll get right on this," Viv assured him. "Thanks again for the help. It was nice to see you again."

They said their good-byes and were escorted out of the embassy.

Once they were completely outside, Jacob spoke up. "What's the real deal with you and Samir?"

Viv arched an eyebrow. "What do you mean?"

"There's clearly a history between you two."

"I told you that we've worked together in the past."

"Is that it?"

"I don't appreciate what you're insinuating."

He was trying to push her buttons to see if he could get anything out of her, but she just looked at him like he had five heads. "I'm not saying the two of you were a thing, but I am saying that there was a tight connection there. Do you trust him?"

She didn't answer immediately. "I trust very few people."

"Now that's something we can agree on."

❖

Viv was known for having a lot of patience, but Jacob Cruz was testing even her at the moment. They'd spent the past two hours in her office at the State Department, going through the documents Samir had provided.

"We're going to need to figure out where these guys are and get some help putting recon on them," Jacob said.

"That seems reasonable to me. And you're right, they're all men." She wasn't surprised. "We'll need to determine if they're here or if some are back in Egypt or elsewhere. If so, we'll need the Agency's help for sure, because we can't assume the person behind this was physically at the dinner. He could've hired someone."

"It's a shame they won't allow an autopsy on Zidan," Jacob said.

"Yes, but we have to respect their religious beliefs. It just means we'll have to work harder to determine if this was really a heart attack or not."

"What do you think?"

She laughed. "You actually care what I think?"

He sighed. "Okay. I deserve that. I know I came in a bit hot when we first met, but I understand the importance of your work on the task force. So yes, I'm asking your opinion."

She smiled. "If I didn't know better, I'd say that sounded like an apology. So I'll take it. And as far as what I think, I find it coincidental." Her cell rang. "I should get this." She put it on speaker. "This is Vivian."

"Hi, it's Delaney. I just got word from the hospital that initial tests on Ambassador King are showing a street version of fentanyl in her system. That drug is about a hundred times stronger than morphine. This wasn't accidental. Someone wanted her dead."

"Are we sure someone gave it to her and that she didn't take the drug herself?"

"Given the concentration and timing, the doctors don't think this was a purposeful ingestion. Plus, her general excellent medical condition is not one of a woman who uses opioids. The doctors feel pretty strongly about that. All of this means someone was definitely trying to kill Ambassador King—and was bold enough to do it on US soil at a diplomatic dinner."

Viv looked at Jacob, who was drumming his fingers on the desk. "Thanks for the update. Are you sure everything is good with her security at the hospital?"

"Yes. We've got multiple agents stationed there, but she's not doing great. The amount of fentanyl in her system mixed with the alcohol is proving to be a near-fatal combination—if not ultimately fatal. They're doing what they can, but she's hanging by a thread, and I fear the damage might have already been done," Delaney said softly.

"Understood." Viv's heart broke hearing those words. She feared that Penelope wasn't going to pull through this, but she didn't want to get emotional in front of Jacob. He already questioned her toughness. "Talk to you later."

The call ended, and she turned her attention to Jacob.

"If she dies," he said, "then this goes up another level."

"One step at a time." She turned to her computer. "I'm going to get these names Samir provided to Rania and have her work her contacts at the CIA to determine the lowdown on these men." She looked at her watch.

"We should call it a day. I'm sure you haven't gotten a good night's sleep yet. We need to get some rest, or we won't be useful to anyone."

She agreed with him. "You're right. Want to regroup here in the morning?"

He nodded. "Sounds good. Do you need anything else from me?"

"Nope. See you tomorrow." What she needed was a break from dealing with his brown eyes staring at her. She felt like he was evaluating her every move, and it was putting her on edge.

He left her office, and she took a deep, steadying breath. Everything about him seemed intense—he had a way of sucking the energy from the room. There was something else too. A fact that she was trying to ignore: she was actually attracted to him. They had a job to do, and the last thing she wanted was to develop a work crush on a former SEAL who had trouble written all over him.

She sighed as she packed up her bag. The problem with a

nonexistent dating life was that when a man like Jacob came around, it had a way of causing problems. She didn't have to worry, though, because while he was acting better than when they'd first met, he still couldn't hide the fact that he wasn't crazy about her.

Maybe she should stop having these concerns and think about what her real problems were. Like the fact that she had no food at her place. She guessed it would be Thai or pizza tonight—or both because, all of a sudden, she was completely ravenous.

Viv walked out of the State Department and took her usual path to the Foggy Bottom Metro stop to pick up the Blue Line train. Since it was after rush hour, she'd have to wait for the train to arrive. Thankfully, the timing worked in her favor, and it was only a few minutes before she hopped on a sparsely populated train.

Taking one of many empty seats, she thought about how much had transpired since Saturday night. What had started as an annoying dinner had turned into something so much more. She remembered Penelope calling her name and reaching for her. That series of events was emblazoned in her memory. She feared the worst, but that didn't keep her from praying for Penelope's healing.

She exited the Rosslyn station to make the quick walk to her condo. It was one of the things her parents had left to her. Free and clear, completely paid off, which was good, because she couldn't have afforded it with her government salary. She was certain when her parents had made their will that they hadn't predicted Viv would be in the condo for many years, if ever. They'd told her she could use it as a rental investment property if she wanted. But one car crash in Europe had brought her and her twin sister's world to a startling halt their second year of college. And now here she was, living in the luxury condo. She would have traded it in a heartbeat to have her parents back in her life, if only for a single day. While she'd dealt with the grief, there were moments, like tonight, where she thought about them and missed them so much it hurt.

Her phone buzzed, and she looked down and saw she had a text message from a number she didn't recognize.

> Hello, Vivian. It's Samir. Thanks for coming today, but I need to talk to you alone. Can you meet me at Café Latte on Embassy Row tonight? There are some things I couldn't tell you in front of your friend. I only trust you right now.

Her breath caught as she read Samir's message. This could be the break they needed, and she understood his hesitation. He'd never met Jacob, and even though she could tell the former SEAL had tried, he gave off a vibe that wasn't inviting.

She texted back quickly.

> I can be there in about half an hour.

She didn't wait for his response but turned around and started walking back to the Metro.

> Great. See you soon. And *shukran*.

She knew that meant *thank you* in Arabic. Her adrenaline started pumping, and all thoughts about her dinner evaporated. Samir knew something. Something he couldn't tell her in front of Jacob, and she had to know what that was.

She tapped her foot impatiently as she waited to get back on the Metro. Finally, after what seemed like forever, she was getting off the train and walking toward Café Latte.

She was about two blocks away from the coffee shop when two men jumped out in front of her, catching her off guard. She tried to sidestep them, but they blocked her way. Her pulse ratcheted up as she realized they weren't just messing around. Then the taller man grabbed her, and she gasped.

Fear shot through her body as she shrieked. The shorter man punched her hard in the face, making her reel. She tasted blood and was stunned by the pain radiating through her cheek. His punch would have knocked her down if the other man wasn't holding her up. His hands squeezed her upper arms.

She started thrashing as much as she could, but it didn't make much of an impact. This was an unfair fight in every sense. Why were these two men attacking her?

A punch to her stomach almost made her vomit from the impact. She screamed as loud as she could, but nothing she did stopped the onslaught. She'd never felt pain like this before. A hard slap across the face knocked her back into the man holding her. He threw her to the ground, and she was barely able to break her fall to prevent her head from crashing into the sidewalk. The man hovered over her, and she feared he was going to hit her again, but instead he ripped her bag off her shoulder. She wasn't going to fight for her stuff—no, she feared she was fighting for her life.

She closed her eyes for a second, crying out to God and readying herself for the next punch.

"Hey, what are you doing?" A loud male voice rang out from behind her.

The two attackers started running away. Viv struggled to get air as pain shot through her body.

"Are you okay?" the new voice asked.

Her entire body shook as the man who had called out

crouched beside her. She looked into his light brown eyes. She couldn't speak.

"I think you're in shock. Do you want me to call someone? The police?" he asked.

She couldn't think. Couldn't stop shaking. The pain was too bad, and she feared she might pass out.

When she didn't answer, he pulled out his phone. She could hear him talking to 911.

"They'll be here in a minute. I'll wait with you to make sure those men don't come back."

"Thank you." Her voice wobbled.

"Of course. I'm Mark."

"I'm Viv," she said. "You saved my life." She choked back tears.

He placed his hand on her shoulder. "You're safe now. The police will be here soon."

"How can I ever thank you?"

"I'm just glad I was here. These streets are usually pretty safe, but you never know what kind of dirtbags are out there."

"They took all my stuff. I don't even have my phone."

"Do you need me to call anyone? Or do you want to use my phone?"

"Yes, please."

She would call Layla. But first she needed to know who her Good Samaritan was. "Do you have a business card?"

He lifted his eyebrow. "I do." He pulled out his wallet and handed her a card. "But I promise there's no need to do anything to thank me."

She didn't agree with that. This man had single-handedly stopped what could have been her brutal murder.

CHAPTER
FOUR

On Tuesday morning, SSA Delaney O'Sullivan looked into her rookie partner's light blue eyes and knew exactly what he was thinking. "Weston, I know you're unhappy about being on this task force, but I can't understand why."

Weston straightened his shoulders. "You already have a great career, but I'm just starting out."

She laughed. "Are you calling me old?"

He shook his head. "No, but your reputation is well-known. You're a top agent. I, on the other hand, am still on shaky ground from that slipup four months ago, and if I mess this up, too, it could be a career killer. It's like the FBI is testing me."

The slipup he was referring to had almost gotten someone killed, but thankfully Delaney had been there to save the day. The young agent had been a rock star at Quantico, but when he'd been assigned to her as a rookie, she'd learned on day one that she had her hands completely full. "Every day we're tested. It's how we handle the challenge that matters."

"Thanks for the pep talk." He grinned. "Where is everyone else?"

"They should be here soon, and you need to get your act together. We can't have your doubt creeping in. I need you on your game. The stakes are too high here. Got it?"

Weston nodded. "I'm in."

She'd discovered the best way to deal with Weston was the direct approach. No babying. He might only be twenty-five, but the weight of the world was now on his shoulders.

After a few minutes, Rania and Cody walked into the war room, carrying some files. "Good morning, everyone." Cody's dark eyes met Delaney's, and he smiled.

Rania handed her and Weston a few folders. "Here's what Vivian and Jacob were able to get from the embassy."

Jacob walked into the room. "Did I hear my name?"

Delaney wasn't sure what to make of Jacob. It was under his watch that this entire mess had gone down, but her experience told her that sometimes security could only do so much if people were intent on inflicting terror. She'd just graduated college when 9/11 happened, and it had changed her entire life. Instead of taking the job in corporate America she had lined up, she applied to work for the FBI. She wanted to make a difference. Two decades later, she'd seen more pain and evil than she cared to admit, but she knew she was living out her life's purpose by being an agent.

"I was just passing out what we've been able to dig up on the names you and Vivian provided," Rania said.

Jacob looked around. "Speaking of Viv, has anyone seen her this morning?"

"No," Delaney said.

Jacob looked at his watch. "That's odd. She's been busting my chops about being late."

"We should get started reviewing the files while we wait on her," Rania said.

They all sat quietly, reading up on the men Samir had told them to investigate.

"Najib Suliman seems like a bad guy," Jacob said.

Rania turned to his bio. "Agreed. He's a troublemaker back in Egypt. He has some powerful family connections, so he's been given a bit of latitude, but the CIA called me early this morning and told me there is new intel linking him to a terrorist offshoot group."

"So he'd be motivated to take down a moderate like Zidan," Delaney said.

"Absolutely," Rania agreed. "The only problem is that our other intel has been that Zidan and Suliman go way back. They studied together for years and supposedly have a strong affection for each other."

Jacob scoffed. "Wouldn't be the first time a terrorist turned on his friend. I think we have to drill deeper."

"I hear you," Rania said. "But my sources on the ground think we would be barking up the wrong tree if we target Suliman."

Delaney tended to trust the local intel, but there were greater issues at play here. "I would usually agree with you, but given the implications, we have to run it down as a possibility."

The door opened, and Director Phillips walked through it. Delaney hadn't expected to see him again so soon.

"We've got a problem," Lang said.

The last thing they needed was more problems.

Lang crossed his arms. "Vivian is in the hospital."

Jacob stood. "What happened to her?"

"I'm still trying to get the full download, but she was going to meet her contact from the Egyptian embassy last night, and on her way there, she was violently attacked."

"Why was she meeting him alone?" Jacob asked. "I didn't know anything about this."

Lang moved toward Jacob. "We're going to figure that out. Jacob, you head down to the hospital in Arlington. Report back, and we'll figure out if this could be part of the bigger picture."

"Yes, sir." Jacob quickly walked out of the room.

"Everyone else, get back to work. Delaney, can I have a word with you outside?"

"Yes, sir."

Weston gave her a troubled look as she walked outside the room with Lang.

"Delaney, I'm not sure where all of this is headed, and I need your best here. Do you understand that?"

"Absolutely, sir. I know the stakes are high."

"They just got a lot higher. We now have the White House calling and asking for updates. If you need access to more agents or resources, just say the word."

"Roger that, sir."

"And I want to be updated no matter how small the development. I'm risking my hide here, too, especially since I'm new to this position. You were highly recommended to me by people I trust, so I'm counting on you. Don't mess this up."

Before she could give any further affirmation, he turned and walked away.

Great, no pressure. It was clear Director Phillips would have her badge if she didn't produce results.

Jacob was not doing a good job of keeping his temper in check as he got out of the hospital elevator and headed toward Viv's room. She had a lot to answer for—including why she had ditched him. They were supposed to be working this case together. He wondered if she had planned it all out, because she definitely hadn't said a word when they'd parted ways last night. How was he supposed to work with her if she kept things from him and skulked around on her own? Did she realize how dangerous that was for someone who was untrained? Obviously not.

When he reached her room, the door was open, so he walked in, ready to chew her out. But when he saw her lying in the bed, he felt like he'd been gut-punched. Her eyes were closed, but they opened as he moved inside. Her face was covered in large purple bruises, and he could also see bruising up and down her arms.

"Jacob," she whispered.

That one little whisper, along with seeing her in such a bad state, was enough to wipe away his immediate anger. No, he was still angry. In fact, that anger had turned into a raging boil, but now it was directed at the guy who did this to her.

"What happened?" He slid a chair up beside her bed and sat down.

"I thought I might die," she croaked.

Real, rabid fear was coming off her in waves, and it almost undid him. She looked so small and beaten down, and she had lost the feisty spark she'd had when they first met. Her light brown hair was tangled, and he could see some caked blood near her temples. He couldn't help himself and reached out to lightly place his hand on hers.

He would have to try to walk her through this, because he needed to know everything. "Start at the beginning."

"Samir texted me last night when I was almost home and asked me to meet him at a coffee shop on Embassy Row."

"Did he say why?"

"He said he had something to tell me that he couldn't tell me at the embassy."

"Because of me?"

"Yes, but I also think he wanted to get outside the embassy to talk more freely."

After he made sure Viv was okay, Jacob's first stop would be the Egyptian embassy to deal with Samir. "Did you hear from him after that?"

She winced. "No. But they took my phone."

"They?"

"I was attacked by two men."

He muttered a few things Viv probably didn't want or need to hear, but he couldn't believe this. "Where?"

"A couple of blocks from the coffee shop. They jumped in front of me. Blocked my path. And then . . ."

There it was again. The fear. "Are you in a lot of pain?"

"Would you believe me if I said no?"

"No." He squeezed her hand. "I'm going to find out who did this to you."

Her eyes filled with tears. "If it wasn't for some guy walking by and stopping them, I don't know what would've happened."

"They stole your bag?"

"Yes, but my wallet was in my jacket, and I guess they didn't know or didn't care. I'm not sure what their exact motivation was. They seemed so vile. Like they wanted to hurt me. Really hurt me."

That didn't add up. Random thieves didn't normally seek to exact such pain on their victims, which made him wonder if this could be a setup by Samir. But Viv was too bad off right now for him to accuse her friend like that. All the more reason he needed to talk to Samir and get some answers ASAP.

"Are you mad at me?" she asked quietly.

He couldn't be after what he'd just heard. "No. I'm mad that this happened to you." He took a deep breath. "But I have to tell you, I think you should take a step back from the task force."

She struggled to sit up. "No. I have to see this through. I need to talk to Samir. He's probably wondering why I stood him up. Especially since I have no phone."

"I'll go talk to him and explain everything," he reassured her.

Viv grimaced in pain. "You can't go off on him. This wasn't his fault."

He wasn't so sure about that. "I have to talk to him. You must understand that."

"Talking is one thing, but threatening is another."

Even in her compromised state, she was still making her wishes known. "I promise I'll handle him appropriately." Appropriate for his standards at least, but maybe not for Viv's diplomatic tact. He still had unanswered questions, though. "Did the men who attacked you say anything? Did you get a good look at them?"

"They didn't speak. One was tall, the other short. Both Caucasian. But nothing stood out to distinguish them. It was dark, and everything happened so fast."

"Any other descriptive things about them?"

"One of them had light hair and the other was bald. And if you're wondering if Samir sent these guys to hurt me, then you're way off base. He wouldn't do that. Samir's a good man."

41

He understood that she wanted to defend her friend, but he wasn't willing to put her life on the line for it. "Let me do some digging. In the meantime, is there anyone you need or want me to call? Friends, boyfriend, family?"

She let out a little laugh. "There's no boyfriend. I've talked to my friends, and one of them is on her way here."

"Good." He was at a loss for words as he looked into her hazel eyes.

"I'll be back to work tomorrow," she said.

"Are you sure that's a good idea?"

"Yes. This investigation means a lot to me. I want justice for what's been done to Ambassador King—and maybe even Ambassador Zidan, if we figure out it's related."

"I'll let you know what I find out from Samir."

"Leave me your number, please. My friend is bringing me a new phone, and I'll text you my number when I have it."

He pulled out his card and set it on her table. "Text me. Call me. Whatever you need. I'm here."

She gave him a slight smile. "Thanks, Jacob."

He stood and glanced over his shoulder before walking out. She was staring out the window, and he wondered what was going through her mind.

Their partnership had just gotten a lot more complicated.

◆

When Layla and Bailey arrived at the hospital, Viv did her best to hold back tears.

Layla took her hand. "We didn't really get to talk about what happened last night because the docs wanted to check you out." Layla had rushed over when Viv called last night, but Viv had ended up sending Layla home, promising to reconvene this morning.

"Tell us everything that happened," Bailey said. She was an FBI agent, and from the looks of it, she was in full agent questioning mode.

Viv took a deep breath and recounted the story to her two best friends, who interrupted only minimally for questions. When she finished, she waited for the real interrogation to begin.

Layla spoke first. "So you don't think this was a setup by your contact at the embassy?"

"No. I definitely don't. Samir and I are on the same page. There's no way he would've done that to me."

"It could be a random violent mugging," Bailey said. "We do see that in the area. I hate to say it, but it happens more than we'd like to believe."

"That's what I think. Jacob is insistent on the tie to the Egyptians."

"Jacob?" Bailey asked. "Who's that?"

"He's in the Diplomatic Security Service. I met him at the dinner, and we're working together on the task force."

Layla's dark eyes lit up. "Wait a minute. Is this the security hunk who was checking you out?"

Viv had known Layla would latch on to this. "Yes, it is."

"It seems like this guy has made quite an impression on you two," Bailey said.

"Just on Layla. I'm not fazed. He hates lawyers and has lots of baggage. But we're working together, so I have to deal with him."

Her friends exchanged knowing glances. "Okay, we get that it's just professional at this point," Layla said.

"Period," Viv insisted.

"Have you talked to Willow?" Bailey asked.

Viv didn't want to worry her twin sister unnecessarily.

"No. I didn't want to bother her. She's still finishing up her humanitarian trip on the border between Turkey and Syria and is really busy."

"You should tell her what happened and give her your new phone number." Layla pulled a phone out of her bag and gave it to Viv. "You can get your number back on a better phone once things calm down, but for now just use this burner."

"Thanks. I did call my carrier to report it stolen, so hopefully that will help." Although the least of her concerns was her phone. That was easily replaceable. "I'm going to reach out to the guy who saved me. What do you think is an appropriate token of appreciation for saving my life? A coffee gift card just seems so trite, given the circumstances."

Layla smiled. "I'm sure he feels good enough knowing he was there to stop something even worse from happening. I think a card would be more than enough. I don't even think it has to be monetary."

"I just thank God he was there," Bailey said.

Me too, Viv thought. She had a feeling she was going to have nightmares for weeks over this. Which brought her to another topic. "I know I've resisted this for years, but I'm thinking of getting a firearm."

"We'll support you in any decision you make," Bailey said. "You know I'd help train you, and I'm sure Layla would too. But I don't want this attack to change your entire way of life, Viv. You're a lawyer. You fight with your words, not guns. And I know how anti-gun you've been in the past. So just think on it."

Layla nodded. "Bailey's right. We'll help you and teach you if you ultimately decide you want to carry, but this one event shouldn't impact your entire life moving forward."

Easy for them to say. They were both highly trained not only in firearms but also in self-defense. She wasn't.

"You're frowning," Bailey said.

"I just felt really ill-equipped to fight them off, and that makes me mad."

Bailey gaped at her. "Viv, it was two on one! Of course you'd be at a disadvantage."

Viv knew her friend was right, but it didn't make her feel any less vulnerable.

"I'm going to reach out to the DC police and see what I can find out," Bailey said.

"I wouldn't hold your breath. My mugging isn't the top crime priority in the city."

Bailey sighed. "I'm still going to call them. What can we do for you?"

"I'm supposed to be released this afternoon. So there's nothing I can do until that happens."

Layla looked at Bailey. "I'm sure one of us will be able to help you get home. If we get tied up, we could call Izzy, and we also found out that Lexi is back in town."

Viv perked up at that piece of good news. "I'd love to see Lexi. I know Izzy is crazy busy with law school, and I don't want to distract her."

"We'll let both of them know what happened," Layla said. Then she looked down at her watch. "I have to run into the office for a meeting that can't get pushed, but I'll check on you later. Maybe you should try to get some rest until they release you."

Bailey laid a hand on Viv's arm. "Yeah, I've got to run too. But we're just a text or phone call away. Let us know when you're released, and we'll make sure one of us comes over."

Viv felt herself getting emotional again. "Thank you both for everything. I don't deserve you."

Layla squeezed her hand. "We're all in this together. You know that."

Viv said her final good-byes, and her friends left the room. Her thoughts went back to Jacob, and she hoped and prayed he wasn't doing anything stupid at the Egyptian embassy. But there was something else she needed to do before she worried about that.

She picked up the burner phone and dialed her twin's number.

"This is Willow," her sister answered.

"It's Viv."

"Oh, hi! I didn't recognize the number."

Viv took a deep breath. "I'm calling on a burner phone. I need to tell you something, but I need you to stay calm, okay?"

"Burner phone? What's going on?" Her sister's voice caught. "Are you all right?"

"I'm okay, but I'm in the hospital. I'll be released soon. I was attacked last night by two men."

Her sister gasped. "What did they do to you? Where were you?"

She explained what happened. "Thankfully, someone came to my rescue, and my injuries are minimal, but they did take my phone, and I wanted to make sure you could get in contact with me until I get the phone situation straightened out."

"Viv, what aren't you telling me?" Her sister's voice cut right through her.

"Things are a bit thorny here, but I'm going to be fine." There was something she absolutely had to say, though. "I love you, Willow. There was a moment last night when I worried if I was going to make it, and I was thinking about you and Mom and Dad."

"You're really scaring me. Do I need to come home?"

"No. There's nothing you could do. You're doing important work there, but it's really good to hear your voice." She tried to keep her own voice from cracking.

"I love you, sis. If you need me, just say the word. You need to be more careful."

"I'm working with a diplomatic security guy, and now he's on high alert. It'll be okay."

"I'll call you later to check on you. And email me when you get out of the hospital, okay? Promise."

"I promise."

Viv ended the call with Willow, and a tear slid down her cheek. She really missed her sister.

CHAPTER
FIVE

By the time Jacob pushed through the red tape to get into the Egyptian embassy, his temper had gone from hot to red hot. He had promised Viv that he would behave, but his number-one priority was getting to the truth.

When Samir finally walked out to greet him, he tried his best not to put on a scowl.

"Agent Cruz, I must admit I'm surprised to see you again so soon. What can I help you with today?" Samir led him into a private room, and they both took a seat.

"I need to know why you were texting Viv last night."

Samir raised an eyebrow. "Excuse me?"

"You sent Viv a text telling her to meet you at Café Latte down the road."

Samir shook his head. "No. You must be mistaken."

Jacob's pulse jumped a few beats. "Are you saying you did *not* text Viv last night?"

"No, I didn't text Ms. Vivian. The last I communicated

with her was when you both were here. I didn't send her any text."

Jacob blew out a breath, trying to gather his thoughts.

"Tell me what's going on. Where is Ms. Vivian?"

Looking into Samir's dark eyes, Jacob had to make a judgment call. He hoped he was making the right one. "Viv is in the hospital."

Samir's eyes widened. "What? Is she all right?"

"Yes, she will be, but last night she received what she thought was a text from you asking her to meet at Café Latte. Before she got there, she was jumped and attacked by two men. They stole her phone and bag and attacked her. She's pretty beat up."

Samir started pacing the room. "This is bad."

"I know."

Samir moved toward him. "Let's go for a walk outside."

Jacob realized Samir wasn't sure if he could speak freely inside the embassy, so he agreed, and a few minutes later they were walking down the sidewalk.

"We have to be careful," Samir said. "I know I didn't send that message, but someone went through the trouble to make it look like I did."

Jacob nodded. "And that means we have to assume that Viv wasn't randomly attacked on the streets of DC. That it was a trap to lure her out to meet you."

"But why? To scare her?"

"Maybe it's a big back-off message. And they took her bag. Maybe they thought there could be something useful on her phone or in her notes. But the big question is who. Who would do this?"

Samir slowed down. "Someone who wants to keep the truth from coming out about Ambassador Zidan's death."

That was the obvious response, but what if there was something else they were overlooking? "Could there be any other reason? Viv said the two of you worked together previously. Could this be connected to that?"

Samir wiped a bead of sweat off his forehead. "I don't think so, but I'm not at liberty to speak about what Ms. Vivian and I worked on together."

Things were getting more interesting by the moment, but since it was clear Jacob was getting stonewalled on the past project with Viv, he needed to reverse course. "Okay, back to the ambassador. Do you think any of those names you gave us could be responsible for what happened to Viv?"

"Unfortunately, I'm afraid so. Those men are not to be trifled with. They have their own agenda for Egypt. They don't like the direction our president is taking the country."

Jacob understood the political turmoil in Egypt, but something wasn't fitting together in his mind. "But why mess with Viv?"

Another bead of sweat dripped down Samir's face. "Maybe someone knows we met at the embassy and they are trying to scare her off from investigating the death. They just want an open-and-shut case with a determination of a heart attack that can't be linked back to opposition forces in Egypt."

"Yeah, but couldn't someone else just fill the void if Viv bailed?" Jacob thought out loud.

Samir took a deep breath. "You'll have to forgive me, but I'm almost sixty years old, and I've seen a lot of things in my lifetime, both in Egypt and elsewhere. I know I'm paranoid. Maybe my paranoia is clouding my vision. If Ms. Vivian had been randomly attacked, maybe I could write that off, but the subterfuge with the text from me puts an entirely different spin on things."

Jacob had to be forthright, as there was a lot on the line. "Samir, whether you like it or not, you're right in the middle of this mess. I can't tell you what to do, but I'd be crazy if I didn't advise you to watch your back."

"Thank you, my friend."

Jacob had just graduated from untrusted outsider to friend. He worried that Samir's trusting nature might have helped get him into this. "If you had to pinpoint any of those men on that list you gave us, who would it be?"

Samir sighed loudly. "That's the problem. I could see any of them being involved—that was the list of people I have no doubt are working against the interests of the current Egyptian government. There's a much longer list of possibilities beyond that."

They would have to figure out a way to put this all together and get a manageable list of suspects.

"Please tell Ms. Vivian I'm sorry, but I think it will be best for all of us if we start limiting our in-person contact."

"I agree with you. What's the best way to reach you?"

"Let me give you the number to my personal cell."

Jacob pulled out his phone, and Samir rattled off his number.

"Be careful, my friend. There are enemies everywhere." Samir shook Jacob's hand and then walked away.

◆

Delaney turned to Weston before they got out of her government-issued black SUV. As part of the investigation, they had to do a full work-up on Ambassador Penelope King, and since her husband was by her side as she fought for her life, they'd decided to talk to others first while they waited to speak to him.

They were parked in front of Nan Kennedy's home in an affluent Arlington suburb. Through their initial research, they'd learned that Nan was a very close friend of Penelope's.

"What's our strategy here?" Weston asked.

His overconfidence when they'd first started working together had taken a turn after he blew that important op, and now Delaney was trying to get his confidence levels back up. "What do you think we should do?"

Weston blinked a couple of times. "Is this a test?"

"No. I'm just asking your opinion. You've got to get over being so sensitive, okay?"

He looked like a scolded puppy as he nodded. "This lady clearly has money and probably is used to people kissing up. I say we start out in that lane and see what she says before we get tougher."

She patted him on the back. "I agree. C'mon."

They made their way up the front steps and rang the doorbell. After a few seconds, an attractive petite woman with long black hair opened the door.

"Hi, I'm SSA O'Sullivan, and this is Agent Weston. We're with the FBI. Are you Nan Kennedy?"

"Yes. You must be here about Penelope."

Delaney nodded. "May we come in?"

"Of course." Nan moved away from the door. "Can I get you agents anything? Coffee, tea, water?"

"No, thank you," Weston replied.

"We can speak in here." Nan led them into a bright and airy living room.

They took a seat on the white couch that was probably custom-made. "Thank you again, Ms. Kennedy, for speaking with us."

"Do you have any idea what really happened to Penelope?" Nan tucked a stray hair behind her ear.

"That's exactly what we're working on," Weston said. "We're hoping we could talk to you about a few things."

She gave them a weak smile. "Whatever you need."

"Do you know of anyone who would want to hurt the ambassador?" Delaney asked.

Nan sighed. "No. I've known Penelope since college. She's always been the life of the party. But also very smart and professional. She knew how to play the game in Washington, and that meant knowing how not to make enemies. Even if she didn't like you, she didn't show it."

"Isn't that a bit disingenuous?" Weston asked.

"Maybe. But in her line of work it was absolutely necessary. She has her circle of true friends, but beyond that she has many acquaintances."

"She never gave you any indication that she was concerned about her safety?" Delaney carefully watched Nan's response.

Nan shook her head. "No. Her job was political, yes, but not dangerous. At least not until now."

"She's been the ambassador to Belgium for three years. Do you know what she was doing before that?"

Nan nodded. "She worked here in the State Department for a number of years. Before that she was abroad in the foreign service. She's very well-traveled and speaks a few languages."

They needed to figure out what lay beneath the surface. "What about the ambassador's personal life?"

Nan frowned for a moment. "What do you mean?"

"We know she's been married for about a decade. How well do you know her husband?"

Nan crossed her hands in her lap. "I know Jeff pretty well. I was her maid of honor in the wedding."

"And? What can you tell us about their relationship?" Weston asked.

"What does that have to do with anything?"

Bingo. There was something more going on here. "It's standard questioning in a situation like this for us to try to understand the ambassador's relationships. Her marriage is a big part of that."

Nan looked away and didn't say anything.

"Ms. Kennedy, it's very important that you're open with us." Delaney felt her voice getting more stern.

"It's really not my place to say." Nan fidgeted in her seat.

"Well, unfortunately, the ambassador can't speak for herself. So as her closest friend, you need to speak for her," Weston said.

"I should say at the outset that there's no way Jeff did this to Penelope."

"We didn't say he did."

Nan's eyes narrowed. "I just wanted to be clear."

"We appreciate that," Delaney said. "But it's obvious there's something going on here that you're not telling us."

Nan looked down again. "I just think you need to talk to Jeff about this if you have more questions."

Weston cleared his throat. "You want us to go to him while he's at his wife's bedside as she fights for her life?"

Weston was turning into the bad cop, but it appeared to be working. Nan looked like she might be ready to fold.

"Their marriage isn't perfect, but no marriage is."

"Go on," Delaney urged.

"There have been some issues in the past with Penelope

54

when she and Jeff weren't living together because of Jeff's job in the States."

"Infidelity issues?" Weston asked.

"Yes. But they worked through those, and like I said, I know Jeff loves her and wouldn't hurt her no matter what."

Nan sounded convinced, but Delaney didn't take her account at face value, especially since it was her friend who had apparently been unfaithful. Still, she could think of a lot of less flashy ways to kill your spouse that would have drawn much less attention to the crime.

Weston was tapping his foot as he often did. "Is there anything else you can think of that might be helpful?"

Nan's face paled. "No. I'm just hoping she can pull through this. I honestly don't know what I'd do without her."

Delaney felt for her. "Ms. Kennedy, we know this is extremely difficult for you, but I have one more question before we go."

"Sure."

"Are you aware of the ambassador using opioids?"

Nan's eyes widened. "No. Absolutely not. Penelope is a health freak. She probably drank a little too much wine, but that was as far as it ever went. Why would you even ask that?"

"Because there was a large amount of a street version of fentanyl in her system."

"You think that's what did this to her? That's possible?" Nan's voice shook.

Delaney nodded. "Unfortunately, the drug is highly lethal, especially if it's mixed with alcohol."

Nan straightened her shoulders. "All I can tell you is that there is zero chance Penelope was taking drugs. I know that with every fiber of my being. I would've known about something like this."

Delaney hadn't wanted to upset Nan, but her reaction was consistent with what the medical experts were saying. It bolstered the working assumption that someone had deliberately put that fentanyl in her drink with the intent to kill her. "I appreciate your candor. It's been very helpful. I can assure you that we will find out who is responsible for this."

Nan sniffed. "Thank you."

Weston stood and handed Nan his card. "If you think of anything else, give us a call. We can see ourselves out."

They walked out of the house and were silent until they got back into the privacy of their SUV. Weston got behind the wheel, and they were off.

"You did well back there," Delaney said.

"Thanks. Do you think she was telling us everything?"

Delaney scoffed. "They never tell us everything. She clearly didn't want to talk about the ambassador's infidelity. We both know that's an easy enough motive for murder."

Weston tapped his fingers on the steering wheel. "Although given how tight these women are, if Nan really thought Jeff could've been responsible, wouldn't she have said so? Wouldn't she want Jeff to be brought to justice for potentially murdering her friend?"

"Regardless, we need to dig further into Jeff King. Statistics put this on him, but you have a good point about Nan. I'll have someone back at HQ pull everything on him, and then we'll work through it with the rest of the team. We know Jeff was at the dinner, although he excused himself early before the ambassador collapsed. He would've had the opportunity to dose his wife's drink. Unfortunately, there are a lot of other people who had access to one of her drinks as well."

"Have you gotten any updates on Vivian?" Weston asked.

"Jacob sent me a text saying that he'd seen her and that she was stable but pretty badly beaten up."

"Is there ever any good news in this job?"

"Rarely."

They rode in silence for a few minutes as she responded to a few messages on her phone.

"Delaney," Weston said.

"Yeah."

"This may be nothing, but there's a black truck tailing us."

She turned and looked over her shoulder, spotting the vehicle. "When did you first notice it?"

"Soon after we left Nan's. Maybe right when we got out of her neighborhood and onto the main road."

"Why didn't you say anything sooner?"

Weston glanced at her. "I wanted to make sure I wasn't overreacting."

"Okay. Let's keep heading back toward the State Department. You keep your eyes glued on the road. Let me worry about the truck."

"Should I speed up?"

"Not yet. I want to monitor the situation for a minute."

Weston was still a rookie, but she trusted his instincts on stuff like this. If he thought they had a tail, then they most likely had a tail. But who? The person who attacked Ambassador King? Or could this be completely unrelated?

She noticed a bead of sweat roll down the side of Weston's face. He was nervous. He'd trained for this type of thing at Quantico, but this was the first time he'd dealt with it in the real world. She wanted to give him some room to operate, but at the same time, as the senior agent, she had to make sure they were safe.

The truck was keeping a reasonable distance. It was time to add to the mix.

"Take a right," she said. "Quick."

Weston obeyed without question, hanging a right at the next road. The truck continued its pursuit.

"What do they want?" he asked.

"Maybe they want to see who we're talking to next. Once they realize we're going back to the State Department, they'll most likely disappear."

"But you can't guarantee that."

She shook her head. "No guarantees in anything about our work. That's why you have to be ready at any time. The moment you let down your guard is the moment you could get killed." She was trying to teach him all the lessons she could.

Weston nodded. "Roger that."

"If the truck started to take more aggressive action, what would you do?" No time like the present for some on-the-job training.

"Evasive maneuvers."

"Right. It's always preferable to get out of the situation instead of engaging. If we had to engage, what would happen then?"

"You'd need to return fire if fired upon, but you would not instigate."

"Good. You can take a deep breath, partner. I don't think this truck is going to hurt us. They just want to know where we're going."

He cut his eyes at her. "I hope you're right."

She did too. But more than likely the people in the truck would have already made their move if they were going to make it. Her bigger question was who was watching them. And why.

◆

Viv had nodded off, and when she woke up, she noticed the bright floral arrangement on the table beside her. Excitedly, she pulled out the card, figuring it had to be from her friends, but once she read it, she knew even more that she had to do something to thank Mark. This guy had single-handedly saved her life, and now he was sending her flowers. She read the card again.

Viv,
   I hope you're feeling much better today. I'm sorry again about what happened to you.

Mark Pullman

She groaned in pain as she leaned over and grabbed her stuff from the table, then pulled out his card. This deserved a phone call. She paused for one moment, but decided it was only right to call him.

Then she had to remind herself that this guy was off limits. He had done the right thing and was following up, but he probably had a wife and kids. She had thought about how cute he was after the fact, but she knew he was probably even more attractive to her because of his good deed. He had wavy jet-black hair and light brown eyes. She remembered those eyes the most, because they held so much kindness. She almost started to cry again but forced herself to get it together.

Viv dialed his number and waited. He picked up on the third ring.

"This is Mark," he said in a curt tone.

"Mark, hi. This is Viv. The woman from last night."

"Oh, hey. Sorry I sounded annoyed. I didn't recognize the number and thought you might be a telemarketer."

She laughed. "I don't blame you."

"How're you feeling today?"

"I'm sore everywhere, but I'll be okay. No permanent damage." She took a breath. "I wanted to call and thank you again, and also thank you for the beautiful flowers. It was so thoughtful of you."

"You're welcome. You had a rough night. I'm just glad you're okay. I assume you talked with the police at length?"

"Yeah, but I'm not very hopeful they'll find those guys." A shiver of fear went through her at the thought of having to face them ever again.

"I'm sure it was just a one-off situation. You're safe now."

She could only pray that he was right. Then another thought hit her. "I'd love to take you to coffee to thank you for everything." She'd blurted it out before she could stop herself.

"You really don't need to do that, though it would be nice. But no rush. I know you're trying to get better."

"Oh, I'm going back to work tomorrow."

"Really? Is that too fast?" he asked.

"No, I think I need to get right back to it."

"That's pretty admirable of you."

"My work is important to me."

"I get that. I'm an attorney, so I'm working all the time."

Now, wasn't that something. "I'm also an attorney. I work on the government side, though. How about you?"

"Law firm. I did the big firm thing for years, then transitioned to a smaller firm for my own sanity."

"Nice. Well, I'll call you about coffee, okay?"

"Sounds like a plan. Please take care of yourself, Viv."

The call ended, and she saw Jacob standing at the door.

"Who were you talking to?" he asked.

"The guy who saved me last night. I want to take him to coffee."

He raised an eyebrow. "Are you sure that's a good idea?"

"He's the only reason I'm talking to you right now and not dead in some alley or beaten to a pulp. I assure you I'll be fine with him."

"Sorry, I'm just taking every precaution, and what I'm about to tell you will make you understand why."

Her stomach dropped. "What is it?"

He slid the chair closer to her and took a seat. "Samir didn't send you that text."

Her mouth dropped open. "What? What do you mean? I definitely got a text from him."

"It's not that I don't believe you. It's something else entirely. Someone wanted you to think Samir sent you that text, but it was not him."

Silence hung in her small hospital room as the enormity of what Jacob had just revealed hit her. "It was a coordinated attack. They drew me out and planned it."

He grimaced. "I'm afraid it looks that way."

"They got my phone, but that was really the only thing of any worth they got from me. And I don't carry classified material on my phone."

"Maybe they were just trying to shake you up. Hurt you to get you to stop working on this case. Or . . ."

"Or what?"

"Okay, hear me out for a minute."

"Go ahead."

"I find it odd that you meet with Samir at the embassy, and then he's used as the vehicle to trap you. Is there any possibility that this could be connected to whatever project you worked on with Samir? He couldn't tell me anything, but I know you can. I have the clearances. No offense, but I probably have a higher clearance level than you do."

She broke eye contact. "I would need to talk to someone about sharing because I was in a support role. It wasn't my op."

"Op?"

"Yeah." She had worked with Samir as part of a CIA op with Layla last year. "I was providing legal guidance, but it was driven by the Agency."

Jacob muttered something as he ran his hand through his hair. "We have to explore it."

"I still think it's more likely connected to the ambassador's death. We were just at the embassy, and then this happens."

He nodded. "That cuts both ways. We know the embassy and the connection to Samir is key. We just don't know whether it's related to Ambassador Zidan's death or this op you can't tell me about. We need to report this new information about Samir not sending you the text to the team." He looked away for a second. "I know we started off on rocky footing, and that's my fault. But given everything we know now, I don't think you should be out and about on your own."

"What are you saying?"

"That I need to provide you with personal protection."

"You?" She could barely believe what he was suggesting.

"Yeah. I know I'm probably the last person you want around, but given we're working together anyway and you want to keep working, I think it makes sense. We'll need to talk to the director about all of this. Your life is potentially in danger, and we're not sure why."

She bit the inside of her cheek. "Believe me. I know. And I'll accept all the help I can get. I was just telling the girls earlier that I wanted to get a gun."

He frowned. "I'm not sure that's the best idea if you aren't trained."

"I would need to get trained. They offered to help me."

"I'm an expert marksman. I can train you if needed, but let's take this to the big man and see how he wants to handle it."

"Jacob, I don't want to be thrown off the task force and locked up in some unknown location while we wait this thing out. I need to keep working. It's the only thing that will keep me sane."

"I hear you loud and clear. I'll make the case to the director, but you'll need to be willing to have me by your side."

As she looked into his smoldering dark eyes, she was surprised by how much that thought frightened her.

CHAPTER SIX

The next morning, Delaney grabbed a booth at the Foggy Bottom Diner and waited for Weston to arrive. They'd agreed to grab coffee before they hunkered down in the war room to prepare for their interview with Jeff King that afternoon.

The truck that had been tailing them yesterday had veered off when they'd gotten closer to State, just as she had predicted. She had reported the incident to the task force because everyone involved should be on high alert in case the surveillance turned into something more sinister.

As she sipped her coffee—extra cream and sugar—she reminded herself how important this case was. Mentoring Weston was challenging, but frankly, it was exactly what she needed.

Ever since her husband, Ryan, was killed two years ago during an FBI drug bust gone wrong, she'd been going through the motions in most of her life. But she had doubled down on her job. Ryan was a brilliant agent. He'd just been in the wrong place at the wrong time, facing down a strung-out druggie who didn't even remember pulling the trigger. He would have wanted her to keep climbing the FBI ladder.

She was finally starting to feel like herself again, but she didn't know how she'd really get over the loss of the only man she had ever truly loved. Living in a constant state of grief had a way of wearing you down and tearing at your soul. So she took it one day at a time because that was all she could do. And thank God for her work, because it was the motivating factor in her life.

She sighed as she saw Weston walking up to the counter to order. Being able to throw everything into her work had saved her. It gave her a purpose. There were days after Ryan's murder when she honestly didn't think she'd be able to move on.

And as far as romance, there had been no one since Ryan. It wasn't because she didn't think he would have been okay with it. She just didn't have those feelings for anyone she'd encountered. Her heart still belonged to him, and she wondered if it always would.

Weston joined her at the table, wearing a goofy smile and carrying his cup of coffee.

"Why are you grinning so big?"

"I just got the number of the barista."

Delaney laughed. "You are seriously always trying to see what woman's heart you can break next."

Weston put his hand on his chest. "Never! I'm just young and trying to find out what I really want in life. You were my age once too, remember? Back when you had a love life."

Delaney looked down. At twenty-five, she'd been a couple of years into her FBI career. Then, at twenty-nine, she'd met Ryan. They got married when she turned thirty-three.

They'd had it all planned out. A family, who was going to take leave when to balance their careers. Unfortunately, after struggling for years, she'd been unable to get pregnant. They were just starting to talk about adoption and were both really excited about the prospect of being parents. But then it all came to a crashing halt.

Weston placed his hand on her arm. "Delaney, I'm so sorry. Sometimes I forget and say the stupidest stuff. I wasn't even thinking." He hadn't known Ryan, but he knew what had happened to him.

"It's okay. I know you didn't mean anything by it."

Weston shrugged. "I'm an idiot. What else can I say?"

"You're not an idiot."

"But since we're already on the topic, there's someone I think would be great for you to meet. He works in private security. He's only a couple years younger than you."

She lifted up her hand. "How many times do I have to tell you that I don't need my partner trying to find me a date?"

Weston leaned in. "Actually, you do. You know how you told me that you would take the tough-love approach with me and make sure I learned everything I could?"

"Yeah."

"Well, as your partner, I feel like I have the right to do the same with you, just on a different topic."

She started to speak, but he cut her off.

"Delaney, you're the best agent I know, but your life should be about more than the job. You deserve happiness again. I know you think I'm overstepping, but it's because I care. You've saved my hide more times than I can count. I work with you every single day. I know you better than you think. I'm just being honest here. I don't want to see you in pain. You should be thriving in all parts of your life, not just your job."

She couldn't be mad at him, because she knew his heart was in the right place, but she still didn't want him trying to play matchmaker. "I appreciate your concern, but I need to handle things my way and in my own time. Do you understand that?"

He gave a reluctant nod. "Remember, I'm here if you change your mind and want to talk. Okay?"

"Enough romance talk for the day. How are you doing after yesterday?"

"I'm good. I know in the moment I didn't look rock solid. I think my adrenaline started to take over, and it was hard to remain calm and not react. Thanks for walking me through it."

"Adrenaline is a great thing, Weston. You'll need it. And as annoying as it is that someone was watching us, it was a good experience for you. But just know that it could take only a second for a situation like that to get out of hand. You always have to be ready to act. You can't be complacent. Being calm is different than complacent. Do you understand?"

He nodded. "I'm lucky to have you as my partner. I'm learning so much from you."

"Let's get moving." She was anxious to get to State and stop picking at the wounds of her past.

◆

After jumping through hoops, Jacob had finally gotten the necessary approvals late in the morning to have this meeting with Viv and her CIA friend Layla.

He instantly recognized the striking olive-skinned woman with long dark hair from the diplomatic dinner. Why wasn't he surprised that the CIA had people there? He'd dealt with plenty of CIA officers, since they poked their heads into SEAL missions far more than he had liked. But he also understood that they did a necessary job, and one that was far from easy. He usually let them think they were running the show, and everyone got along fine.

Layla's dark eyes locked on to him. "I have permission to read you into this op, but I still need you to keep this completely confidential. What I'm about to tell you doesn't leave this room. Do you understand?"

"I know how it works." He was trying not to get frustrated, but he'd been a Navy SEAL for years. He knew all about how important it was to keep the country's secrets. He had sacrificed more than he wanted to admit doing just that.

"One more thing," Layla said. "I know you fully understand this, but I have to repeat it. My cover is as a State Department analyst, and I need to keep that intact."

"Understood." He glanced at Viv, who sat with a frown on her bruised face. Every time he looked at her and saw the damage those men had inflicted, his anger returned. Those feelings only fueled him to redouble his efforts to find out who hurt her. Now that they'd dealt with all the bureaucratic stuff, hopefully he'd get some real details about this operation.

Layla leaned in. "We had a joint CIA-Egyptian operation that dealt with the transfer of high-value detainees out of CIA custody and into Egyptian custody."

This was a page out of the CIA playbook that he was very familiar with. "Let me guess. You wanted the Egyptians to have them because they are harsher with their interrogation techniques than we are."

Layla sighed. "I'd be lying if I said that wasn't part of it, but it actually wasn't the main driver this time. Under CIA interrogation, we were able to identify a few detainees with specific links to the anti-democratic forces in Egypt. The opposition movement wanted to overthrow the president because they felt he's too moderate. Once we shared that intel with the Egyptians, they came up with a plan to receive the detainees back in Egypt. The thought was that if we turned over the detainees, the Egyptians could put them under surveillance to help identify those in the president's inner circle who might be working against democratic interests in Egypt."

"Ah, so you used them as bait," he said.

Viv jumped in. "These are known terrorists we're talking about here, Jacob. They are not innocent civilians, and that's where my role came in. I had to provide legal advice to make sure we were doing everything by the book and not violating any international laws."

"C'mon, Viv. As soon as those guys got to Egyptian custody, you knew how they would be treated. I think you're both forgetting that I was a Navy SEAL. I've seen more than the two of you could even imagine, and that's good, because I wouldn't wish what I have seen and done on anyone. But let's not play the legality card here."

Viv bit her bottom lip. "I'm not playing any card. I'm just saying I was given a job, and I took it seriously. Not only did we play by the book with the detainee transfer, our efforts worked. Once back in Egypt, the detainees were released, and that allowed the Egyptian intelligence services to monitor their every move. Because of that, they were able to find the men from the Egyptian president's inner circle. It turns out they were planning a terrorist plot to kill him *and* countless innocent civilians. We can't lose sight of the bigger picture here."

"I'm not. It sounds like it was a highly successful op." The tension between them was palpable, but he couldn't help but think it didn't have much to do with what they were currently talking about and everything to do with the fact that they were about to be joined at the hip.

"I think you have everything you need from me for the moment. Viv can provide other details, and you two need some time to talk about next steps." Layla picked up her bag and exited the conference room, leaving him alone with Viv.

They sat in silence for a few moments before Viv touched his arm, catching him off guard and making him painfully aware of how close she was to him.

"Jacob, I'm sorry. I shouldn't be combative. Let's work through this and focus on what's really important here."

On that he agreed. "Yes. Which is figuring out why you were targeted."

She shook her head. "The most important thing is figuring out who attacked our ambassador and possibly the Egyptian ambassador. This isn't about me."

Let her think that, but her personal safety was just as important to him. Maybe that was why he was so wound up.

"Do you want to talk about whatever is really bothering you?" she asked.

"I don't know what you mean."

"There's something bubbling underneath. I'm not sure what it is, but it's clearly impacting you. Maybe if you talked about it, you would feel better."

He ran a hand through his hair. He wasn't ready to open up to someone about his problems. He wasn't sure if he ever would be. "I highly doubt that. Let's not get preoccupied with psychoanalyzing me, all right? We've got a lot of problems to deal with, and we both need to be laser-focused to handle all of this."

She gave him a weak smile. "I'm a good listener if you ever do want to talk to anyone. And as a lawyer, I know how to keep secrets. It's in my job description."

He appreciated her offer even if he wouldn't take it. "Thanks, Viv."

"I need you on my team, not debating and questioning every small detail. You would think as a lawyer that would be my role."

That made him chuckle. "You're right. Honestly, I'm hyped up about your attack. I hate not knowing all the facts of a situation, and I feel like I'm flying blind. Does that make sense?"

"Yes. You like to gather all the information and then make the best decision you can, but we both know we don't have that luxury here. We're going on pieces of intel, half-truths, word of mouth, and who knows what else."

"I'm used to operating in the dark, but that doesn't mean I like it. We are at a tactical and strategic disadvantage. The sooner we can narrow down where the threats are coming from, the better."

"We have a team meeting in the morning, but for the purposes of the task force, let's keep the focus on the current cases and not this past op with the CIA, okay?"

"That's fine with me." He wasn't convinced the FBI or anyone else on the team would really be able to help Viv. He was going to have to help her.

"What's wrong?"

"What do you mean?"

"You're scowling again."

He shrugged. "Sorry. Maybe you think I'm scowling when I'm just thinking."

That softened her up some, and she touched his arm again.

The contact sent a jolt of awareness through him. He looked up at her and tried not to react, but he was concerned that Viv was starting to get under his skin in more ways than one.

◆

Delaney wasn't looking forward to interviewing the ambassador's husband, but they'd given him as much time as they possibly could. The ambassador was still fighting for her life, so they had agreed to do the interview in the hospital cafeteria. Weston had secured a section of the cafeteria so they could talk in private, and now they sat across from Jeff King.

Data from millions of murders told her that this man was probably behind all of this, especially given the infidelity piece. But they had no evidence against him, and this was a highly delicate situation, given all the facts. Yes, he'd had opportunity, since he was with Penelope King at the dinner, and he had motive because of the infidelity in the past, but they would need a lot more than that. She wanted to be able to look him in the eyes and make her own determination.

"Thank you again, Mr. King, for speaking with us. We know this is a very difficult time for you."

Jeff King's dark hair was streaked with a bit of gray. It looked like he hadn't shaved in days. He presented more like a grieving husband than a killer.

"It's awful. I wouldn't wish something like this on anyone. The doctors tell me she isn't suffering anymore because they have her heavily sedated, but I know at some point she definitely was. Are you guys any closer to finding out who is responsible for this?" He choked up. "There's less than a ten percent chance that she's going to pull through."

Delaney jumped in. "I know you're hurting, Mr. King,

and you can rest assured we are working around the clock to bring whoever did this to justice. That's the reason we wanted to talk to you."

Jeff's eyes were bloodshot. "Anything I can do, just ask."

She glanced at Weston before starting. They'd had a talk earlier and had come to an agreement on strategy. "I'd prefer to get the most difficult questions out of the way first, if that's okay with you, Mr. King."

"Looks like you've done your homework, Agent O'Sullivan. You're going to ask about the affairs."

Plural. "Yes. Please tell us about that. I know it's hard, but we have to gather all the facts."

Jeff looked directly at her. "Penelope has had a number of relationships with other men, but most of that was my fault."

"You weren't upset?" Weston asked.

"Of course I was. I'm a man and I've got an ego, but we were living apart for quite a while, and I wanted to save our relationship. I do really love her, and I know she loves me. We decided to make changes to see each other more, and then ultimately I shifted jobs so I could live with her abroad. That made a big difference."

"When was the last affair?" Delaney asked.

"Probably about a year or so ago."

"We're going to need the names of those people," she said.

Jeff looked down. "I'll do my best on names. As you can imagine, I wasn't getting complete profiles on these guys."

"I understand," she said. "Just your best shot." As she studied him, she saw a man who was clearly exhausted.

"Mr. King, let's shift topics," Weston said.

"Thank you." Jeff took a sip of water. Obviously talking about the affairs wasn't easy, but it was necessary.

"I know the doctors told you about the street fentanyl in your wife's system and that being the cause of all this."

Jeff lifted a hand. "Yes, and Penelope would've never overdosed. First, she doesn't do drugs, and second, there's no way she would've tried to kill herself. That's not in her DNA. I'm telling you absolutely no way. Never."

"We just had to ask."

"I get it," Jeff said. "But someone drugged my wife."

"You were at the dinner with her for a while, correct?" she asked.

"Yes. I started getting a migraine as we were having the main course. She knows how badly those impact me, so she was fine with me bailing early. Although now I obviously wish I'd been there to help her."

"Did you notice anyone around her who could've had access to her drinks?"

Jeff let out a little laugh. "Penelope was always surrounded by people. I know she had some drinks before dinner started. I think I got her a drink, but the others she either got herself or someone else brought them to her."

"Do you know of anyone who would want to hurt your wife?" Weston asked.

Jeff blew out a breath. "Penelope is extremely political, so I know she could rub some the wrong way to get what she wanted. But I don't know of anyone who would've taken it so far as to drug her."

Delaney shifted in her chair. "Mr. King, there's just one other thing I'd like to discuss. Do you think that something your wife was doing for her job as ambassador to Belgium could have anything to do with this? Had she mentioned any problems at work?"

Jeff shook his head. "The Belgium post was pretty posh. It

was a far cry from when she worked in Africa or the Middle East at the beginning of her career when she was in the Foreign Service. But Brussels is the center of a lot of diplomatic action in Europe, and she was right in the middle of all of it. Penelope is so smart and driven. She likes to be where the political action and heavy hitters are."

Penelope King sounded like an interesting and complex woman. The more Delaney learned, the more she feared that Penelope was not afraid to rock the boat, and that could have led to trouble.

"Do you know if she knew the Egyptian ambassador, Ali Zidan?"

"Penelope knows everyone, but I wasn't aware that the two of them were close or had any working relationship. She never lived in Egypt or worked there." Jeff looked at his watch. "I'd really like to get back to her. Is that okay?" His voice started to crack.

"Absolutely." He was either an amazing actor or he hadn't tried to hurt his wife.

Weston stood and shook Jeff's hand. "If you think of anything else, let us know. Here's my card with my email and phone."

"Will do." Jeff turned and quickly walked away.

"I don't know, Delaney. He doesn't seem guilty to me," Weston said.

This was another good teachable moment for the young agent. "I'm a big believer in gut feelings in our job, but we have to weigh that against evidence. You're also the type of person who likes to see the good in people. That's a great quality, but you have to accept the hard reality that there are people who tell us one thing to our faces and do just the opposite. We see the dark side of people. The evil that is often hidden."

Weston blew out a breath. "Getting deep on me today, Delaney."

"I just want you to always question. Never accept at face value. Even if suspects cry or seem genuinely upset. That doesn't mean they're innocent. It also doesn't mean they're guilty, but that's why we have to dig and get the facts and the evidence."

Weston nodded. "I hear you loud and clear." His phone buzzed, and he looked down at it and frowned.

"What?"

"I just got a text that they've found some suspicious financial activity for the ambassador."

She blew out a breath. "Have them send us everything. We'll go back to the office and review it now."

Exactly what had Penelope King gotten herself into, and would she pay for it with her life?

CHAPTER
SEVEN

Viv sat relaxing on her couch after a long day. She was debating what to eat for dinner. Jacob had insisted on escorting her to her Metro stop. She couldn't help but feel the tension. If she didn't know better, she'd say there was some sort of spark kindling between them. But her first priority was helping out in the investigation the best way she could. She wasn't a Fed, but she was smart and resourceful and very good at connecting the dots.

Her phone rang, and she answered.

"Viv, hi, it's Mark. Mark Pullman."

She smiled at the sound of his voice and that he thought he needed to say his last name. "Hi there. How're you doing?"

"That's the question I should be asking you. Did you get out of the hospital?"

She stood and walked into the kitchen to grab a soda. "Yes. I'm at home and back at work."

"I just wanted to check on you. I'm so glad you're doing okay."

"Thank you. It's been quite a whirlwind." She paused. "I still want to do coffee. Why don't we go ahead and set something up?"

"Are you sure? We can wait until you're fully recovered."

I'm never going to be fully recovered, she thought. The fear would always be with her. "No. Let's do it. How about tomorrow, midmorning? Would it be possible for you to get away around ten o'clock?"

"Sure. Where do you want to meet?" he asked.

"If you can get to Foggy Bottom, that would be great. I have a favorite coffee place called Coffee Cups. Does that work?"

"Sure. I'll see you then. Try to get some rest."

"Thanks." She hung up and thanked God once again that Mark had been there to save her.

She had just finished a peanut butter sandwich—the only thing she had the energy to fix—when the doorbell rang.

Looking through the peephole, she let out a little screech of joy when she saw who was on the other side.

"Lexi!" She pulled her friend into a big hug.

"I'm so glad to see you." The blond JAG attorney had just gotten home from a lengthy overseas assignment and was finally going to be working again in the DC area. "Let me look at you." Lexi frowned as she surveyed Viv.

Viv knew the bruises still looked bad, but there was nothing she could do about that.

Lexi put her arm around Viv's shoulder. "Are you in pain? The girls told me what happened, but it's just so hard to comprehend. You're not supposed to be in the line of fire. You're a diplomatic attorney."

If only it was that cut-and-dried. "Yeah, it's been surreal, and not in a good way, but it could've been so much worse if a Good Samaritan hadn't stepped in and stopped them."

"Do you have any leads on the guys behind this?"

"We're working on it, but it might be more than just a random attack. I can't go into all the details right now, but it's a mess."

Lexi gave her a knowing look. "Does this have something to do with the attack on our ambassador?"

Viv remained silent.

Lexi's eyes narrowed. "Okay, I get it. But you need to be careful. What're you doing about your personal security?"

"I'm working with a former SEAL who now works for the Diplomatic Security Service. His plan is to watch me like a hawk. We need to talk to the FBI director, since he's running the task force we're working on, to make sure he's on board with that. We have a meeting with the task force at eight in the morning."

"A SEAL?"

"Yes."

Sadness touched Lexi's eyes. She had represented a Navy SEAL who had ended up getting murdered.

"I'm sorry, Lexi." Viv touched her friend's arm.

"Nothing to apologize for. Hopefully you will get the SEAL as personal protection. They're the best, and I'd feel a lot better knowing you had one of them watching your back."

"Jacob is quite something. He hates lawyers, for starters."

Lexi laughed. "Well, that isn't so unique. As a fellow attorney, I can empathize."

"I know. I've been trying to get him to open up to me by showing him that not all lawyers are like the stereotypical versions he seems to have dealt with."

Lexi patted Viv's shoulder. "The fact that he wants to protect you says a lot about the kind of guy he is. In my experience, guys like that have wounds and battle scars that go beyond the physical."

That was becoming more evident every day. "Thanks for the advice. How're you doing? Are you glad to be back?"

Lexi threw her head back. "Yes. So glad to be back home. It was a challenging assignment, but I also gained a lot of good experience, and it was an important set of cases."

"I assume you can't talk about them?" Viv understood protocol.

Lexi shook her head. "These specific cases, no. But I was in Afghanistan working with special ops. There was a high-level investigation related to a couple of missions that went sideways. They were under tight security protocols—that gives you an idea of the stakes involved."

"It's great that you're so passionate about your work. I know I feel fortunate every day to go to work. Not many people thrive in their jobs like that."

Lexi nodded. "I'm thankful too. We both get to serve our country, and that is a feeling that can't be matched, even with private-sector money."

"You'll be back in town for the foreseeable future, then?"

"Yes."

Viv smiled. "So does that mean you'll be seeing Derek?"

Lexi groaned. "You know we left things kind of open-ended."

"That doesn't answer my question." It was nice to put the heat on someone else about their love life instead of having the attention directed at her.

Lexi looked away. "I want to see him, but I'm nervous that he's moved on. I was gone for six months."

"Did you talk to him while you were gone?"

"Very little. Given the security situation, communications were pretty much on lockdown except for emergencies because they didn't want the possibility of any leaks in the investigation. I told him that before I left, and he seemed to understand, but it's a lot different when it actually happens, you know?"

Viv squeezed Lexi's hand. "You need to reach out to him and let him know you're back. At least give him a chance. Maybe he's anxiously awaiting your return. Don't wait any longer to call him."

Lexi sighed. "You're right. Thanks for the tough love. Let me know if there's anything I can do to help you. I'll be here in an instant if you need me."

They caught up for a while longer before calling it a night. Viv gave her friend a big hug at the door, so glad to have her back in her life.

Before she could go to bed, her phone rang, and she recognized that it was her sister calling.

"Hey, sis."

"How're you feeling?" Willow asked.

"I'm doing better."

Willow sighed. "I'm really worried about you. I feel like you're keeping me in the dark about something."

Her sister knew her all too well. "I can't tell you everything because of the security clearance issues."

"Just what I feared. This attack against you wasn't random but had to do with work."

"Please don't push me on things you know I can't answer."

"I just want to make sure you're safe."

"I am. That diplomatic security agent I told you about is a former SEAL. He's not letting me out of his sight. And when I'm at home, I'm all locked up and secure and have my alarm system."

"A SEAL?" Willow asked. "Tell me more about him."

"Don't get any ideas. It's not like that."

"Like what?" Willow laughed. "I'm just curious about who this guy is, and you assumed I was asking about romance. You were always the romantic between us."

"And look at me. I'm alone."

"Stop that. You're alone by choice."

Her sister was giving her too much credit. "How is Rohan?"

Willow groaned. "We broke up."

"When? Why didn't you tell me?" They told each other everything.

"I didn't want to get interrogated over it. Really, it was an amicable split. We just decided we weren't right for each other. We're still friends, and I see him a lot with our work."

"Everything going okay with work?" Her sister worked with an NGO that helped refugees.

"Yes. It's pretty grueling but worth it. There's so much we have to be thankful for, Viv. I know we lost a huge part of us when Mom and Dad died, but the people I'm helping here on the Syrian-Turkish border . . . they have nothing except the clothes on their backs. The situation in Syria is beyond tragic. They've often lost family members. Kids have been through the unspeakable. They're just trying to find somewhere safe away from brutal dictatorships or terrorist threats."

Viv couldn't be more proud of Willow. "You're doing amazing work. Really making an impact on people's lives."

"Thanks for saying that. I also noticed how you expertly shifted topics away from the SEAL."

"Enough of that. I'm tired and am going to bed. But we'll talk again soon."

"Seriously, sis. Please be careful. I love you."

"Love you too."

◆

Early the next morning, the team had a meeting scheduled in the war room at State. Delaney was the first one to arrive, followed by Cody. The lanky, dark-haired European analyst seemed highly competent, and that was what they needed.

"How're you?" Cody asked.

"Hanging in there." She paused. "How long have you been working at State?"

He drummed his fingers on the table. "Since I finished grad school."

"What was your degree in?"

"European studies."

"You're basically tailor-made for the job, then. I'm guessing you speak a lot of languages?"

"Italian, French, and German are my specialties."

She smiled. "I've got nothing beyond English."

He laughed. "Well, special agents in the FBI don't need a lot of language skills to excel in their jobs. From what I hear, you're one of the best."

At the compliment, she felt her cheeks redden. She wasn't sure why his words made her blush.

Thankfully, she was saved by the arrival of the others. She watched as everyone filed into the room, including the last two team members to enter—Jacob and Vivian—who both wore extremely grim facial expressions.

While the director had told them that Vivian was in the hospital, the details were highly sketchy. Delaney figured they'd get the download in a few minutes. She waited anxiously for her turn to update the group on what she and

Weston were working on. There were some unexpected findings related to Ambassador King, and they had to figure out what was really going on.

Director Phillips strode into the room, full of confidence as usual, and slammed some folders on the table before setting down his extra-large coffee mug. "I better hear some good updates this morning. Talk to me." He looked out at the room, awaiting an answer.

The room was silent for a moment, as no one necessarily wanted to be the first to speak. Jacob finally broke the silence. "Sir, as you know, we've had some major developments. For the benefit of the whole group, we should probably brief them, if that's okay with you."

Lang nodded. "Go ahead."

Jacob surveyed the room. "The other night Viv was attacked by two men when she thought she was going to meet Samir from the Egyptian embassy for coffee. We now know that Viv was contacted via text message by someone posing as Samir to draw her out. Samir denied all responsibility, and we believe him. What we don't know is why these two men went through the trouble to concoct this ruse and attack Viv."

Delaney looked at Vivian and now saw the unmistakable bruising on her face that she hadn't initially noticed at a quick glance. Delaney had gotten a vague text from the director the other night, but she hadn't understood how serious this was until now. And she had a lot of questions.

"Let me get this straight. You're saying that someone posed as a contact from the Egyptian embassy to lure you out and assault you?" Delaney asked. "Did they steal anything from you? Did they say anything?"

Viv nodded. "They took my phone. My wallet was in

my jacket pocket, so they didn't get that, but I was wearing a crossbody bag, and they literally ripped that off of me."

Delaney glanced at Jacob, who looked like he was about to blow.

Viv kept going. "They didn't say anything at all to me, not a single word, but they were extremely violent—both of them. I was no match for two men. If it hadn't been for some guy walking by and stopping them, I truly don't know what would've happened. I might not be sitting here with you."

Jacob stood. "And that's what bothers me the most. If this was a hit job and they failed, that means someone will most likely be back to finish it, but we don't know who was behind it."

"What if they were just trying to shake Vivian up? Send some sort of message?" Weston asked. "If they wanted to kill her, it's clear they could've just shot her or slit her throat or something. It was two against one."

"Unless they wanted her to die a slow, painful death," Jacob said flatly.

Vivian's face drained of all its color, but she didn't speak.

Lang cleared his throat. "What we've got is a lot of theories and speculation, but we're really thin on facts. However, given the evident threat level, I've told Jacob that he is going to be on protective duty for Vivian. I've also spoken to Vivian, and to her credit she does not want to stop working the case. For now I'll allow that, but of course I'm subject to changing my mind if the facts on the ground alter."

Delaney thought it might be a bad idea for Vivian to stay on the task force as an active team member, but she would never challenge the director. Instead, she took a different tack. "We have to assume, don't we, that this is connected, right? The Egyptian ambassador supposedly has a heart attack,

Vivian starts investigating, including reaching out to her contact at the embassy, and then the attack happens. Maybe there's some type of cover-up at play. A big one, and they don't want Vivian poking around. How deep do we want to get into internal Egyptian politics?"

"As deep as we have to get," Lang responded.

Viv nodded. "It's possible it could be some of the anti-democratic forces within Egypt. The same people we've been targeting as suspects from the list Samir gave us. Maybe they somehow knew that Samir gave us leads and wanted to stop everything right then and there."

Jacob paced around the room. "Anyone else have any ideas?"

Rania tapped her pen on the desk. "I've been working closely with my contacts at the CIA, and we've been able to track some of the men pretty closely on Samir's list—most of whom are not currently in the US. I think this theory we're weaving makes a lot of sense, given the current political climate in Egypt. The country may seem somewhat stable on the surface, but underneath it's a powder keg. And we might've gotten involved in it more than we realized. When Vivian made a very public visit to the embassy, that could've set off red flags. Maybe whoever is behind this thought the heart attack angle would easily hold and doesn't want the US government poking its nose in."

"What about me?" Jacob asked.

"They could've assumed you're just the muscle," Rania said. "No offense, but you definitely give off that vibe, and you're in diplomatic security. They might not see you as actually being operational."

"Well, I want all hands on deck on this. We still need answers to tell the Egyptians, but we also have to cover our own hides," Lang said. "I'm juggling quite a few balls in the air here. As you can imagine, the White House has an interest in this, given our close relationship with Egypt."

"Understood, sir," Jacob said. "We'll get to the bottom of this, and I'll make sure Viv is safe in the meantime."

Lang looked up. "Delaney, what do you have? Hopefully something promising to go on?"

Delaney took a breath. "Depends on how you define promising, sir. We've been conducting interviews with many of Ambassador King's friends and family, including one of the ambassador's oldest friends and her husband. We found out there has been a history of infidelity on the ambassador's side. We ran down the men Jeff King knew about, but none of them seem like possible suspects here. Jeff's knowledge of the repeated affairs makes us think he could be a suspect as the scorned and jealous husband. When we interviewed him, however, we thought he could be clean."

Lang scoffed. "And let me guess, that didn't pan out?"

"It's a bit more complicated than that, sir. We've uncovered some financial transactions that look very suspicious in the ambassador's personal offshore bank account. A series of large deposits over the past few months. We don't know why she would've been getting that influx of cash or from whom."

Lang frowned. "The last thing I want is us making accusations about our ambassador as she lies in the hospital. Continue trying to get the answers, but keep this close to your vests. I expect zero leaks coming out of this room. Does everyone understand that?"

"Yes, sir," Delaney answered.

"But I want the truth even if it's ugly," Lang continued. "Let me be the one who has to handle any fallout."

"We're working hard here on all the leads you guys are sending us. Nothing too small. Remember that." Cody looked at Delaney.

Unfortunately, she was already giving the team everything they had. It just wasn't much. She could only hope and pray that it would be enough to crack these cases before it was too late and someone else got hurt or, worse, ended up dead.

CHAPTER
EIGHT

"**I've got a plan of attack** for the day." Jacob walked by Viv's side as they exited the war room.

She looked at her watch and realized she needed to head to the coffee shop to meet Mark. "There's actually something I need to do now."

Jacob raised an eyebrow. "What?"

"I'm meeting Mark—the guy who saved me—for coffee. It's just at Coffee Cups. I'll be fine. I'll be back around eleven."

Jacob grabbed her arm and pulled her to a stop. "I don't think you understand this protective detail thing at all. If you go, I go."

She thought he was being a bit paranoid. "Jacob, it's two blocks from here. I go there all the time. It's safe. It's broad daylight."

He sighed. "Nothing is safe for you right now. *Nothing.*"

She stared into his dark eyes. "Really?" Her voice cracked.

"I am trying not to freak you out. I know you went through

a pretty severe attack, but if I have to scare you by speaking the truth, then I will. We have to make sure you are safe. We don't know what the end game is yet, but I know for certain that you play a role in it."

"All right. Well, I can't stand the guy up. He saved my life." There was no way she would bail on him like that.

"I'll come with you. It'll be fine. I'll sit at a different table. You won't even realize I'm there."

She highly doubted that. His presence was obvious in every situation.

They didn't speak much on the short walk to Coffee Cups, and for that she was grateful. Sometimes quiet was good. It gave her time to think.

"There he is." She discreetly pointed.

Jacob placed his hand on her shoulder. "Okay. I'll be over here if you need anything."

"I'll be fine."

She walked toward Mark, and he smiled when he saw her. In the daylight and not in a time of shock, she could see more of his features. She remembered those almond-brown eyes instantly.

"Viv, so good to see you." Mark stretched out his hand, and she took it.

"Great to see you too."

"You're looking better than the last time I saw you. How're you feeling?"

"Let's grab coffee, and we can talk. My treat, of course." There was no way she would let him pay. This was her tangible thank-you.

After a few minutes, they had coffee and croissants and sat down at a corner table still clearly within Jacob's line of sight.

"Hey, Viv, do you know that guy over there on the other side of the shop? He's watching you like a hawk."

She sighed. So much for Jacob being inconspicuous. "Yes. I work with him, and right now he's doing double duty as my security detail, for lack of a better word."

Mark's eyes widened. "They're taking this really seriously then, huh?"

"Yeah."

He took a sip of coffee. "That must mean they don't think it was random."

She looked down, trying to figure out how much to tell him. "I'm really not at liberty to say much, but there is a possibility that the attack was linked to my work at the State Department. We don't know yet."

"Wow. Who knew State Department lawyers were at risk like that? I know I didn't."

She gave him a little smile. "Well, honestly, we aren't normally. My job is usually under the radar and far from glamorous."

He chuckled. "I get that. I feel like half of my job is being locked in my office, reading and writing briefs and motions."

"You actually get to litigate though, right?" She enjoyed talking lawyer shop.

He nodded. "I do. My practice is general commercial litigation. Since I left the big firm years ago, though, the dollar value of my cases is a bit lower. Still large, but not the astronomical amounts they were at the firm. Do you miss not being able to try cases?"

She shook her head. "No. I always knew I was going to do some sort of public-policy job. Battling it out in the courtroom isn't my strong suit. I hate arguing." She laughed.

He gave her a big smile. "It's good to see you laughing.

I won't lie, you had me really worried that night. I've never experienced anything like that."

The memories hit her hard. "I'm sorry about that."

He grabbed her hand. "There's no need to apologize. I didn't mean it like that at all." He pulled his hand away. "I just meant it was a really scary situation, and I'm thankful you've pushed through it."

Even without him bringing it up, she relived the attack far too often. She wondered if that would get better with time. "And I'm thankful you were there at just the right time." She blew out a breath. "It was easier talking about our jobs."

Mark laughed. "If I've learned one thing over the years, it's that lawyers love to talk about being lawyers."

She appreciated that he was trying to lighten the mood. "Honestly, buying you coffee and a croissant doesn't seem like enough for what you did."

"I would've done it regardless of the thank-you or lack of one. I just acted on pure instinct. Watching it unfold right in front of me was scary for me too."

"I get what you're saying about instinct. I've learned to trust my gut more and more."

"In your work or in your life?"

She considered that for a moment. "Both, actually. I think with age we learn to trust ourselves more."

He laughed again. "It's not like you're that old, Viv."

"I'm older than I look. I've always had a young face." She looked down at her watch.

"I know you're incredibly busy and need to get back to work, and so do I." He took his last sip of coffee before standing up. "And your muscle is on the move."

She grinned as she looked over her shoulder and saw Jacob at the ready. "Thanks again for everything. If there's anything I can ever do to help you out, please don't hesitate to ask."

Mark touched her arm. "Maybe we'll see each other again sometime."

"I'd like that." What was she supposed to say? Had this just gone from a thank-you coffee to a date?

Thankfully, Jacob approached, and Mark waved and walked away.

"Well, that looked like a lot more than coffee to me," Jacob said.

She batted that idea away even though she had started to think the same thing. "Don't be silly. It's not like that."

His eyes narrowed. "Maybe not for you, but definitely for him."

"It's beside the point. I thanked him for what he did, and now we can get back to work."

"Do you know anything about this guy?"

"He's a lawyer."

"Great." Jacob didn't hide his sarcasm.

"Hey now, remember Mark's one of the good guys. Regardless, I doubt I'll see him again anytime soon. I'm too busy for anything like that anyway."

Jacob didn't look convinced, but he let it go.

She had a lot bigger problems than her nonexistent love life.

◆

Jacob sat with Viv in her office and thought about what had just happened. He hadn't liked the looks of that Mark guy. The way he kept laughing and touching Viv. But then it hit him that he shouldn't care the least bit about their flirtation. So why did he?

Whether he wanted to admit it to himself or not, Viv had gotten under his skin. He'd done a good job of keeping her at arm's length even after the attack, but he wasn't sure how to process what he was starting to feel for her. The more time he spent with her, the more she had, without even trying, started to pull down his walls. And that was what bothered him the most. It was like she was oblivious to how she impacted others, and surprisingly for a lawyer, she didn't appear to have a mean bone in her body.

After her attack, he'd jumped into protector mode, but now he was wondering if he was the one who needed protecting from her.

"What are you staring at?" Viv asked him.

"That picture of you." He pointed. "I can't put my finger on it, but it seems off to me."

Viv smiled.

"What?" he asked.

"You're the first person ever to notice."

He was confused. "Notice what?"

"That's not me."

He leaned over and pulled the framed picture into his hands. "Who is it?"

"My twin sister, Willow."

"You have a twin?"

She grinned. "Yes, I do."

"Is she as difficult to deal with as you are?" he half joked.

"Actually, she's much worse." Viv laughed.

"Then I don't know how I could handle her." As he watched her laugh and smile, he checked himself again.

"She is quite something, but she has a huge heart."

He smirked. "She's not a lawyer, then."

She shook her head. "No way. She works for a nonprofit

on humanitarian missions all over the place. She's a save-the-world type through and through. Right now, she's working with refugees on the border between Turkey and Syria."

"Are you close?" He asked the question before he could think it through.

Viv looked down. "Yes, even though we don't talk all the time, given our crazy schedules. We lost our parents, so it's just the two of us."

He softened, as he could tell this was a painful topic for her. "I'm sorry about that." He wanted to shift the conversation back. "To me, it seems like you're a save-the-world type too."

"Maybe. But she is much bolder in her approach than I'll ever be."

"Don't sell yourself short."

Her eyes opened wide. "Wait a minute. Are you actually defending me? I never thought I'd see the day."

He smiled. "I know I'm the one who got us sidetracked, but let's get back to the plan."

She arched an eyebrow. "Which is?"

"We still need to talk about your CIA op." That was front and center in his mind.

Viv leaned forward. "You heard the director. The first order of business is trying to find out if the attack was linked to the ambassador's death."

They'd had a private talk with him offline, given the sensitive nature of the operation, and Jacob had heard the director loud and clear, but he wanted to keep all options open. "We need to talk to Samir again. I just need to figure out the best secure way to make that happen. Maybe we should invite him here."

She shook her head. "He'll have an entourage. They won't let him come here alone."

"We'll just have to deal with that. I'm sure we can separate him somehow. Leave that to me." He had to ask, though. "If Samir is on the side of the Egyptian president and his supporters, why would he have to be watched so closely?"

"Because the president is really paranoid and doesn't trust anyone. Don't get me wrong—he still has his staunch allies, and he would protect them. Samir is in that group, but the president doesn't take chances. And he especially won't now after Ambassador Zidan's death."

"Another question."

"Shoot."

He needed more operational details to really evaluate what was going on here. "How many other people were involved in the Egyptian op?"

Viv bit her bottom lip. "We kept it really small. Layla planned the op and ran logistics from Langley. There was a CIA security team on the ground with me, plus translators."

He lifted a hand. "Wait a minute. You were in the field?"

She nodded. "I had to supervise the transfer of the detainees. I thought it was paramount that legal counsel be there. That was the whole point."

"People saw your face." This was getting worse by the minute.

"I wasn't trying to hide my role, Jacob. I'm an attorney, not CIA. I have a public role with the State Department."

He blew out a breath. "That's not the point. Do you realize how many CIA officers have public State Department covers?"

She frowned. "Yeah, I guess I did know that. Just like Layla."

"Did you have direct interaction with any of the detainees?"

"Of course I did. I spoke to each of them, sometimes with a translator, since I don't speak Arabic."

"Who was the translator?"

Viv shrugged. "I'm not sure. It was a CIA contractor. A guy. What're you getting at?"

Jacob thought before he spoke, because once he put it out there, it was one more thing for Viv to be worried about. But he couldn't hold back. Not on something like this. "I'm concerned that someone has identified you as being part of the op and is now seeking retribution."

She sat silently for a moment. "Like I said, I was there in a purely legal capacity. I did my job as a lawyer."

"C'mon, Viv. These guys couldn't care less about that. What they do know is that you were involved, and their grand plan got disrupted. Get it?"

"Yeah," she said softly.

"Play this out with me, okay?"

She nodded.

"You go and visit your old buddy Samir at the embassy, and someone there recognizes you. They let whoever is in charge know that you were there to see Samir. They positively identify you as being involved in the detainee transfer and then decide to come after you."

"Why not just kill me, though, if it's all about revenge?"

"Maybe there's a bigger play here we're not seeing."

"Or we're seeing things that don't even exist. Maybe whoever is behind the attack on the ambassador found out I was talking to Samir, and they wanted to get me out of commission because they think I have some sort of special knowledge about the case." She trailed off.

"Which is why it's critical we talk to Samir again."

"I can call him." She picked up her phone and dialed his number. "It's his voicemail."

"Ask him to call you back." He listened as Viv left the voice message.

"Now what?" she asked.

"I want you to go through the documents we have on the men from Samir's files and see if you recognize any of them as the detainees you were with."

"That I can handle, but I assume we don't have pictures of everyone Samir named."

Jacob shook his head. "No, or not very good ones, but let's review what we have."

After two hours poring over documents and pictures, they hadn't made much progress.

"I don't know. It's really hard to be sure. You have to remember that when I was with those men, I wasn't focusing on trying to remember their every feature. I was thinking about how they were being treated and whether we were following all necessary protocols."

Eyewitness identification was tricky under any circumstances, and this was a lot more problematic than most. "I understand. We'll figure this out." Nothing seemed easy about this investigation.

Viv's office phone rang, and she picked it up.

After a second, she frowned and pushed the speaker button. "It's Layla. She has something to tell us. Go on, Layla."

"I have bad news. I just got a call from my contact at the Egyptian embassy. There's no easy way to say this."

"Just spit it out," Jacob said.

"Samir has been murdered."

CHAPTER
NINE

Viv felt numb as she sat in her office and looked at Layla and Jacob. "Are you sure your sources are right, Layla?" Her friend had rushed over to State to share more details in person.

Layla nodded. "I'm so sorry, Viv. Samir was killed in his home last night."

"How?"

Layla didn't immediately respond, and Viv felt the sickness growing in the pit of her stomach.

"That bad?" Jacob asked.

"His throat was slit," Layla said flatly. "And it appears he was tortured before his death."

Viv's eyes filled with tears. "This is madness."

"Is the Egyptian president stepping up his security?" Jacob asked.

Layla nodded. "Yes, and unfortunately, I fear he's going to be a bit draconian in his approach to try to ferret out traitors.

Two of his biggest allies in the government are dead, and he has to wonder if he's next."

Viv could barely put her thoughts together. Samir had always been such a kind man. And now he was dead. Why?

"Viv, you're pale," Layla said. "Are you okay?"

"No! I'm not okay. None of this is okay. This is crazy. We have to stop this."

Jacob cleared his throat. "Layla, could I talk to Viv for a moment alone?"

Layla raised an eyebrow but didn't object. "I'll run to the break room and get some coffee." She walked out of the office and shut the door behind her.

Jacob turned to Viv. "Look. You're not cut out for this type of thing."

She let out a little laugh that didn't hold any humor. "Of course I'm not, but it appears I'm right in the middle of it, doesn't it?" She tried to keep her emotions in check, but she was failing. How had her world gone from relatively mundane to deadly so quickly?

Jacob touched her arm. "That's exactly my point. We need to get you out of this ASAP. I'm going to suggest to the director that you get pulled from the task force and placed in protective custody."

She moved away from him. "No. I have to see this through. I can't go the rest of my life looking over my shoulder. I worked really hard to build this career. We need to get to the bottom of this so we have answers. Definitive answers. My hiding in a hole somewhere isn't going to get us to the truth."

"At the risk of losing your life? Of being tortured like your friend Samir?"

She recoiled. "You didn't have to say that."

His eyes narrowed. "Actually, I did, because after all of this, I still don't think you realize how dangerous this situation is—especially to you personally. These guys aren't messing around."

She didn't want to think of it like that. "We don't know for sure that it's all connected."

"You're in denial," he shot back.

She had to find a middle road fast before Jacob got her removed from the task force. "There has to be a way I can keep working. Please. I can't turn away from this."

Jacob ran a hand through his hair. "Are you dead set on this?" He cut her off before she could answer. "Of course you are."

"You're getting to know me pretty well."

He gave her a halfhearted smile. "We still need to step up the security at your condo. And that's just a start. We should ask Layla to come back." He stood and returned a couple of minutes later with her friend.

"I was just talking to Viv about stepping up her security," he was saying as they came in the door, "and you should warn anyone else who was on the ground for the op. Based on everything I'm seeing, I think this could all be connected."

"I want to say something." Viv looked them both in the eyes. "There is still a chance this isn't related to our detainee operation, but that the radical forces in Egypt killed Ambassador Zidan and are now trying to take out the other moderating forces."

"And your attack?" Jacob asked.

"They don't want the US government messing in their business. They saw me at the embassy. They want me to back off. What better way to send a pretty drastic signal?"

Layla looked at her. "I think both theories have merit,

and Jacob is right. You need to be on high alert. I'm going to debrief my boss so he knows the latest."

Viv didn't want anything to happen to her best friend. She gave Layla a hug. "Please be careful."

Layla smiled. "I've got this covered. I'm not the one with the target on my back." She turned to Jacob. "Watch out for her. You got it?"

"Roger that."

Viv wondered what the next days would hold and if anyone else was going to end up dead.

◆

Delaney dreaded confronting Jeff King about what they'd found in his wife's finances, but they had no other choice.

"Do you want me to take the lead?" Weston asked.

"Sure." Not only would it give him experience, it would be good for her, too, as she could watch Jeff's reactions closely. She wasn't sure what his role was in this tangled mess. There were too many unknowns at this point. Did Jeff know about these deposits in his wife's account?

This wasn't a run-of-the-mill case, and the political implications had not escaped her. If the ambassador had gotten herself involved in something questionable, it would be bad for everyone.

She'd made the decision to talk to Jeff at the hospital again so as not to drag him away from Penelope. They were back down in the cafeteria when Jeff arrived and took a seat.

"You said it was important. Have you had a breakthrough in the case?" His eyes widened.

"Not exactly," Delaney said. She looked at Weston, giving him the okay to proceed.

"Mr. King."

"Please just call me Jeff."

"Jeff." Weston shifted in his seat. "We have some information we need to share with you that is quite troubling."

Jeff's face fell. "I was hoping for some good news. I could really use it. Things are looking desperate for my wife."

Weston opened a large manila folder, took out a couple of pages, and slid them across the table. "Do you recognize this as one of your wife's bank accounts?"

"How did you get this?" Jeff suddenly went on the defensive.

"Through purely legal means." Weston leaned in. "Please answer my question."

Weston was already ratcheting up the tension, and Delaney was interested to see how this was going to play out.

Jeff rubbed his chin and scanned the document. "I recognize the account, yes, but there has to be some mistake. I have no idea where these deposits came from."

Delaney couldn't help herself. She had to jump in. "Just to be perfectly clear, you're saying that you knew your wife kept an offshore bank account in her name only, but you had no knowledge about these influxes of cash?"

Jeff's eyes met hers. "Right. Penelope kept this as a savings account." He paused. "Or at least that's what she told me."

"You sound like you're doubting your wife," Weston said.

Jeff bit his bottom lip. "I thought things were much better between us, but given what you're showing me, I'm wondering if I was wrong. What was she hiding?"

Delaney wanted to empathize with him, but she also had a job to do. "We need you to think. Is there anything your wife could've been involved in that would explain these deposits over the last couple of months?"

Jeff's eyes narrowed. "Are you insinuating that Penelope was involved in something illegal?"

He'd made the jump for her. "That's what we're trying to find out. If she was, then that could provide the motive for whoever tried to kill her."

Jeff stared off into space. "I'm not sure what to say. You've thrown me for a loop."

"Let's take a step back, then. You said you moved to Brussels with her?" Weston asked.

"About six months ago. So she was there two and a half years without me."

"And she never mentioned that she experienced any problems or came into contact with any unsavory characters who were looking for favors?" Delaney asked.

Jeff frowned. "No. She really didn't discuss her work with me. As I told you before, living in Brussels was nice. It was a far cry from her earlier jobs. I didn't think there were any problems, but after all of this, I'm wondering if I missed something big."

"Was she secretive at all beyond the necessary discretion for her work?" Weston asked.

Jeff blew out a breath. "Penelope was always stepping away to take calls, but I understood that went with the territory. Honestly, I didn't give it a second thought."

"We're going to need some time to look into all of this." Delaney wanted to make one thing clear. "But if you remember anything that could be relevant, we need to know ASAP."

Jeff's shoulders slumped. "I'm basically living here, so you'll know where to find me." He still looked defeated as he walked away from them.

She turned to Weston. "Do you believe him?"

"Maybe he knows the truth but doesn't want to admit it. Money doesn't just appear out of thin air."

"We're missing something. That money had to come from somewhere, and I'm guessing it's nowhere good."

Weston tapped his fingers on the table. "The million-dollar question is, Who is behind it?"

"We should set up a meeting with Cody. We're going to need his help digging into this Brussels avenue and seeing what she could've been up to over there. I don't know about you, but I know very little about Belgium."

Weston nodded. "Same here."

She stood and buttoned her suit jacket. "Let's talk to the expert, then."

◆

"I'm going to need to do a full security work-up of your place." Jacob looked at a weary Viv as they headed toward her condo.

"I understand. You can knock yourself out. I have a basic alarm system."

As they stood in front of her building, Jacob gave a low whistle. "You didn't tell me you were loaded."

Viv laughed. "I'm not. My parents bought this place with a chunk of their savings a month before they died, and they left it to me. Living here somehow makes me feel closer to them."

"What did your twin get?"

She looked up at him. "Money. They knew she would put it to good use and that real estate wasn't her thing. I could definitely make money off this place if I rented it out, but I just didn't want to do that. You probably think it's silly."

He softened. "No. Not silly at all."

"Let's go in."

"You have a doorman."

She smiled at him. "I know."

"That's good. I'll take any additional security we can get."

He followed her lead as they went up to the seventeenth floor.

"This is me." She unlocked the door, and he followed right behind her as she shut off the alarm.

He took a moment and let himself adjust to his surroundings. This was a far cry from the places he'd lived. "This is amazing."

"The view is one of the best parts. Let me show you." She grabbed his hand to lead him deeper into the condo. He didn't break away even though he should have. In fact, he was a little bummed when she eventually let go.

He stared out the large living room window with an amazing view of the Potomac and Key Bridge. "Wow. The view is out of this world. You really could make a killing on this place." He paused, thinking that was a bad choice of words given the circumstances, but she didn't seem fazed.

"I know, but I love it." She sighed.

He could see that the condo was much more than a material possession for her. "I don't blame you. It makes you feel connected to your parents. Show me the rest of it."

She took him on the tour, and he found two bedrooms, a large office, two baths, plus the living and dining room spaces. They ended in the enormous kitchen.

"This island is the size of my entire kitchen," he said.

Viv laughed. "I know it's a bit much for one person, but hopefully I won't be alone forever."

"Why would you even think that?" Viv was definitely not the type of woman who needed to worry about finding someone special.

She groaned. "Well, I'm thirty-one and I haven't found anyone yet."

"No one serious?"

"Not really. It's embarrassing to admit, but after a couple of dates, things just usually fade. Or the guys end up being total jerks. My two best friends have found someone, so now I'm the last woman standing." She laughed again.

He couldn't believe they were having this conversation. Why had he opened this door? What was wrong with him?

"What about you?" she asked.

This was his fault for bringing this up to begin with, so he couldn't blame her for making polite conversation. "As you could probably surmise, I'm not exactly good relationship material. I've got a lot of baggage."

"We all do," she said softly.

He needed to redirect this quickly. "Do you mind if I keep looking around for a minute? I just want to think about the new security plan."

"Sure." She smiled. "Make yourself at home."

While he did want to evaluate the condo's security, he also needed to put a little distance between the two of them. He wasn't getting any vibes from her that she felt attracted to him—and that was all the more reason to box up these crazy feelings and focus on additional security for her place.

He took his time moving from room to room. He was concerned about exit strategies. The high floor was a blessing and a curse. Clearly there was no going out the window, but that also meant it would be almost impossible to get in that way too.

By the time he was finished, he found her sitting on the sofa in the living room with her feet tucked underneath her and the news on the TV.

"So? What do you think?" she asked.

"In many ways, I like it."

She raised an eyebrow. "But?"

"I worry about safe and quick exit options. Are you familiar with the stairs?"

She laughed. "Yes, but I usually use the elevator."

"I want to upgrade your security system. I'm not sure if we can get the government to cover the cost or not."

She nodded. "Probably not, but regardless, it's an investment, so I'm willing to pay for it."

"Okay. I can get you some estimates. I'll install it myself, so there won't be any charge there."

"What if I made you dinner to thank you? Are you hungry?"

Actually, he was starving, but he was having a great internal debate over whether to stay or go.

"Please, let me," Viv said.

The *please* slayed him. He was doomed.

Viv couldn't believe she'd asked Jacob to stay for dinner. Thankfully, she had some chicken in the fridge and was able to whip up her parmesan lemon chicken with angel hair pasta. Jacob devoured the food as if he hadn't eaten in days. Good thing she'd made a lot in hopes that he'd have a large appetite.

"What now?" she asked.

"We should probably call it a night." He looked away.

"No, I meant next steps for the investigation."

"Oh yeah, right. First thing tomorrow, I'm going to work on the security system upgrades. Then we're going to figure out if there's anyone else on the Egyptian side we can trust.

We need visibility into what's going on now that Samir is gone."

"Very true. Are you doing okay, Jacob?"

He looked at her. "Yeah, why do you ask?"

"You've seemed a bit off tonight, that's all." She wasn't sure if he was getting tired of playing babysitter already or what. While he wasn't hostile toward her, he'd definitely turned cool. And she'd thought they had started to make progress on being able to be in the same room without wanting to kill each other.

"Sorry. Just a lot on my mind, that's all. I have to thank you for dinner. I know I ate like a monster, but it was so good."

She smiled. "I'm glad you enjoyed it."

"I know my way around the kitchen, but I'm not that great."

"You're welcome for dinner anytime."

A knock on the door made Jacob jump out of his chair. "I'll go check on that. I assume you're not expecting any-one?"

"No." She followed close behind him.

"Who is it?" Jacob asked.

"Delivery for Ms. Steele."

She watched as Jacob looked through the peephole and then opened the door and stepped into the hall.

He returned with a large vase of flowers. "I guess these are for you." He handed them to her.

"I can't imagine who would've sent them."

The bright tulips were beautiful, and she eagerly pulled the card off and read the message.

Dinner tomorrow night at 7? I'll call you and hope you say yes.

—Mark

Jacob leaned over her shoulder. "See, I told you that guy was interested."

"It's not practical right now."

"I'm not saying it's the best idea in the world, but if you want to go, I can be your wingman. I'll make sure you're safe."

Viv felt very conflicted. "It was very sweet of him, but I need to sleep on it."

Jacob checked everything one last time, even though she knew it was unnecessary, and then he left her alone. As flattered as she was by Mark's invitation, she wasn't sure she felt that kind of connection to him. There weren't any sparks or butterflies. None of the type of chemistry she wanted.

Suddenly, she realized what she was doing. Comparing Mark to Jacob. How had that happened? When had she started to have feelings for Jacob?

◆

That night after work, Delaney set out on her daily run on Mount Vernon Trail. This was her own time. Her time to think about her cases or just not to think at all. To blast music and try to escape the reality of her personal situation that many days threatened to overtake her.

Although tonight she was annoyed because she'd left her headphones at home by accident, so she was forced to deal with the sounds around her and the harsh truth. She was alone. She missed Ryan every single day. She no longer cried all the time like she had at first, but that didn't mean she was free of pain or grief.

She wondered if there would come a time when it wouldn't hurt. Two years later, it still was painful, but she had made a lot of progress working through her grief. Ryan's murder was so senseless, but he had been doing what he loved to do. There was no way he would have given up his job as an FBI agent, even if someone had told him what was going to happen to him. Ryan faced things head on. It was one of his many wonderful qualities.

But here she was, unsure whether she was going to spend the rest of her life alone or not. There was no replacing Ryan. It was utterly impossible. But she was beginning to question whether there was space in her heart and life for companionship with someone else. Ryan wouldn't have wanted her to be single forever—and that wasn't just conjecture. Given both of their jobs, they'd had the talk right after they married about what if something happened to either of them. They had both agreed that they would want the other to find someone else to spend their life with when the time was right. The big question for her was whether there would ever be a right time.

She heard a noise behind her and glanced over her shoulder. It was still barely light, and she didn't see anything out of the ordinary, so she kept running. And thinking. Getting lost in her own thoughts was dangerous but something she did far too often.

After a few more minutes, she couldn't shake the feeling that something was wrong. She stopped for a moment to catch her breath and survey her surroundings. There were other runners, dog walkers, and a few casual walkers. No threats that she could identify. So why did she feel so off-kilter all of a sudden? She couldn't disregard the uneasy feeling that someone was watching her. And after the experience with the truck tailing them, she couldn't just write it off.

Given where she was on the trail, she had no choice but to keep running. But she also needed to play this smart. She pulled her phone out of the pocket of her jogging pants and called Weston.

"Delaney, what's up?"

"Hey. I'm on Mount Vernon Trail for my jog, and I feel like someone is watching me."

"Where exactly are you? I can be there in a few minutes."

"Just meet me back at my place."

"How far out are you?"

"Probably twenty minutes." She could cut that down if she really sped up, but she didn't know if that was necessary.

"I'll meet you there. Do you want to keep the line open?" Weston asked.

She considered it for a moment, but it seemed like overkill. "No. I'll be okay. See you in a few."

Taking a deep breath, she pushed her body to run faster. And reminded herself that she wasn't out here all alone. Other people were around. Nothing was going to happen.

But if something did, she'd be in trouble because her sidearm was at home. She wasn't going to go running unarmed anymore.

By the time she made it home, Weston was parked outside her house. He got out of the car and jogged over to her. "Are you okay?"

She bent over, trying to catch her breath. "Yeah. My gun is in my safe, though. Can we check out my place just in case?"

"Definitely." He drew his gun. "You should wait in my car. I'll clear your place and then come get you."

"No. I'm coming with you."

He shook his head. "Not without a weapon, you aren't."

She moved closer to him. "Give me your backup. I know you have it in your ankle holster."

Weston frowned, but he retrieved his other gun and gave it to her. "I'm still going in first."

She wasn't used to this take-charge attitude from Weston, but it was good to see. He had a lot of potential.

She followed him up her porch. "Door is unlocked," he said.

"That can't be right." She pushed forward with him, expecting the worst as she entered her house, but it looked normal.

She checked the alarm system. It had been disabled. "Whoever was in here knew what they were doing."

They cleared her home room by room. "Weston, nothing looks disturbed." She even checked her safe, and everything was intact.

"Why would someone break into your home and leave it untouched?"

She thought for a minute. "Because they want me to know they were here. First, the truck tailing us, and now this. What if someone is trying to communicate?"

Weston raised an eyebrow. "Strange way of doing it. Why not just talk face-to-face?"

"Because for some reason they can't."

Weston started pacing around her living room. "You think this has to do with Ambassador King?"

"Don't you?" she asked.

He stopped and faced her. "What if it's not? What if you have a stalker or something? You need to take this as a threat and report it to the director."

"I understand your concern, but we have to be open to my theory as well. If I'm right, I need to figure out a way to open the lines of communication with this person."

"And how would that happen?" he asked.

Good question. "I'll think about it."

Weston scowled. "I don't know, Delaney. Someone broke into your home. They invaded your space. I don't like it. Do you want me to stay here tonight?"

"That won't be necessary. I'll be fine. I've got my gun."

Weston put his hand on her shoulder. "I'd feel a lot better. Please. Let me do this for you as a friend. And as your partner."

She was worried he wouldn't accept no for an answer, and she had more than enough room for him. "Okay. Sure."

"See, I knew that go bag you told me to have would come in handy at some point."

She couldn't help but smile. She really cared for Weston. He was like family—the little brother she never had. It felt good to know someone had her back.

CHAPTER
TEN

The next morning, Delaney sat with Weston and Cody in the war room. They had just finished filling him in on what had happened to her last night.

Cody was frowning deeply. "This is out of my wheelhouse, to say the least, but shouldn't you have a stronger reaction to someone following you and being inside your home?"

It was a perfectly reasonable question. "I'm being careful. Weston stayed at my place last night as an extra precaution, and I've reported everything to the director."

"I'm worried that Delaney has a stalker," Weston said, "but she's convinced that some phantom is trying to communicate with her about the case."

Cody drummed his fingers on the desk. "If Delaney is right, there would have to be a reason for this person to operate in the shadows."

Delaney opened her notebook. "That brings us to our latest thoughts on the case that we need to share with you." She got him up to speed on their working theories on the ambassador.

"You think the ambassador got herself into some type of trouble in Brussels?" Cody typed quickly on his laptop.

"Possibly," Delaney said. "But Weston and I are totally out of our area of expertise here because we don't know anything about the situation on the ground in Brussels. We need you to give us some background so we can figure out the best roads to go down. That money didn't just magically appear in her offshore bank account, and in my experience, the explanation usually isn't aboveboard. We've got our financial analysts working on tracing it, but in the meantime, we need to explore other avenues."

His dark eyes met hers. "Got it. Off the top of my head, the most likely thing that could fit this scenario is organized crime."

"That's a big thing in Belgium?" Weston asked.

Cody typed again for a moment, and then a map appeared on the screen on the wall. "Belgium is a small country. Landlocked in the center of Europe. It's actually one of the European hot spots of organized crime."

"What kind are we talking?" Weston stood and looked at the map.

Cody glanced at her before looking at Weston. "Drugs are at the top of the list, followed by arms trafficking."

Delaney was trying to get her head around this. "Let's play this scenario out. What could the US ambassador to Belgium have gotten into with an organized-crime group?"

Cody leaned in. "Ambassadors wield a lot of power and influence. Maybe they approached her for some type of assistance, and then she got something in return."

"Like a kickback," Weston said.

"Yeah. You scratch my back, I'll scratch yours," Cody said. "But maybe she got in too deep."

Delaney wasn't sure about this. "But what would the ambassador be able to provide? Political favors?"

"Yes. For example, organized-crime groups often have legitimate front businesses. She could've been called on to help in that way," Cody offered.

Delaney had another thought. "Is it possible she could've been working with any other authorities as an informant or something like that?"

Cody frowned. "It would be highly unusual for a US ambassador to work with a foreign law enforcement authority and the US not know about it. And to take money on top of that would be a big no-no."

"True, but we need to reach out to our Interpol contacts and check." If this investigation was showing her anything, it was that the normal assumptions might not apply, and they simply couldn't afford to get this wrong.

"It's good to check, but I can't really see a world in which she could've been doing that. If so, why would she have hidden it?" Cody asked. "As much as I hate to admit it, the facts are looking more like the ambassador is the problem here."

She knew Cody was right, but she could always hold out hope. "I understand."

Weston stood. "I'll go make some calls to people at the FBI with key Interpol contacts."

Delaney was glad to see Weston taking the initiative. "Good."

He exited, leaving her alone with Cody.

"You're frowning," Cody said.

"One of the things I love most about my job is putting together the pieces and connecting the dots, but something about this case is driving me up the wall."

Cody leaned in. "How so?"

"If the ambassador did get tangled up with organized crime, then why kill her in the US? Wouldn't it have been less risky to do it in Brussels?"

"Maybe they thought there'd be less connection to them if they did it here," Cody suggested.

"True, but I still feel like there's a puzzle piece—a big one—that we're not seeing just yet. I'm not sold on this organized-crime theory."

"We'll figure it out." Cody paused. "I hope I'm not talking out of turn here, but Weston has a point. You should be careful. We can't just assume that whatever happened to you last night is connected to this case."

"Thanks for the concern. I promise I'll be careful. I know I don't have any evidence, but I'm going on a hunch."

He smiled. "I know you can take care of yourself. All of this just has me a bit on edge."

"That's understandable. We're all on edge, but we're going to get to the bottom of this."

"I've seen how you all operate. I have the utmost confidence in the FBI."

She hated not knowing all the facts, but that was often the story of her life. "We need everything we can get from you to help make that happen."

"I'm all in. This job is pretty much my life." He looked down.

"Me too. I don't know that it's a healthy way to live, but it's the way I'm living."

He nodded. "Do you have kids?"

A simple question she got asked frequently, but it still felt like a punch to the gut every time. "No. It's just me. You?"

He shook his head. "I wanted kids, but my ex didn't. She

decided after a while that she didn't want me either, so she left."

Her heart broke for him. "I'm so sorry. Was this recent?"

"No. About three years ago. Honestly, it was really rough, but in hindsight, I see it was all for the best."

She definitely couldn't say the same about Ryan's death. Yes, she was stronger now because she had to be, but she would give anything to have him back in her life. She didn't want to bring up what had happened to him. It was easier just to say she was alone.

Weston opened the door and walked back into the room. "I've got some names."

She let out a breath. "Let's start making the calls."

◆

That evening, Viv was trying to stay composed. Jacob had done a complete security work-up on her place, and she'd given him the go-ahead to proceed. He had just finished the new install and was running some tests.

She walked into the living room, where Jacob was tinkering with an additional security device. "I can cancel on Mark."

"That's not necessary," Jacob said. "You'll just need to explain to him why I'm the third wheel."

"I already told him about that."

"Then he shouldn't have any issues."

They'd agreed to go somewhere within walking distance from her place and that Jacob would follow them there. She hadn't given Mark all the details on that yet, but he understood there were still security concerns. And she couldn't even tell him about the newest threats.

"I shouldn't have said yes to this," she muttered to herself.

Jacob walked over to her. "Viv, you don't owe this guy

anything. If you don't want to go to dinner with him, then you don't have to."

"I should've said no initially. It would be extremely rude to do so now. I'll just make it clear that I'm not up for going out anymore right now."

"It's completely up to you."

As if on cue, the doorbell rang. "That has to be him."

Jacob caught her by the arm. "Let me check."

She relented, but mainly because she needed an additional moment.

Jacob opened the door. "Hi, Mark. I'm Special Agent Jacob Cruz."

They shook hands. "Yes, I remember you from the café. You're the one in charge of protecting Viv, right?"

"Yes, sir, I am. I'll try not to be intrusive into your evening, but I know you understand why we need to take these extra precautions."

"Absolutely. Whatever you need to do to keep her safe." Mark looked at her, and she walked over to greet him.

"Thanks again for the flowers." It sounded awkward, but this whole situation was just downright weird.

"You're welcome."

"Let's head out," she said.

Jacob moved toward them. "You two go ahead. I'll be behind you."

Once they got out of the building and out of Jacob's earshot, she tried to loosen up. "Sorry, Mark, I know this is completely weird. It's like we have a chaperone."

He laughed. "It is quite unlike any other date I've been on, but we met in a strange way, so I'm rolling with it. I'm just glad you have a professional looking out for you. He's military, right?"

"Former SEAL. He's currently with the Diplomatic Security Service."

Mark raised an eyebrow. "Sounds important."

"I'm just grateful, like you said. Things have gotten a bit tense in my life lately."

He took her hand. "For tonight, maybe let's try not to talk about those stressful topics. How does that sound?"

"Wonderful, actually."

They made small talk throughout dinner and then moved on to dessert and coffee. Mark was kind and definitely attractive, but when she glanced over her shoulder and saw Jacob sitting a few tables away, she couldn't help but feel something that wasn't as nice and easy. But it was strong, compelling, and exciting. A connection that had started out rocky but now made her feel tied to him somehow.

"Viv, did you hear me?" Mark asked.

"Sorry. My mind went somewhere else for a minute." *Yeah, like to my bodyguard over there.*

Mark smiled. "I think maybe I've been a bit pushy, and I wanted to apologize for that."

She shook her head. "No, you haven't at all. You've been perfect. It's just that I'm going through a lot." She lifted her hands. "I mean, I had to bring a bodyguard on a date."

Mark chuckled. "I get it. Do you have any sense of when you'll be able to breathe easily again?"

She took a sip of coffee before answering. "I wish I did. We're still trying to figure out exactly why I was attacked, and unfortunately, someone I was close to was killed."

Mark's eyes grew wide. "Are you serious?"

"Yes."

He reached out and took her hand. "Do the police think it's all interrelated?"

She paused, considering how to share information without giving away too much. "Some stuff has happened with my work, and no one really knows what the source is, just that there's a threat out there."

"Are you afraid?" Mark asked.

"Of course, but I also want to keep doing my job. There was some talk about me stopping my current assignment, but I'm not on board with that."

"Wouldn't you be safer?"

"Yes, but it's not just about me."

Mark ran his hand through his hair. "Reading between the lines here, I feel like you've gotten yourself involved in something big. Are you sure you're a State Department lawyer and not a CIA agent?" He laughed loudly.

She made herself laugh as well, but this was getting too close to home. "I know it sounds crazy, but yes, I'm just a lawyer. Sometimes trouble follows us too. I'm sure you've had some experiences that—while not quite the same—mean you can still relate."

He nodded. "That's very true. I haven't been assaulted on the streets of DC, but I get your point. We're not just paper pushers."

She was beginning to get anxious for the night to end. "Thank you for dinner. It was really lovely."

"Are you sure there's nothing I can do to help you? I know some great private investigators. They aren't the government, but maybe they could help get answers for you."

She shook her head. "I'm sorry. There are too many security clearance issues to be concerned about."

His eyes widened. "Wait a minute. Are you working on the attack on the ambassadors at that diplomatic dinner?"

Viv bit her bottom lip. How had she given herself away?

Mark sighed. "No wonder you have a bodyguard. Viv, this is really serious." He paused. "But what's your connection to that? Why would they come after you?"

"I can't say, but believe me, we're trying to figure that out. I know you understand confidentiality as a lawyer, so you realize that I can't divulge the details of the investigation."

He leaned in. "Absolutely. I just want you to be okay. I have to admit I'm curious why you'd be targeted, but I know you can't reveal why."

As much as she wanted to confide in him, she just couldn't. "It may not be connected. We just don't know yet."

"Then what would it be connected to?"

"I really can't say."

He raised an eyebrow. "You're getting more mysterious by the minute."

She laughed, trying to lighten the mood. "That's really not me, usually."

"We all get ourselves into trouble sometimes."

She didn't respond directly to that but instead tried to wrap things up. "It's getting late."

"Let me get the check." Mark waved at the server, and within a few minutes, they were walking back to her place.

She was acutely aware of Jacob trailing behind them, and she was ready to end this date without an awkward good-night kiss—especially since she didn't feel that way about Mark.

They walked close to each other but not too close. She was still thankful that Mark had come into her life to save her from those evil men. Maybe she should stop obsessing over things and just go with the flow. It was a beautiful night in Rosslyn, and she tried to enjoy the fresh air and not overthink everything that was happening.

All of that changed when she heard the loud squealing of tires coming from behind her.

"What's going on?" She turned to look over her shoulder.

Her world started to move in slow motion. Seconds ticked by like hours as her brain tried to catch up to what was happening around them. The sound of screeching tires drew closer, but her legs felt like tree trunks planted in the ground.

"Get down!" Jacob yelled.

Loud gunshots pierced the air, and Mark shoved her hard to the sidewalk. She screamed as pain radiated through her body, and she wondered if she had been hit or if it was just the impact of his body crashing down on top of hers.

The sound of tires faded. After a moment, Mark rolled away, and she turned over, trying to catch her breath.

"Are you okay?" he asked.

She took a deep breath and looked into his eyes.

"You just saved my life. Again."

CHAPTER
ELEVEN

It had all happened so quickly. Once Jacob saw the dark SUV approaching on his left side, he'd begun to run, but because he had been trying to give Viv some privacy, even when he hit a full-on sprint, he hadn't reached her in time. The best he could do was yell a warning.

Fortunately, Mark had acted quickly, and they both hit the deck. As thankful as Jacob was for what Mark had done, his priority was Viv.

"I need to get her out of here," Jacob said.

"What about Mark?" Viv's voice was unsteady.

"No, Jacob's right." Mark placed his hand on her shoulder. "I think, given everything, you were the target here, not me. I'll be fine." He turned to Jacob. "You'll take care of her, right?"

"Absolutely. But we should move. I don't like being out here in the open like this." They needed protective covering—and fast. "Are you okay to walk?" he asked her.

"Yes," she said softly. She moved toward Mark and gave him a hug. "Thanks again for saving me."

Jacob was annoyed at the affection between them even though he realized he had every reason to be grateful for Mark's quick action.

The three of them walked briskly back to the condo. When they arrived, Mark gave Viv a quick kiss on the cheek before going to retrieve his car.

Jacob escorted Viv upstairs and, after clearing her condo, was satisfied that she was safe.

She turned to him. "You were a little rude to the man who just saved my life. We didn't even invite him in."

"He understood, Viv. The threat is against you. Not him. And my job is to protect you."

"*Mark* protected me back there." Her voice got louder.

That stung. Mainly because she was one hundred percent right. "Yes, I made the mistake of not being close enough. That won't happen again." He had been too accommodating, and Viv could have been killed.

She ran her hand through her hair. "I'm sorry. I know none of this is your fault. I'm just not used to dodging bullets." She flopped down on the couch. "What am I going to do?"

"I've got to talk to Director Phillips. I just sent him an urgent text."

She scrambled up and grabbed his arm. "But I don't want to get pulled from the task force."

"Viv, I don't think you understand. This is a lot bigger than the task force. This is your life we're talking about. Someone is out to kill you."

She shuddered. "I get it, but I can't hide away forever."

"No one is talking about forever. We'll figure something out, but the immediate issue is your safety."

"Why didn't they just kill me when they attacked me?"

He had no good answer for that. "Unclear. But we have to consider that maybe they got something out of Samir that changed their opinion of you, and the result is tonight's attack."

She shook her head. "Samir had nothing to tell them about me."

"Men will say a lot of things while being tortured—many of them untrue."

Her eyes widened. "No. I refuse to believe that. There has to be something else."

"We'll figure it out, but I'm almost certain the director is going to want to move you. Probably ASAP."

She raised an eyebrow. "Move me where?"

He would be fighting her each step of the way at this rate. "Somewhere safe. They obviously know where you live."

Viv lowered her head into her hands. "This is a nightmare. Just when I think things can't get any worse. I could be dead right now."

"But you're not. That's what you have to focus on. You're a fighter. We'll get through this."

"I'm not so sure."

"I know I made a mistake by being too far behind you tonight. I give you my word that I won't let that happen again. No matter what. I'm here."

And he would give his life to protect hers.

◆

Viv tried to stop shaking as Jacob and two FBI agents led her into a safe house in a suburb of Arlington late Friday night. She sat on the sofa while a flurry of activity buzzed around her. The past couple of hours had been a blur, but at least she was safe. For now.

Agents were going to be combing her place, just in case there was anything to find, and it had been made clear to her that the safe house was currently her only option.

When she heard the FBI director's deep southern drawl bellowing through the safe house, she groaned. It couldn't be good that he had shown up.

"Vivian, Jacob, we need to talk." Director Phillips didn't bother with any niceties as he walked into the living room. "Everyone else, y'all please give us the room."

The other FBI agents quickly dispersed. She glanced at Jacob, who had on his signature scowl.

"I've been on the phone with the CIA director. Frankly, I was beginning to have some questions about whether I'd been told everything about the op you worked with them, Vivian."

This didn't sound good at all. She braced herself for the worst.

"After threatening Director Mince within a half inch of his life, I finally got some answers, and I'm afraid you aren't going to like what I have to say."

Jacob cleared his throat. "Director, Viv has had a really rough night. Do you think we could wait until the morning to have this conversation?"

Before the director could answer, Viv jumped in. "No. I want to talk about it now. I'm ready. If there's more bad news, let's just put it all on the table."

Lang looked at her. "Okay. It was my understanding, and I think it was yours, too, that you were on that CIA mission as the State legal representative to make sure we didn't violate any international laws and played by the book. The story I was initially told was that everything went off smoothly. The detainees were transferred over to the Egyptians, and the op was a success because once the detainees were in Egyptian custody, they were able to use them to ferret out the radical forces that were hidden within the government."

"Yes, that was my understanding as well," Viv said.

Lang cleared his throat. "What I didn't know, and I'm guessing you didn't either, is that it wasn't a one-way prisoner swap."

"What do you mean?"

Lang shifted in his chair. "The CIA took in some high-value detainees who were in Egyptian custody. From what I could drag out of Director Mince, these detainees were important members of Al-Nidal fighting against US interests. You might not remember seeing them because they weren't in prison dress. To keep as much secrecy as possible, they were forced to blend in with the Egyptian staff working the op. The Egyptian intelligence services assigned Samir to be their handler until they were transferred to US custody."

She racked her memory, but nothing was coming to her. "Samir never told me about that."

Director Phillips nodded. "Samir was sworn to silence. Everything about this op was shrouded in secrecy. Different moving pieces, and no one really knew all of them except the high-ups at Langley."

She wondered what Layla knew. Had her best friend been forced to keep information from her?

Jacob started pacing. "What I am missing here? We have these bad guys in custody. How could they be behind all of this? What's the connection?"

"That's what the Agency didn't want to tell us," the director said. "Two of the men escaped CIA custody about a month ago."

She sucked in a breath. "Are you sure?"

"Positive. Like I said, it took a while to get a straight answer, but they are gone. Which means they're free and probably not only out for revenge but out for other things as well."

"Like what?" she asked.

"I'm convinced they think being a State lawyer is just your cover and you're really Agency, and that you might be able to get them the location of the other detainees who are still being held by the CIA. If I'm right, you have a big target on your back."

This was insane. "But I'm not. I'm a lawyer. I'm not with the CIA."

Lang shook his head. "It doesn't matter what the truth is. It matters what they believe, and you're not going to convince them of anything else. They saw you with their own eyes. To them you're the enemy, regardless of what your official position is."

Jacob stopped pacing. "Langley didn't think they should've alerted those at risk immediately after these guys busted out of custody? And how did that happen in the first place?"

Lang lifted a hand. "I get that you're upset about this. I am too. Especially when it puts someone in danger who has no business being involved in this type of work, but here we are. The CIA is trying to find answers on how these men were able to break out of custody, but our top priority has to be Vivian's safety."

"What about the task force?" she asked.

"We'll set you up to work here, but I can't have you out there right now. It's too dangerous. I spoke to your boss a few minutes ago and gave him the sanitized version, and he got the picture. Delaney and Weston have the Ambassador King angle fully under control. We have to consider whether there's any chance that these detainees were behind the death of Ambassador Zidan. From what I was told by Director Mince, they are fierce opponents of the Egyptian president and his allies."

"Can we get their names?" Jacob asked.

The director frowned. "I'm trying to push Langley, but I'm not having any success so far. They claim there are other things in play that they have to protect. But believe me, I'm going to make another run at them."

"So I'm going to be here for a while?" Viv asked.

"For the time being, yes," Lang responded. "Jacob is taking the lead on managing your security. I guarantee you will not be left alone, not even for one second."

Her stomach clenched. She wasn't sure how she felt about that statement because it meant he believed she was in real danger. "Thank you."

"Jacob, walk me out," Lang said.

She knew the director wanted to talk to Jacob without her present. She was so tired of all the secrets.

Closing her eyes, she let the director's words sink in. She went back to the day of the transfer and tried to remember any of those men. They would have been near Samir. There had been so many unfamiliar faces. And her job was to ensure that the prisoners being transferred *from* US custody were treated fairly and in accordance with international law. Right under her nose, the CIA had brought in prisoners from Egypt, and she hadn't even known it. She remembered there had been a couple of separate flights for all the personnel involved. The incoming prisoners must have been on a different flight to the United States.

Jacob walked back into the room and took a seat beside her on the sofa. She expected him to say something right away, but he didn't. They just sat in silence for a moment before she spoke.

"I'm not sure what to say or do."

He turned toward her. "I'm so sorry this has happened to you. I'm a SEAL. I'm used to living every moment of my life wondering if it could be the last, but it's not fair to put that on someone who isn't prepared. You didn't ask for this. You were doing your job, and because the CIA kept too many secrets, your life has been put at risk." He took her hand. "Viv, this is serious. Those men who escaped are powerful. Look what they did to Samir."

She pulled away. "You don't have to remind me of that, Jacob. I have nightmares about his throat being slit and my being there, unable to do anything to stop it." Her voice started to shake.

He put his arm around her. "Hey, I wasn't trying to upset you. I really don't want that. You have my word that I will protect you."

She looked up into his dark eyes. "You don't even like me. Why are you going through all this?"

He sighed. "I didn't like you at first, no. But you've grown on me." He squeezed her shoulder, and one corner of his mouth quirked up.

She did feel safe with him, but as she looked into his eyes, she wondered what else she was feeling.

◆

Jacob stared into Viv's hazel eyes, and his gut clenched. There was so much going on in his head, but the main thing he wanted was to protect Viv.

"You look like you want to say something else," he said softly.

"I don't even know where to start." She paused. "Who all is going to be staying here?"

"You, of course. I'll also be here, leading the security team. There will be two agents in addition to me here at all times. The director meant it when he said you wouldn't be alone. The two agents on first shift are outside. I'll be in constant contact with them."

"We rushed out of my place so quickly. What about clothes and my personal items and things like that?"

"A female agent is at your place now, packing up things for you. She'll be here soon. I figured you'd be more comfortable with another woman rummaging through your stuff, but they had to do the evidence collection first. I'll be honest with you, I'm not expecting them to find prints or anything like that. We didn't find anything indicating that someone had actually been inside your condo. But these guys are good, and I believe they've connected with a network of professionals to get things done."

Her eyes widened. "You mean like assassins?"

"Hit men, mercenaries, private contractors, and yes, assassins. All of the above. They have a funding source and are using it. I don't think the escaped terrorists are the ones who killed Samir. I think they hired someone. The terrorists are probably lying low until they're ready to strike."

"Do you think they hired someone to attack me on my way to see Samir?"

"Yes, I do."

"And do you think it was the same story tonight? The person shooting was a murderer-for-hire type?"

He grimaced. "Yeah. At first I thought they wanted you alive to figure out what you know, but given what happened tonight, it seems revenge might be trumping knowledge at this point." He felt her shiver. "I've got you, Viv. Nothing is going to happen to you tonight."

"I pray that you're right."

He paused. "That's the first time I've heard you mention prayer."

"I'm not that vocal about my beliefs, but I do have them."

"Me too. Although I'll tell you, this is one of the times when I'm asking God why He's letting something like this happen."

She gave him a weak smile. "We don't know all the answers, but I do know that He is faithful, and that's what I have to hold on to. After my parents died, I was so confused about why God had taken them from me. Finally, I realized that I'd never fully understand why they died, but that I had to be thankful for the time I had with them. And if God thinks this is my time, I will have to be at peace with that."

"No. We're not going to be defeatist in our thinking. It's fine to believe that God has a plan and when it's your time to leave this earth, you're okay with that. But it's another thing just to accept defeat. We will fight. I will fight for you. There is no doubt in my mind. The God I worship is bigger than any of this, Viv."

Her eyes misted up. "I know that, but I also can't hide my fear."

"There's nothing wrong with that either. Lean on me, okay? I'm built for things like this."

She hesitated, looking at him thoughtfully. "You never told me why you left the SEALs."

He hated talking about this.

"If you don't want to tell me, I understand." She looked down.

"I didn't leave by choice."

"What happened?"

"We were on an op. Everything was going right until it wasn't. I got shot in the shoulder. I did full rehab and everything, but they still thought I wasn't up for going back in the field. My CO and I had a huge blowup over it. I said some things. He said some things. I'd been in the military my entire adult life, and suddenly I couldn't do what I was meant to do."

"You believe you're still strong enough to be out there, don't you?"

"I do. But they have all these rules and regs and this test and that test, and I got poked and prodded by all the doctors. At the end of the day, it was out of my hands."

"That explains a lot."

"What do you mean?"

"Why you always seem so sad. You left what you truly loved doing. You said yourself you were in the military your whole adult life. It shaped your entire sense of identity. And then they stripped that away from you—you believe unfairly. That would take a toll on anyone."

He nodded. "Yeah. It was one of the worst times of my life." He thought about how much more he wanted to say.

"You're still hurting. Have you talked to someone about it?"

"The Navy made me talk to someone right after I got shot, but that was it. If you haven't figured it out yet, talking about my feelings isn't my strong suit."

She looked up at him. "Jacob, I can feel your pain. It's apparent in everything you do."

"You make me sound so transparent."

Viv shook her head. "No. I just meant as we spend time together, I can sense it. I know you're hurting. You hide it, of course, but it impacts your life."

135

No one had ever called him out so completely and honestly—yet with no judgment whatsoever.

She took his hand. "You're helping me. I'd like to help you. Whatever I can do, just say it."

"You're already helping just by listening." How had his feelings changed so dramatically for her? He'd had so many preconceived notions about what she would be like, but she had busted all of them. She was kind, caring, and smart. And he was incredibly attracted to her, but he wasn't sure that making a move would be what she wanted. And it probably wasn't the best idea, given the circumstances.

Viv squeezed his hand. "It's a deal, then. We'll get through this together."

CHAPTER
TWELVE

Jacob had spent most of the night talking to all the agents assigned to Viv's security detail. He'd pulled in two people from DSS to supplement the FBI team. Given the circumstances, he hadn't had any trouble getting his boss to approve the additional resources.

Thankfully, his military training allowed him to operate on power naps and little sleep. He didn't feel that tired in the morning. He felt energized. On edge. What the director had told them had shaken him hard, but he had to put on a strong face for Viv. The fact that she was the target of a terrorist group instilled fear into even his heart.

He was mad at the CIA for bringing Viv into this assignment to begin with. They should have read her into the op and at least given her the chance to turn it down. They took that choice away from her and instead thrust her into a dangerous situation. And the worst part was that he was still concerned the Agency could be holding out on them. He hoped the FBI director would be able to get all the information available, but he wasn't naïve. He knew there were still certain lines drawn between the CIA and the FBI.

One of the other agents at DSS had brought him a bag from his place. This safe house was going to be home for the foreseeable future. If he had any inkling that they were no longer safe here, though, he'd have zero hesitation taking Viv somewhere else.

"Hey." Viv walked into the kitchen. "Did you stay up all night?"

"I took a couple of power naps. I'm good." This wasn't about him. "Did you get any sleep?"

She nodded. "Yeah, some. Not the best night, but it could've been worse, so I'll take it. I have to admit, knowing you guys were here made a big difference."

"That's good. I made coffee too."

Viv smiled widely. "You really are my hero. You don't want to have to deal with me in the morning without coffee. I'm a mess." She started rummaging through the cabinets.

"Last one on the left," he said.

"Thanks." She found a mug, filled it, and took a seat beside him. "I was thinking about Layla. Has she been told about this?"

"Yes. The Agency is dealing with her. Unfortunately, she can't come here. None of your friends can. It's too dangerous."

She bit her bottom lip. "I get it. I don't want them to get hurt."

It was even more important for her safety, but he didn't say that.

"Did they drop off the computers for me to use?"

"Yes. We've got laptops and burner phones." He'd taken

her phone away from her last night, much to her disappointment, and discarded the SIM card.

"Good." She took a sip of coffee. "I need to work my way through this."

"I've got pictures of the escaped detainees that I can show you whenever you're up for it."

"Oh, I'm up for it." She paused. "I know I've had some moments of weakness lately, but I don't want you to think I can't handle this. Yeah, I'm not a trained fighter, and I can't take on the enemy in hand-to-hand combat, but I'll do what I can to the best of my ability."

He couldn't help but smile. "You are a fighter. It may not be with your hands, but definitely with your head and heart."

She touched his arm. "Thank you. That means a lot coming from a warrior like you. We need to look at how these guys busted out. What if it's an inside job?"

"That's exactly one of the reasons the director did not tell anyone at the Agency about this safe house. It's completely on a need-to-know basis, and only a very small number of people know. I did pull in some guys from my team at DSS, but I trust them. I wanted to make sure you were fully covered."

Viv nodded. "I'm ready to get to work when you are."

❖

Delaney sat in the secure conference room, waiting to talk to Murray Hertz, Penelope's right-hand man. In the room with her were Weston and Cody. Weekends still meant work when you were on a task force like this.

Nothing else had happened to her since the incident on Thursday night, but she was still on high alert. She'd told Weston he didn't need to stay with her anymore, and although he didn't like it, he had relented. She couldn't have her partner trying to babysit her twenty-four hours a day.

She picked up her extra-large coffee cup, which was needed this morning. It had been a long night after she'd found out that Vivian had been the target of a drive-by shooting. There was even more going on than the director was telling her, but Vivian was now in a safe house and would be working from there. The fact that the director was keeping Delaney in the dark made her think Vivian's problems were really bad—and highly sensitive in nature. She knew better than to push to get info that a superior didn't want to give to her, and when that superior was the director of the FBI, she definitely understood her place. He'd made it abundantly clear that her only focus was the Ambassador King case.

Cody picked up the remote to turn on the video screen. "Murray should be on momentarily."

They'd decided to talk to Murray since he was the ambassador's chief of staff, hoping to get anything they could out of him that might shed some light on what the ambassador had been up to in Brussels that had made her a target. "Are we on mute now?" she asked.

"Yes." Cody pointed to the red light on the sound box.

"I'm going to start out, but, Weston, feel free to jump in if you need to."

"You got it," Weston replied.

"Cody, if there's something we need to know, please interrupt. We'll just make Murray wait while we chat privately." She intended to use his knowledge the best way they could.

"We have the ability not only to mute but to blank the screen for private conference, so we should be good." He smiled.

There was something about the way he looked at her with

those big brown eyes that gave her pause. He was handsome, though not her usual type. But since when was she even thinking about types? She'd only gone on a few dates since Ryan died, and those were all setups by her friends and came to a screeching halt before they really started.

After a few more sips of coffee, Murray Hertz appeared on the screen. She immediately sized him up. She'd read his file. In his forties, the stocky, dark-haired man wore glasses and an ill-fitting gray suit. He'd spent the past five years in Brussels and was assigned as the ambassador's chief of staff upon her arrival at the post.

"Mr. Hertz, thanks for talking to us. I know you spoke to some of my colleagues earlier, but we appreciate you taking the time to do some follow-up with us. I'm SSA Delaney O'Sullivan, and this is Special Agent Weston Lee. I think you already know Cody Rico."

"Hello, everyone," Murray said. "Please call me Murray. No need to stand on formalities around here. Is there any new word on the ambassador?"

She shook her head. "Unfortunately not. She's still in critical condition."

Murray looked down. "I hate to hear that."

She decided to start with an easy question. "How long have you worked with the ambassador?"

"Since she made the move to Brussels about three years ago."

Delaney thought about rehashing the topics he'd discussed with the other agents, since she'd read their interview memos carefully, but there was another option. "You told the other agents you spoke to that you had no reason to think anyone would've been targeting the ambassador. Is that still your response?"

Murray raised an eyebrow. "Is there something I don't know?"

She leaned forward. "You tell me."

Murray blew out a breath. "I don't know anything new. Penelope was well liked. Highly political and very connected. She purposely didn't try to cross people. She was more of a coalition builder than a double-crosser. A deal maker. People wanted her in the room. Does that make sense?"

"It does," she answered. "Are you aware of any relationship the ambassador had that might have caused her trouble?" She specifically asked the question vaguely to see how he'd take it.

"Look, I'm not comfortable talking about the ambassador's personal life."

Back to the elephant in the room. "I'm not referring to any romantic relationships."

"Oh." Murray frowned. "Then I'm not understanding your question."

"Any other relationships that might not have been aboveboard?"

Murray's eyes narrowed. "No. Penelope was aboveboard."

"I know you wouldn't want to rat out your boss," Weston said. "But now is the time to tell us if you know anything. There's a good chance she won't make it, and then we'll be talking about a murder investigation instead of attempted murder. And I'd hope you would want the person who did this to pay."

Murray looked uncomfortable as he tugged at his tie. "I really wish I could help, but I don't have anything for you. I feel like you know something and think I do, too, but it's just not like that."

"Give us a minute, please, Murray." She looked at Cody, who muted and blanked the screen.

"He knows something," Weston said.

142

"I agree, but he's not going to open up unless we start exerting some pressure. Cody, what do you think?"

Cody opened the folder in front of him. "I've scoured his files and asked some sources about him. They couldn't give me anything."

"We just need to make him think we already know things." She thought a moment. "Cody, can you get out of his line of sight? I'm going to tell him that I asked you to leave. Maybe he'll talk more openly if he thinks there aren't any State Department reps in the room."

"Understood." Cody stood. "Just push that button when you're ready."

She waited for Cody to go to the back of the room, outside of the camera shot, and then she pushed the button to resume the videoconference. "Murray, we're back. Sorry about that."

Murray shifted. "I'm still here."

"I asked Cody to give us some privacy. I thought that might make you more comfortable engaging in some of these tough topics."

"All right. But like I said, I don't know anything."

"That's the thing," Weston said. "You do know something, and we're trying to give you the opportunity to tell us what it is. Work with us here, Murray."

Murray sighed. "The ambassador is not only my boss but also my friend."

They were starting to get somewhere. "I understand that you're in a difficult position here, but your friend is fighting for her life. We're trying to determine who is responsible. If you know anything, no matter how small, even if it's just conjecture, we'll take it."

Moments passed in silence, and she didn't say anything, waiting on Murray to make the next move.

He stood and took off his gray suit jacket before return-ing to his seat. "The ambassador is a complicated woman."

Uh-oh. She didn't like the sound of that.

"In what way?" Weston asked.

Murray let out a dramatic sigh. "I'm sure at this point you've found out about the issues she's had with her hus-band."

Back to the infidelity. "Yes, we're well aware, but is there anything else you can tell us to shed light on things?"

Murray clenched his hands on the table in front of him. "You said conjecture, so here it is. The ambassador seemed to have a close and friendly relationship with Sergei Popov."

"Who is Popov?" she asked.

"He's one of the diplomats who works at the Russian embassy in Brussels."

Delaney needed to get this straight. "When you say close and friendly relationship, are you insinuating something ro-mantic or something more on a transactional basis?"

Murray looked down. "I'm thinking more romantic, but honestly, I can't say for sure either way." He squirmed in his seat as perspiration formed on his forehead. "Look, I did see them kiss once. It was late and at the end of a long party, so I can't say whether it was serious, though there was a sense of familiarity that gave me pause. But it really wasn't my business."

The introduction of a Russian diplomat just made this case even more of a powder keg. "Do you know if Popov is currently in Brussels?"

"He's stationed here, but he travels quite a bit, so I can't be certain he's here at this moment."

"Did you ever ask the ambassador about her relationship with Popov?"

Murray shook his head. "That would not have been my place at all, Agent O'Sullivan. The ambassador runs in many social circles, and I never question who she chooses to spend her personal time with."

"Even if it's a *Russian* diplomat?"

"Even if." Murray started to dig in his heels. "And like I told you before, I'm not certain how serious she was about him. It just seemed that she had more affection for him than many of the other men I've noticed her socializing with, but I wouldn't base anything off of what I'm telling you without doing your own independent research. And even if there was something going on between them, I can't imagine how Popov could be involved. He's a very well-respected diplomat and was obviously fond of the ambassador."

"Popov's possible involvement is for us to figure out, Murray," she told him. "We appreciate you being forthcoming today. If you think of anything else, please don't hesitate to reach out."

Weston provided his contact information to Murray before disconnecting the call.

Cody rejoined them at the table. "I just sent a note to the Russia desk asking about Popov."

"We should reach out to our CIA contacts as well." Delaney wasn't going to leave any stone unturned after hearing this revelation. "We've got a recent influx of cash into the ambassador's offshore account and now a Russian diplomat. Is anyone else really concerned?"

Weston and Cody looked at her, but before they could respond, her phone rang. It was the director. "This is Delaney."

"I've got bad news," Lang said.

Her stomach dropped. "What now?"

"Ambassador King went into cardiac arrest. She's dead."

CHAPTER
THIRTEEN

Jacob watched as Viv frowned at her laptop.

"These are the guys who escaped? Are you sure?" she asked.

"Yes. Why are you so hesitant?"

She stared at the screen another minute before turning back to him. "Unfortunately, I don't remember these men. But there was a lot going on, and I was focused on the detainees we were transferring to the Egyptians."

"That was your job. You were doing what you were supposed to do. You didn't even know who these men were." He paused. "I assume there's no way these two were the ones who attacked you?"

"They are definitely not the ones. I'm one hundred percent certain. If I saw the attackers again, I would recognize them. Can you tell me more about these guys?"

"Members of the Al-Nidal terrorist cell. Extremely valuable targets with intel we need to help thwart attacks in the

US and around the world. Highly dangerous. Since the CIA won't give up their identities, that's all we know."

"I'm not an expert on the Al-Nidal terrorist network. That's much more Layla's expertise. We should talk to her and see if she can shed any light on this."

He didn't want to get her hopes up. "I hate to say this, but I'm betting the Agency has gagged her. They probably won't let her talk any more about this topic."

"I'm her best friend. I get that she'll do what she needs to do to protect national security and follow the rules, but I think we at least have to try. We've got nothing to lose."

"We'll need to set up a secure line. She can't come here."

"Yeah, I remember."

His phone started beeping, and he looked down and saw the bad news. "Viv, I hate to tell you this, but Ambassador King passed away."

Viv froze for a few seconds, then stood. "I'm sorry. I need a moment." She walked out of the room, and he didn't follow.

He understood she was friendly with the ambassador. Add that news on top of everything else, and Viv was probably close to a breaking point. Jacob couldn't let that happen. He had to keep her spirits up.

After a few minutes, she returned to the room. Her eyes were red, but otherwise she seemed okay, given the circumstances. "You don't think her death is linked to all of this, do you?"

"Delaney and Weston are working hard and haven't found anything to connect Penelope to what's going on with the Egyptian side. Most likely there's no link at all between the two events. We still can't rule out a heart attack for Ambassador Zidan. Regardless, though, his death has set off a chain reaction of events."

She sat down. "Is this really a revenge mission on the part of these Al-Nidal guys? There has to be more to this than revenge, right?"

Sadly, she was wrong. "I'm afraid not. These men are terrorists. They wouldn't think twice about killing someone as an act of revenge. Their whole purpose is to inflict pain. These aren't political dissidents. This isn't diplomacy, like you're used to dealing with. They're straight-up bad guys. Understand?"

Viv blew out a breath. "I know. I'm just having a hard time wrapping my head around it."

"That's because you see the light in people, not the darkness. I specialize in seeing the darkness and fighting it."

"That's a hard way to live," she whispered.

"It's all I know." He paused. "Back to your original question, I think we're dealing with separate events here. Penelope's death seems to be a completely different scenario. There's no reason she would've been targeted above any other US diplomat if the threat was from Al-Nidal. What we don't know is whether these guys were responsible for Zidan's death or whether that was just the catalyst for them to act."

◆

That evening, Viv realized she had to reach out to Mark since he didn't have her new phone number. She didn't want Jacob involved in the conversation, so she went to her bedroom in the safe house and made the call. Thankfully, she'd kept Mark's business card in her purse, so she had his number.

He answered after a few rings. "Hello."

"Mark, hey, it's Viv."

"Viv! I've been worried sick about you. I kept trying your phone, and it went straight to voicemail, and you weren't answering my texts. I started to get worried."

"I'm so sorry, Mark. It's been a whirlwind."

"What happened?"

"I'm at a safe house while they evaluate the situation."

"Wow. I'm glad they're taking this so seriously. It's really important that you're safe. You know you probably shouldn't be calling me."

"I'll be fast. I had to let you know I was all right because I knew you would worry. It's just been jarring." She paused. "I still can't get last night out of my mind. You were so quick to react, and you have now saved my life twice. I feel indebted to you, but saying thank you just seems trite, given the implications."

"Viv, please don't think like that. I know we haven't known each other that long, but I care about you, and I'm so thankful I was able to stop them from hurting you."

"I put you in harm's way, and I can't stand that."

"Don't worry about me. I'm tougher than I look." He chuckled.

"You're looking pretty tough to me these days."

"Am I going to be able to see you again?"

"I don't know. This lockdown is really tight, and they told me I can't tell anyone where I am."

"I get it. That's for the best. They're taking every precaution. Are they saying anything about finding those responsible? Do they still think it's part of what happened to the ambassadors?"

"We're still trying to figure that out. Unfortunately, I don't really have answers, and I don't think anyone else does either."

"What can I do? Just name it."

"Mark, you've already done so much."

"If anything comes up, let me know. I'm here for whatever you need."

A knock on her door startled her. "I need to run, but thank you again."

"Call me soon and let me know how you are. Or if you can't call, just email me to let me know you're still doing okay." He rattled off his email address.

"Will do."

She hung up, then opened her bedroom door. Jacob was on the other side.

"Who were you talking to?"

"Mark," she said.

"Give me your phone."

"What?"

"Give me your phone."

She handed it to him, and he pulled the SIM card out of the back and then cracked it.

"Hey! Why did you do that?"

"Because we can't have anyone tracking your number and having it lead to the safe house."

She couldn't help but laugh. "Oh, just the man who saved my life last night. I wasn't supposed to call and let him know how I was doing?" Her frustration level was rising.

"I understand why you wanted to do that, but you'll need to cut off communication for now."

She looked up at him. "I don't like the sound of any of this."

He hung his head. "I'm just trying to keep you alive."

Her heart softened a bit as she looked at him. He was clearly worn out and stressed. She had to be more considerate, given all the circumstances.

"There's something else," he said.

"What?" Her stomach dropped, fearing more bad news.

"We've been summoned to Langley."

"On a Saturday evening? Why?" What more could there possibly be? She didn't think she could take it.

"No idea. But we need to go. They said ASAP."

◆

Viv's stomach was tied in knots by the time they entered a SCIF at the CIA to have their secure conversation. She wasn't sure who all would be involved, but she got some of her answers as Jacob escorted her to her seat.

Director Phillips was there, and CIA Director Mince sat at the head of the table. She started feeling nauseated. Then she saw Layla on the other side of the table and let out a breath. It was so reassuring to see her face, but Layla wasn't smiling or giving off any good vibes. Just the opposite. Seeing how serious Layla was only made Viv feel worse. What could they tell her that would make this situation any more dire?

Viv stole a glance at Jacob and saw he also had his game face on.

Director Phillips stood, commanding the attention of the room. "I think we have everyone. I called this meeting be-cause it has come to my attention that there is more informa-tion to be shared regarding this ongoing operation. Director Mince graciously agreed to provide some valuable intel, and he also has some pictures to share with you, Vivian." He spoke slowly, his southern drawl on full display. "We'd like to see if you recognize any of the men."

Director Mince walked over to her and offered his hand. "Vivian, I don't believe we've met before, but I've been fully briefed by Lang. We are prepared to reveal the identities of these two men, but before that happens, I want to direct your attention to the screen as we go through some video footage and photos. We'd like to see if you recognize any of these men from the diplomatic dinner, the prisoner exchange, or any other time, for that matter. Is that okay with you?"

"Yes, thank you, Director." What else was she supposed to say? She looked at Layla, who gave her an encouraging nod. She still wasn't sure how involved Layla's role was in all of this, and deep in the pit of her stomach she worried that Layla knew more than she'd revealed.

"Roll the tape," Director Phillips said.

Viv clenched her hands together under the table and tried to keep cool. She reminded herself that no one could hurt her while she was locked in a secure room at the CIA with her own personal bodyguard. She needed to focus her energy on the screen and see if she could be of any assistance.

She watched the screen closely as they scrolled through photo after photo of various men that she didn't recognize. Racking her brain, she tried to put faces to the nebulous figures in her memory of the men around Samir at the detainee swap, but nothing was coming to her.

Taking a few deep breaths, she watched the slideshow for several minutes. Then a picture flashed up on the large screen that made her stomach drop, and she jumped out of her seat. "Wait! Stop."

Director Mince looked at her. "Do you know that man?"

She stared at the screen and felt like the world was collapsing on top of her. How had this all gone so terribly wrong? She glanced at Jacob to see if she was crazy, but his shock seemed to match her own. "Who is that?"

"Who do you think it is?" Director Phillips asked.

"I know that man as Mark Pullman. He's the Good Samaritan who saved me from the attack." She took another breath. "And the man who saved me from being shot to death last night."

The room was deathly silent. All she could hear was the buzz of the fan unit in the ceiling.

Director Mince walked toward the screen and pointed to the man she knew as Mark. "Are you sure? Are you absolutely sure?"

"I can confirm this," Jacob said. "That is definitely Mark Pullman. Viv, you might want to tell them about your contact with him as recently as right before we left to come here."

Viv began pacing. "First, I want to know who he is. Who he *really* is. I deserve to know."

Director Mince unbuttoned his jacket and took a seat. "That is Paul Joubert. French national. He's one of the chief financiers of Al-Nidal. He was radicalized in the mid-2000s in France. He's taken on multiple aliases in his line of work, but we believe that Paul Joubert is his true name. But don't let his financial cover fool you. He's as deadly as they come. We've been able to trace his work for the past five years, and he is directly responsible for financing multiple terrorist operations in Europe and in the Middle East. He has the blood of thousands of innocent civilians on his hands."

Viv had to sit down. Stars started to appear before her eyes as confusion swirled in her brain. She worried that she might pass out. "But he saved me. He saved me." She repeated the words over and over as if to help herself figure out what was going on.

Jacob walked to the front of the room. "Let's think this through. Viv gets a text from someone claiming to be Samir, luring her to a meeting. Two men attack her, but by chance a Good Samaritan shows up at the perfect time to swoop in and save her." He pointed to the screen. "We now know that it is Joubert who jumps in and comes to the rescue. Then, naturally, Viv follows up, they form a connection, and he once again saves her from danger last night."

It was starting to come together in Viv's mind. "It was all planned. They planted him there to save me so I would trust him. He was trying to get close to me. But why? Why the elaborate ruse?"

Layla finally spoke. "You need to tell us exactly what happened when you saw him after the attack."

She glanced again at Jacob. "I've seen him twice. The first time was when I took him to coffee to thank him, and the second was when he took me to dinner last night. And as Jacob said, I just spoke with him on the phone before we headed over here."

More awkward silence filled the room.

Uneasy tension moved from her back up to her neck. "Obviously, I had no idea."

Director Mince straightened in his seat. "It's vitally important, Vivian, that you think back to every conversation you had with this man. What did you tell him, if anything, about your work and what happened to you?"

She tested her memory, trying to think about what she specifically said. She knew she'd held back information from him, but at the time, she was thinking more from a purely classified information standpoint as opposed to him being the enemy. In her mind, he had been a friend. Someone who had saved her from certain assault and likely death.

Before she could answer, Director Phillips jumped in. "Vivian, now is not the time to hold back. If you did tell him more than you should have, it's understandable, given you were still in shock after the attack and he's the one who saved you. So just get everything out in the open, and then we can handle it."

"Why is everyone assuming Viv spilled her guts to this guy?" Jacob asked. "Why don't we let her tell her side of the story before we jump to any conclusions?"

Once again Jacob was protecting her. She gave him a weak smile. But she did need to describe everything she had told Mark, because it was probably more than she should have said.

"Okay, we had the first coffee meeting, and that's when we made small talk. Mark told me he was a lawyer, which gave us an immediate connection. I did tell him I worked for the State Department. I don't think there was much more discussion about me at that coffee meeting." She kept trying to remember. "Wait, at coffee I did mention that we weren't sure if the attack was related to my work, but that was about it. But when we went to dinner last night, he knew something was up because we had Jacob as our escort. He asked more questions, but I thought it was out of concern or curiosity as opposed to him being the enemy!"

Layla moved into the seat beside her. "None of this is your fault, Viv. You haven't done anything wrong."

Viv appreciated her friend taking up for her. Especially in front of the two directors. "He asked if he could refer me to a private investigator. I told him security clearance issues wouldn't permit that. That's when he asked if I was working on the attacks on the ambassadors. I did not volunteer that information. Looking back on it now, it does seem a little odd for him to ask, but I thought he was focused on the fact that I was in danger and that I worked at the State Department, and he was putting two and two together. I told him I couldn't say and that we were still trying to figure out why

I was being targeted. He did make a joke about whether I was CIA, and I thought it was just that—a joke. He may have prodded a little more, but I don't recall giving him any information. I tried to change the topic so as to avoid any more awkward questions." She paused. "Oh, I told him that since he was a lawyer, he understood the confidentiality concerns I had to deal with."

Director Mince tapped his pen on the table hard. "Are you sure that's it?"

She sat quietly, thinking. "No." She groaned as the memory came back. "I told him that someone I was close to was murdered, but I didn't give any names. That's all I can remember. If I think of anything else, I'll let you know ASAP. When I spoke to him this evening, he wanted to make sure I was okay. He asked if we knew yet who was behind everything, and I said no." She took another deep breath. "It seems like such a complicated effort for a couple of dates."

"They were fishing." Layla pushed her hair behind her ear. "I think they wanted to figure out who you are and what you might know. That CIA comment wasn't really a joke. He was trying to read you. Then he saves your life a second time, and that really makes you put your trust in him. If I had to bet, they want to use you to figure out the location of the other detainees and who knows what else."

Director Phillips nodded. "I definitely think that's part of it. Plus, if he could develop a relationship with Vivian, he could keep tabs on how things were going with the investigation. Maybe he thought if he got close enough, you would open up and say something you shouldn't. Let's not fool ourselves into thinking that kind of thing doesn't happen. He's shown himself to be trustworthy, protective, and caring. It's a pretty impressive move on their part. And if they're digging about the investigation, that lends credence to the theory that there could be foul play related to Ambassador Zidan's death."

Director Mince rubbed his chin. "As much as I hate to say this, we may need to think about how we can use this to our advantage. We may not get an opportunity like this again."

"You can't do that to Viv," Jacob said. "She's already been put through enough and has a big target on her back. Now you want her to, what, pretend to be in a relationship with this guy to get information? That may work for the spies at the CIA, but it isn't going to work for her."

"I'm sorry, but do I get a say in the matter?" Viv asked.

No one answered her. She looked at Layla, who shook her head. It was clear her friend didn't think this was a good idea. But of course the Director of the CIA thought it was a great one.

Layla leaned in. "Viv is not trained for this. You absolutely cannot ask it of her."

Director Mince cleared his throat. "Everyone just slow down for a moment so we can think this through. The way I understand it, Joubert already expects Viv to have some security detail, so we could keep that up, which would maintain her safety and still allow her to work him for information. He may think he's playing her, but we'll be playing him. He may be our best lead in tracking down the two escaped detainees."

"Speaking of that," Jacob said, "when are you going to tell us who those two guys are? I showed the pictures to Viv, and she didn't recognize them. But you have other pictures. I think it would be a good idea for her to see those too."

"Before we get to that, I would like to resolve the Mark issue. Or Joubert or whatever we're going to call him." Viv felt so naïve. She'd really been played, and that made her angry.

This man had preyed on her and then stepped in like a knight in shining armor, but really he was a wolf in sheep's clothing. "I would at least like to know what my options are."

Director Mince looked at Director Phillips and then back at her. "Will you give us a couple minutes to talk in private?"

"Of course," Layla said. "Come on, you two. I'll get us some coffee."

Layla led them out of the SCIF and down the hall to a break room.

"Layla, you didn't know any of this about Mark, right?" Viv asked.

Her friend shook her head. "No, I didn't. I have had to hold things back from you, and I didn't like it. But if I had known that, there's no way I would've kept it to myself. I would've gone to the director to make sure we could tell you what was going on."

Jacob filled a cup with coffee and turned to Layla. "You knew about the escaped detainees and didn't say anything." It was more of an accusation than a statement.

"My hands were tied. I couldn't say anything. And as long as I knew Viv was safe with you looking out for her, I was less concerned. This is so much bigger than me." Layla turned to Viv. "At the time of the exchange, I had no idea what was happening. I thought we were doing a one-way swap. It wasn't until recently that I got read into the full op. And I was mad, too, but being angry will not solve anyone's problems or get you out of danger. We need to be smart to get these guys."

"Doesn't that support my acting like I don't know who he is and continuing to see him?" Viv asked.

Layla and Jacob exchanged a glance before he spoke. "It's like Layla said, you haven't been trained at the Farm. You're a diplomatic attorney. What do you know about subterfuge and cover stories and spy craft? I assume nothing. And that's the way we should keep it. That's the best way to keep you safe. That's my opinion on the matter."

Viv looked over Layla. "But you could teach me."

"Of course I'd help you if you needed my help, but I would love it if there is another way to work this thing out. One that doesn't involve you facing down danger directly."

"I'd like to fully understand my options. This whole thing has been a complete nightmare. If there's any way I can help end it once and for all, I want to consider it."

"At the expense of your life, though?" Jacob asked. "This isn't a game you see on TV. These are big bad terrorists who will stop at nothing to meet their goals. And if you're not willing to be one-hundred-percent committed to doing things you would never otherwise do, I just don't think this is an option we should even have on the table."

"Unfortunately, knowing Director Mince and everything that's at stake here, he's going to push hard for this." Layla looked at her.

Viv had figured as much.

Lang stuck his head into the break room. "We're ready for y'all."

Viv's stomach sank as she wondered whether they were going to put her in or hold her back on the sidelines.

◆

Jacob couldn't believe this was happening. The freaking director of the CIA was going to ask a State Department lawyer to run a spy op with a known terrorist financier. Viv was in way over her head, but the last thing he wanted to do was say it like that. She'd already been through so much, and he just wanted to protect her. But he feared this would be much too good for either director to pass up. Getting those detainees back in custody was priority number one. And Joubert most likely knew exactly where they were. So it was all an interconnected web, and Viv had an invaluable way in.

They settled back into their seats, except for Director Mince, who stood at the front of the room. "I talked this over with Lang, and, Vivian, we want you to do this, but we can't force you. We'd like you to think about it overnight. Talk to Layla. Understand what this would entail, and then let us know tomorrow whether you are in or out. If you're out, we will understand. You are a lawyer, not a trained operative, but we also know that you understand how important this mission is, and we believe that you have the skills and smarts to pull this off."

Jacob hated that they were putting this on her. Making this her problem when really it wasn't. The Agency had lost the guys to begin with. That was another issue he was annoyed about.

"Thank you. I'll think about it and let you know." There was determination in Viv's hazel eyes. And that determination scared him, because he felt he already knew she wasn't going to say no to this.

"Thank you, Vivian," Director Phillips said. "If you decide you want to do this, I will talk to your boss at State to make sure he's fully briefed. I'm sure he's going to hate the idea, but let us deal with him if it comes to that."

They spent the next hour going through additional photos of Al-Nidal members, including the two men who had escaped—Omar Hassan and Ali Abboud. From the briefing, they learned these two were even worse than he had imagined.

Jacob had one job. Make sure—no matter what happened—that Viv got out of this alive.

CHAPTER
FOURTEEN

Later that evening, Viv sat on the couch beside Layla in the living room at the safe house. They'd determined it was fine to allow Layla to know the safe house location since she could also be a trusted backstop if something happened to the security team. Jacob was upstairs so Viv could speak freely with Layla. He hadn't seemed bothered by her request at all. He understood how tight she and Layla were.

Layla took both of Viv's hands in hers. "Before we talk about anything else, I'm sorry about withholding information from you once I knew it. But I was given strict orders, and they came straight from the director. You have to believe that if I really thought you were in immediate danger, I would have moved heaven and earth to make sure you were okay."

Viv's heart felt full as she listened to her friend's words. "I know that, Layla. You've been my rock for years. I would've never doubted you, and you don't have to apologize. But I need your help. Can we talk this through?"

Layla nodded. "Let's start with the decision itself. I know they were putting pressure on you, but you can say no. I want you to understand that. This isn't your job, and you are not under any duty to do this."

Viv stared into Layla's dark eyes and wondered if she actually did have a duty to do this. "It definitely isn't in my job description as an attorney for State, but look at what is on the line here. Am I supposed to turn away because I'm afraid? Or because I'm ill-equipped to take on this challenge?"

Layla sighed. "If only it were so easy. In the abstract, of course it sounds good to do the right thing. Do the brave thing. Fight for your country. But I'm here to tell you the cold hard facts. What this will really look like if you decide to take it on, and not some prettied-up version that you might get from others. You are too important to me to do anything else."

Viv knew Layla was telling her the truth. She tried to keep an open mind. "All right. You have my full attention. Tell me what I need to know."

Layla fidgeted on the couch. "*If* you decide to do this, you have to shift your relationship with Mark quickly. You do not want this to turn into a romance."

Viv felt her eyes widen. "You can't be serious. You think I would actually fall for this guy, now that I know who he is?" There was no way that would happen. Not in a million years.

Layla shook her head. "That isn't what I meant. I'm talking about shifting the game. Shift the foundation of your relationship. You should tell him there is too much going on in your life and that you just want to be friends. This will do a couple things. First, it alleviates the need for you to become romantically involved. Which I know is something you do not want to do. Things can quickly get very uncomfortable if that were to happen. Second, it also provides him a way out of having to turn to romance, because he doesn't know any of this. So he can stay in the friend zone with you and keep trying to milk you for information. He'll be open to the idea. Believe me. You just can't seem too overeager. You open the door for remaining friends, then let him make the next move. I'm certain he will."

"And you don't think he would push back, wanting more?" Viv was very concerned about that.

Layla shook her head. "Remember, this guy's on a mission. If he thought romance was the best way to get the job done, then he would definitely go down that path. But if it's friendship, then he'll be fine with that. This isn't some random guy trying to have a fling. This is a trained operative fighting a battle, and he will do whatever it takes to win. Does that make sense?"

A shiver went down Viv's back. "It sounds a little scary when you say it that way."

"I told you I wouldn't sugarcoat things, and I meant it. You need to know this will be difficult. This will probably be the hardest thing you've ever done. And you have to understand this one thing above any other." She paused. "The moment he realizes you know who he is, you could be dead."

Viv sucked in a breath. "I'm not sure what to say to that."

"Just let that sink in. If he believes you've made him, your life is in danger. As long as he thinks you can provide useful information, you'll stay alive. That has to be the goal."

She had so many questions. "If I decided I wanted to do this, how would I make him believe all this stuff?"

"We don't have time to train you. Real training for the Agency lasts months. But we do have knowledge on our side. He has no idea that we know who he is. You'll have to look at yourself in the mirror, though, and seriously question whether you can pull this off. Can you be close to him, hang out with him, and not let him know that you're afraid? Can you put on a face and act your way through it? Pretend like he is the good man who saved you instead of the monster that lies beneath? Can you lie when needed? Can you reel him in? These are all things you and only you can answer. I have my own opinions, but this is about you and how you feel. I want you to have that conversation with yourself."

Viv closed her eyes and wondered what the right thing to do was. "I'm really not sure."

"You don't have to give me an answer tonight, but they will want an answer tomorrow, because if we're going to make this work, you must reengage quickly. Time is not on our side. But, once again, you should make that decision. If you decide to do it, I'll be here for whatever you need. I can role-play, talk you through certain things. Sometimes the best way to deal with situations like this is to keep things as close to the truth as possible. The more lies you weave outside what you know, the more likely you are to slip up. If you keep things very close to the truth instead, then there's less room for error. But you have to be aware of the danger. Even with Jacob near you as backup, if you're blown, Mark could kill you before Jacob can get to you. Are you able to accept that risk?"

Viv wondered if she could and whether she should be taking this on. "I'd like to think I could pull it off, but I've never done anything like this in my life. My legal training and being a State attorney is all about rules and regulations, the law and justice. It's not about subterfuge. And I'm not sure how good of a game face I have, as you put it."

"I felt the same way about the work I've been required to

do. But my faith has been critical in helping get me through it. And I'm sure it will be the same for you. Regardless of what decision you make."

"I know the Lord is always with me, but that doesn't mean I need to make a bad choice. I want to weigh the pros and cons. And, like you said, really determine if I can do this."

"That's the right call. Also, while I'm thinking about it, I know we revealed his true name today, but don't think of him like that. Think of him as Mark and Mark only. One surefire way to blow the whole thing is to call him by his real name."

"That's a good point. So if I go down this route, I would make initial contact and talk about being friends. Then what happens?"

"You let him make the next move. I'm guessing he'll reach out for coffee or dinner or lunch. And then we have to decide how much and what we're going to tell him. He's going to be looking for more information from you. That's his job. We can feed him false intel, but it can't be too far off, or he may figure it out. The story line you would weave would not be all of your own invention. We would have a team at the Agency working on it." Layla looked down and then back up. "And in full transparency I should tell you they are working on it right now. Since this isn't your area of expertise, you'll have a lot more support on the back end than a normal CIA officer would in the field. Does that make sense?"

"It does." But she still had a lot more concerns and questions.

"Even with all the back-end support, you will still be out there by yourself. I promise there will come a time when Mark asks you something or starts a conversation and you're not sure how to handle it. That's when you have to go with your gut and do your best. We'll present you with as much info as possible, so you'll be prepared for a variety of situations. I'll prep you as much as I can and provide options for different scenarios."

Viv wasn't sure her shoulders were strong enough. She'd gone through a lot in her life, but nothing like this. She thought about Willow and what she would do if Viv got killed. That would be so unfair to her twin, who'd already lost so much. A nagging feeling in her gut tortured her, and she felt her eyes well up with tears. "I'm sorry, Layla. I'm a mess."

Layla pulled her into a hug. "It's okay to break down. Right now, in this safe space, is the exact time to do it. Because once you're out there on this mission, you will have to be strong. There is no room for doubt. If you go forward, you're all in, okay? There is no halfway here. Halfway gets you killed."

Viv let Layla's words settle. "I understand. Thank you for all you're doing to help. I don't know what I would do without you. I also don't know how you deal with this every day. I feel like I'm about to break out in hives just thinking about all of this."

"Now you know why I wanted to remain an analyst, but I had to make the adjustments that were required of me. These ops are hard, but they're also vitally important. I care about the mission of the Agency, and I love this country. So even when I'm afraid, I'm willing to take a chance."

"You're just the inspiration I need."

"But remember that they trained me for this. I have a foundation to work from. This would be a very dangerous operation even for a highly skilled operative."

Those words were haunting.

"I want you to think about all of this. If you need me

tonight, just give me a call. But take some time to digest everything we've gone over."

Viv nodded and said good-bye to her best friend. It had been a very long day and was going to be an even longer night.

◆

Jacob found Viv sitting alone on the sofa in the dark.

"Are you all right?" he asked.

"Yes. Just thinking."

"Can I join you?"

"Sure."

He took a seat beside her. "You're going to do it, aren't you?"

She looked at him. "Do I really have a choice? It's the right thing to do, and it's our best and only lead on catching these men."

He put his hand on her knee. "I get it, but you're going to be put in a very precarious situation with this guy. A guy we know is behind multiple terrorist attacks. The level of danger to your life is off the charts."

"I know," she mumbled. "The only thing holding me back at all is Willow."

"Your sister."

"I don't want her to be alone if something happens to me, but I know that if she knew the facts, she would one hundred percent want me to do it. That's just the way she is."

"Did talking to Layla help?" he asked.

She nodded. "She told me the truth, which is what I needed. I think we can work through this. It means going back to my condo, though."

"Another thing I don't like, but I'm good at adapting. In

the field, we make plans, and usually they never go the way you want them to. In my mind, I'm treating this like a field op, and my main focus is keeping my asset alive."

She smiled. "I'm your asset?"

"In this context, yes."

"No man has ever said anything so sweet to me." She laughed.

He knew she was trying to lighten the mood, but he wasn't ready to laugh any of this off. He took her hands in his. "You will have to get in the zone, Viv. If Mark thinks something is off, he could act quickly against you. I'll be as close as I can, but if I get too close, he'll become suspicious."

"I know. Layla and I already went over that. It's a tall order, and I realize it all depends on me and my ability to play this guy. I've never done anything like this, but I've also never had the stakes be so high that I needed to. I understand how desperate the situation is, and when my back is up against a wall, I will fight back."

He squeezed her hands before letting go. "I don't doubt that. You're also smarter than this guy, and that's how you'll be able to get to him."

"Thanks for the vote of confidence." She paused. "I need you to do something for me, though."

"Name it." He was ready for any request.

"If something happens to me, I need you to make sure my sister understands. I don't want her to get a cleaned-up version of events. It will be important for her to hear the truth to be able to heal."

Jacob placed his hand on her shoulder. "It's not going to come to that, Viv."

"You can't make that guarantee, so I'm asking you to help me with this. It will give me some peace of mind, knowing you'll talk to Willow about everything. I don't care about security clearances. I realize I'm asking you to break protocol, but if I die, I need that to happen. Can you make me that promise?"

He looked down. "Viv, I'm not going to let you die."

She grabbed his face and pulled it close to hers. "I know you're going to do everything you can, but please, I need to know Willow will be told the truth. I'm counting on you alone for that. Promise me?"

He realized just how close she was to him. What he really wanted to do was kiss her, but that was clearly the last thing on her mind. "I promise. If something happens to you, I will personally talk to Willow. You have my word."

She rested her forehead against his. "Thank you," she whispered.

The intimacy of the moment was unexpected, and it felt only natural to wrap his arms around her. She didn't say a word, just laid her head on his shoulder.

What Viv needed was his support and protection. And that was exactly what he planned to give her.

CHAPTER
FIFTEEN

Delaney gave a tissue to a distraught Jeff King as they sat in the swanky Georgetown apartment the Kings lived in while in the United States. Weston sat on the other side of him.

"Sorry," Jeff said. "I thought I had pulled myself together today. Yesterday was a disaster. But when I started talking to you, everything just hit me again."

She hated to be doing this questioning so soon, but with the latest revelations after talking to Murray, they didn't really have a choice. "I know it's really hard to focus on our questions, but now more than ever we need to get to the bottom of this and get justice for Penelope. Do you understand?"

Jeff sniffled. "I do."

She looked at Weston to signal it was his turn to take over.

"Jeff, does the name Sergei Popov mean anything to you?" Weston asked.

Jeff blew his nose before he responded. "Yeah. Sergei is

a Russian diplomat in Brussels. He was good friends with Penelope."

"What type of friend?" Weston asked.

A frown pulled at Jeff's lips. "You're right to wonder if it was romantic, given Penelope's history, but they were just friends. She certainly wasn't trying to hide her friendship with him."

"And how many times did you see Sergei?" Delaney asked.

Jeff took a sip of water. "Oh, I don't know. Maybe I saw him ten or so times. He was always present at the ritzy diplomatic events in town, as were most of those who worked at the embassies. Socializing was a big part of Penelope's job, and the spouses were expected to put in some face time as well."

"And you think Sergei and Penelope were just friends?" She hated pushing, but she had to.

He nodded. "They ran in the same diplomatic circles. It's a pretty tight-knit community, and Penelope made sure she knew all the diplomats, especially from the powerful countries."

"This isn't easy to say, given the circumstances . . ." Delaney prefaced her next statement.

"Nothing is easy right now, Agent O'Sullivan," Jeff said flatly.

She decided to rip off the bandage. "We believe your wife may have been romantically involved with Sergei Popov. And if that isn't enough, we have to determine if the money placed into her account had anything to do with Popov or the Russians."

Jeff ran his hand through his hair. "I'm not sure what to say. I didn't realize that Penelope was stepping out on me again, but given the history, I can't rule it out." He paused.

"But I'm not sure what an affair would have to do with the money."

Weston leaned in. "We're working through all of that."

Jeff rubbed his chin. "Are you concerned that Sergei could be connected to the attack on Penelope?"

Delaney looked at him. "At this point, we're not ruling anything out, which is why we wanted to see if you had any further insight about their relationship."

Jeff muttered something under his breath, then continued. "I hadn't even considered the possibility of a romantic relationship until you put the idea into my head."

She hated this part. "I know, and I'm sorry about that, but as you can imagine, given the sensitivities in the relationship between the US and Russia, this could be much bigger than romance. That's what we have to determine."

His shoulders slumped. "I'll do whatever I can to help. I need to start making funeral arrangements, but I'm going to wait for Penelope's mom to get here tomorrow."

"If you think of anything else, please call us. We'll be in touch."

Once outside, Delaney turned to her partner. "Thoughts?"

"I feel sorry for him," Weston said, starting the SUV and pulling away from the curb. "What a complete nightmare for the guy."

"It's tough to find out you've been betrayed multiple times, but we have to consider that Jeff did know about Popov, and it was the straw that broke the camel's back."

"We don't have any evidence yet to show him tied to this, though," Weston shot back.

"A lack of evidence doesn't mean it isn't there. It just means we might not have found it yet. Keeping an open mind is critical in cases like this." She wanted to drive home that message. This was about more than this one case. It was teaching him how to view all investigations in the future.

"Uh, Delaney?"

"Yeah?"

"That truck is tailing us again."

She was quickly losing patience with this surveillance. "They're not doing a very good job of remaining undetected."

"Does that mean we're dealing with an amateur? Or maybe a member of the press trying to get the scoop for the big story?"

"I hadn't thought about the media angle. That could make sense, given the news coverage surrounding the ambassador."

"What do you want me to do?" Weston asked.

She internally debated their options for a minute before responding. "Call their bluff. Next opportunity you get to stop safely on the side of the road, let's do it."

They drove for a while longer before Weston pulled over.

"Okay, let's see what the truck does." She turned and watched.

The black truck didn't speed up or slow down. It kept its pace. She could see as it approached that the windows were darkly tinted. They wouldn't be able to get a good look inside.

The truck passed by them without any fanfare. She wrote down the license plate number to run it, although she wasn't optimistic about what she'd find.

"Well, that was weird," Weston said.

"Yeah." She had a bad feeling deep in the pit of her stomach that something bigger was going on here. "Someone has a vested interest in keeping tabs on us."

"Or maybe just you," Weston said. "No one has been at my house or followed me on jogging trails. I know it's likely connected to the investigation, but I'm still worried about the possibility of a stalker."

Delaney frowned. "I doubt that's the case."

"Still. You need to be vigilant. I'm going to make sure you get home okay today."

She decided not to push back. Maybe Weston was right. There was no need to take any chances.

Her phone rang, and she saw it was Cody, so she put it on speaker.

"Hey, you've got me and Weston."

"I've got some news," Cody said. "Big news. Our people at State and the CIA believe there's a chance that Sergei Popov isn't just a diplomat."

"What do you mean?" Weston asked.

Delaney already knew the answer.

"They believe he could be GRU. Basically, a Russian spy," Cody said.

Weston whistled. "Well, that certainly sheds some light on the situation."

Delaney still didn't want to jump to any conclusions, but this information was vitally important. "We need to tap our resources and see if we can get more evidence of the ambassador and Popov together. If Murray had suspicions about a romantic relationship, was this on the Agency's radar? And if it was, then why in the world haven't they said something?"

"I'm already on it," Cody said. "Also, last known sighting of Popov in Brussels was about two weeks ago."

"Which means he could have been here the night Ambassador King was poisoned."

◆

On Sunday afternoon, Viv walked back into her condo. She knew what she had to do, and now it was just a matter of doing it. Jacob had conducted the security sweep and was standing guard outside. She'd told him that she felt more comfortable talking to Mark without him in the room. This was going to be hard enough without having an audience.

And not just any audience. She'd had a moment with Jacob last night. She wasn't sure when things had shifted for her, but there was no doubt in her mind that she was starting to have feelings for him. There'd been a minute last night when she wondered if he had started to feel the same way, but then he'd pulled back and gone into his standard SEAL protective mode.

Staring at her phone, she tried to put aside thoughts of Jacob and think about Mark. The man she'd thought had saved her life, but it was just a big lie. How was she going to fake her way through this? Mark was an evil terrorist mastermind, and she had to play buddy-buddy with him. *Dear Lord, please help me.* That prayer was becoming all too familiar lately.

She knew she needed to face this head on. She selected Mark's contact entry and hit Call.

After a couple of rings, Mark answered.

"Mark, it's Viv."

"Hey," he said brightly. "How're you doing?"

Taking a breath, she got ready for the spiel. "Well, believe it or not, they let me come back to my condo."

"Why? I thought they wanted you to stay at the safe house."

She had to spin this story and try to make it convincing, given the fact that she'd already told him about the safe house. "I pushed back hard. I didn't want to be in the safe house. Once I made a big fuss, they relented and said they were comfortable with fortifying my condo."

"How do you feel about that?"

"I'm very glad to be home. I'd rather ride out any danger here in my own surroundings. The safe house felt so cold and impersonal. Being home gives me some comfort, if that makes sense."

"It sure does. Is there anything I can do?" Mark asked.

"That's the main reason I'm calling. I had a really nice time at dinner, but with everything going on, I'm not in the position to start a new relationship." She paused. "What I really need more than anything is a friend. Someone I can trust." She waited, hoping he would take the bait.

"You're going through a traumatic time, and I get that romance isn't at the top of your list. But if you need a friend, you can count on me. I promise I won't push you outside the friend zone. I can tell that isn't what you need."

"I appreciate your understanding." She took another pause. "Honestly, there aren't many people I can really and truly trust. But you're a safe space for me. I know that sounds silly, but I feel connected to you because of what happened. You were there when no one else was, and you stepped in when you didn't have to. That means a lot. That means everything, really."

"I would do it again in a heartbeat. I'm just thankful I was able to react quickly Friday night."

"You and me both."

"Are you still working?" he asked.

"I'm trying to, yes, but it all has to be done remotely."

"Do you want me to come over? Do you need anything? Food or anything else?

"I'm not sure. . . ." They'd instructed her not to be too eager, but she was also working against a clock. "But if you're free later and want to have pizza or something, that might be nice."

176

"That sounds perfect. How about I grab a pizza and come over around six, and we can talk more?"

"Sounds good."

"I'm glad you called, Viv. You'll get through this. I'll be there for you."

They said good-bye, and then she doubled over and grabbed a chair for support. She'd never had a panic attack before, but she felt like she might have one now. That had been intense.

After a few moments, she straightened up. She had done it. They'd said the first call might be the hardest, and she'd come through. But in her mind, she knew this call wasn't going to be the most difficult part. Seeing him in person was something altogether different, and she could only pray that she was up for the immense challenge ahead of her.

She went to the door and let Jacob back in.

"How'd it go?" he asked.

"Like clockwork." She surprised herself with that characterization, but it had gone very smoothly. "He's coming over with pizza at six."

Jacob frowned. "Do you think he got the friend message clearly enough?"

"Yes. He jumped right on it. I emphasized the trust aspect and not wanting or needing a romance. I'm hopeful that, at least initially, I'll be okay on that front." If this went on longer than expected, she was concerned that he would go back to his romantic strategy to coax her into opening up more, but she would cross that bridge if they came to it. Layla had drilled into her to take things one step at a time.

Jacob moved closer to her. "When Mark gets here, I'll stand guard outside the door, but we've put in surveillance everywhere, so I'll be able to hear everything."

"You didn't tell me that before the phone call."

"I didn't want to make you nervous, but I'll be listening to everything. We also need a code word or phrase if you feel in imminent harm. What would you like that to be?"

"It has to be something that wouldn't be commonly used, right?"

"Exactly. But not so weird as to immediately tip him off."

She thought for a moment. "What about 'I need a vacation'?"

"That works. Remember, you'll only use that if you think you're in danger but you're trying to keep your cover, just in case you're off base. If you're positive that you're blown, then scream, shout, do whatever. No need to play games at that point."

"Understood." She looked down at her watch. "A few hours to prepare for this."

He rested his hands on her shoulders. "Don't get inside your head, Viv. I've been on enough missions to know that's the last thing you should do. Once you've put in the preparation, you must let it go. If you obsess every minute for the rest of the afternoon, you'll be a wreck by the time he gets here. This first face-to-face is critical. It sets the tone for everything to come."

"Oh, I know. Any tips for not getting in my head, as you call it?" She was wide open for suggestions. It wasn't like she'd ever done anything like this before.

"Is there a fitness center in the building?" he asked.

"Yes."

"What about getting in a jog or doing some weights?"

"Are you saying I need to hit the gym?" She laughed.

He shook his head. "I'm saying that exercise helps relieve stress. It might be good for you. I don't know what your exercise of choice is."

She smiled. "You're making the assumption that I exercise."

"I have a good eye for those kinds of things."

Suddenly, she felt self-conscious. She had always worried about those last ten pounds she could never seem to shed no matter how many times she hit the gym. "I'm more of a cardio machine and weights kind of girl. I'm not a marathon runner or anything like that."

He cocked his head to the side. "That's fine. Why don't you change, and we'll go? I promise it will make you feel better."

A few minutes later, she found herself in the gym with Jacob. They were the only two there. She'd chosen a T-shirt and yoga pants and had pulled her hair up into a ponytail. He'd also changed into shorts and a T-shirt. It appeared she was going to have a workout buddy. Never in her life had she thought she'd be working out with a Navy SEAL. She hoped he wouldn't judge her fitness level.

"Don't mind me," he said. "Do whatever you'd like to do."

She jumped on one of the elliptical machines, put in her earbuds, and got into her groove. After making a couple of rounds of the room, Jacob hopped on a treadmill. As much as she tried not to, she kept looking at him. He started out at a light jog that probably would've been her fastest run on the best day. When he punched up the speed and barely seemed to lose his breath, she was reminded that this man was a warrior. It gave her a lot of comfort to know he was the one protecting her.

After putting in about forty-five minutes of cardio, she decided to move to the punching bag. It was one of her favorite things to do. As she started to punch it out, Jacob walked over.

"I'll hold the bag," he said.

She threw another punch, and with him holding the bag, it didn't budge an inch.

"Let it out," he told her.

And she did. She envisioned the punching bag as Mark's face, and she punched and jabbed and kicked. Everything she'd learned in her favorite kickboxing class. As she pummeled the bag, an image of Samir floated through her head. She was so angry about his death. She kept pounding at the bag until she realized she had tears flowing down her face.

"That's enough," Jacob said softly.

When she didn't quit, he walked around the bag and pulled her into his arms.

"It's okay. Let it all out."

She felt so safe with him, and it was natural to lean into him and let him hold her while she cried. After a few moments, the tears stopped. Her anger was still bubbling beneath the surface, but she'd gotten her emotions in check.

"I'm all sweaty." She tried to pull back from him, but he only held on to her more tightly.

"I am too. And that was good for you. Not just the exercise but also getting out the emotions."

She found that ironic, considering how tightly he kept his feelings boxed up inside of him, but she wasn't going to call him out. He was being so supportive of her, and she appreciated his strong arms holding her up.

She looked up into his dark eyes. He brushed a piece of hair that had fallen out of her ponytail back behind her ear.

"Jacob," she whispered.

He leaned down until their lips were almost touching. She closed her eyes, waiting for his lips to touch hers. When nothing happened, she opened her eyes. He was looking at her but hadn't made a move.

"What's wrong?" she asked.

"I don't want to hurt you," he said softly.

"You're not hurting me."

"But I will if we don't stop this now."

"Why?"

"Because that's just what I do, Viv."

"Just because that's been your MO in the past doesn't mean it has to be your future." She'd had enough of his fear and excuses. She rose up on her toes and kissed him.

At first he seemed surprised, and she wondered if she had misread him. But after a moment, he pulled her closer to him.

She wasn't sure what she had expected from kissing Jacob, but the reality of the kiss was much better than she could have anticipated. As safe as she felt in his arms, she didn't feel like he was holding back—just the opposite. The kiss went from sweet to intense in a matter of moments. She let loose of all her emotions and got lost in the connection. They'd seemed to clash immediately from the first time they met, but now there was no denying the intense chemistry between them.

Finally, she took a break and moved back. The way he was looking at her sent chills down her back. But at least these were the good kind.

"I told you we shouldn't have done that," he said.

"And I think we should have." She couldn't help but smile before she leaned in and kissed him again. This time it was lighter and easier than before, and after a minute, he was the one to pull away.

"We probably need to stop and get you ready for the dinner meeting."

"You're the one who told me to let it all go and forget."

"I did, but I wasn't expecting you to kiss me as the result." He laughed.

She grabbed his hands. "Jacob, I don't know what is happening right now. My life is a complete mess. Who knows if I'll even make it out of this alive. But here in this room, being with you—" She took a breath. "Kissing you felt like the most right thing I've done in a long time. Please don't deny it."

He looked down and then back up at her.

"What?" she asked.

He pulled her close to him again. "That's the problem, Viv. I can't deny it. You are amazing, and I have a way of screwing up all the good things that have ever been in my life."

She refused to let this line of thought go any further. "Then we're going to stop that right here and now. I'm opening myself up to you, Jacob. I'm being completely honest about my feelings. I hope you try to do the same."

She thought he was going to fight her on it, but instead he kissed her again.

"I'm better at showing than telling," he murmured against her mouth.

Her heart felt like it was about to explode—and not just from the hard workout. Looking at him, she felt the confidence she needed to face down Mark and whatever he might throw at her.

CHAPTER
SIXTEEN

Viv had showered and put on one of the most boring outfits she could find in her closet. She didn't want to send a message to Mark that this could be a date of any sort. The jeans and oversized sweater couldn't have been more appropriate for pizza night with a friend.

As she finished putting on a little makeup, her mind drifted back to Jacob. She couldn't believe she had made the first move. In fact, that was probably the first time in her life she'd ever done that. But it had just seemed like the right thing to do at the time. He was being stubborn, and she had to be the one to break the impasse—and she was so glad she had.

She didn't think any man had truly looked at her the way Jacob had, and it made her stomach do cartwheels. She knew he would try to pull away, but she was persistent. Yes, she was a hopeless romantic, but what if Jacob was the one she'd been searching for all these years, and it took this crisis to bring them together?

She hoped and prayed he wouldn't completely stonewall her, because she felt so much stronger knowing he was by her side. Not just as part of his job but also as something more. She could feel herself falling headlong for him, but she had to keep the depth of her emotions in check so she wouldn't scare him away.

Her relationship history had been pretty dismal, to say the least. Either she felt it and the other guy didn't, or vice versa. She'd never had a serious relationship where they were both all in. It was a bit of an embarrassing fact for her, but her friends had never judged her.

She studied herself in the mirror and was satisfied that she looked appropriate for the mission. And that was exactly what tonight was.

Walking out of her bedroom, her breath caught when she saw Jacob standing at the large living room window. He'd showered, too, and wore a blue button-down and khakis.

He turned around and frowned.

"What?" she said. "Is there something wrong with what I'm wearing? I still have time to change."

He walked over to her. "No. That was my standard scowl, as you call it. Your outfit is fine."

"It says 'friend zone,' right?"

He looked at her, and when their eyes met, there was no hint of a friend zone there. She thought he might kiss her again, but he did just the opposite and turned back to the window. "Yeah. Are you ready?"

She noticed he'd shifted the topic quickly. "Yes. Ready as I'll ever be."

"Remember the code word."

"Yes. I need a vacation."

"Remember his name."

"Mark." She had drilled that one into her head a million times. If she used his real name, it was all over. She'd be signing her death warrant.

"I'll be right outside, but remember I'm listening in. If you need me, I'll be here in a split second." He pulled his gun off the coffee table and holstered it. "I'll stay inside until he gets here. Then I'll move outside."

"That works." She went into the kitchen and pulled a bottle of water from the fridge. "That workout was intense."

He glanced at her. "It was."

"How many miles did you run?"

"A few."

She offered him a water. "You're being modest."

He took the bottle from her. "PT is part of my life. I enjoy running, though. It helps me clear my head, and it doesn't impact my shoulder at all."

"That's what you hurt, right?"

He frowned again. "Yeah. But my running time is still intact."

"I could tell." She laughed.

He closed the space between them and grabbed her arm. "Viv, please tell me that you're ready for this and that what happened between us before isn't going to cloud your thinking."

He was concerned, but she wasn't. At least not about that last point. "What happened between us has no impact on how this is going to go with Mark. If anything, I feel more confident and in a better headspace now. So thank you for that."

Jacob raised an eyebrow.

Before she could respond, the doorbell rang.

He leaned down and whispered in her ear, "You can do this, Viv. I've got you."

She walked over to the door, and Jacob opened it.

Mark walked in carrying a few pizzas. "Hey, Viv. I brought extra because I thought you might still be around, Jacob."

Mark offered his hand, and Jacob took it. "Thanks, man. I'll be right outside to give you two some privacy to talk."

"Take this with you." Mark offered him a pizza.

Viv thought Jacob might not take it, but he did, and he closed the door, leaving her alone with Mark.

"How are you doing?" Mark asked.

"Let's sit and eat, and we can talk." She was starving, and having the food to focus on would help her balance out the conversation.

"This place is so amazing," Mark said.

"Thanks. My parents left it to me." She'd planned out that she could open up to him about things he would already know.

"Oh, I'm sorry." He took a seat at the table.

She brought out plates and napkins. "Want a soda or tea?"

"Soda would be great."

She gave him a bottle and grabbed a tea for herself.

"Any updates?" He picked up a slice.

"We're still trying to figure it all out." She paused. "Mark, there are so many moving pieces here. And like I told you on the phone, I'm having a hard time knowing who I can trust. Do you think I'm paranoid?"

He shook his head. "Absolutely not. You need to be vigilant. You were attacked. Then you're shot at, and you told me something about a friend of yours being killed too, right?"

She sighed and thought about Samir. "Yeah." She took a sip of tea. "He was an Egyptian diplomat. I really can't say more than that, but he's gone." She didn't have to fake the emotion that came to her.

He picked up his soda. "You two must have been close."

"Yes. He was a really good man. You know how some people are just good people to the core? That was Samir." She gasped and covered her mouth with her hand. It was all a ploy to make him think that she had accidentally revealed Samir's name. "Please don't repeat his name. You won't, will you?" She met his gaze.

He leaned in. "I told you, Viv. You can trust me completely with anything. I'm a lawyer like you, so I know how to keep my mouth shut."

She let out a feigned sigh of relief. "Thank you." She leaned back in her chair and took a few more bites of pizza, waiting for him to make the next move.

"Is the State Department providing you with any additional security, or is it just Jacob?"

"Right now, it's just him. He's good at his job, though, so I feel safe."

Mark nodded. "He seems more than competent. Any leads on your attackers?"

She groaned. "Not one. I doubt they'll ever find those guys."

"What are the police telling you?"

She made a show of hesitating. "I can share something with you, right?"

He moved closer. "Yes."

She took a dramatic breath. "The local police have completely turned things over to the FBI."

"The FBI?"

She nodded. "They're investigating why my friend was killed. Trying to figure out why I was attacked and who tried to gun us down."

He narrowed his eyes. "And you don't have any clue?"

"I wish I did. I'm all ears, if you have any theories."

He rubbed his chin. "Well, from a lawyer you may find this hard to believe, but it's hard to opine without all the facts."

"What else would you need to know?"

"I don't know what I don't know." He laughed.

She was glad he laughed, because things had gotten a little intense. "They think this is all tied to the Egyptian ambassador's death."

He frowned in confusion. "I thought he died of a heart attack."

"I've probably said too much." Everything she was saying had been laid out for her by the Agency. This was the story they wanted him to believe. Definitely nothing about the op or the real underlying threat.

He frowned. "You look sad. Let's talk about something else."

"That would be nice."

Mark talked about his work, which Viv wondered if he was actually doing as part of his cover or if it was all fabricated. But she didn't dare push it. She just smiled and nodded and asked questions when appropriate.

She'd been given strict orders not to go outside the lines tonight. This was the first meeting, and the goal was just to make him believe that she wanted him as a confidant. That would keep her alive for the time being and maybe give them a chance to get intel out of him later. But they had to be patient for now.

"Enough of me droning on about myself. What else can I do to help you?" Mark asked.

"Just being here is helping. Being able to talk to you about all of this. I know I can't share every detail, but you understand where I'm coming from. You witnessed what happened to me firsthand. You were there both times. Those monsters. I'm just a lawyer. I am not a threat to anyone."

Mark frowned. "Viv, I hate to say this, but is it possible those wanting to hurt you believe that you're more than a lawyer?"

She raised her eyebrows. "What else would I be?"

"Like a spy or something."

She laughed. "Mark, do I look like a spy to you? I went to Georgetown Law, and I've been a lawyer at State since I graduated. I know people in the intelligence community, and believe me, I am nothing like them."

He cocked his head to the side. "What makes you say that?"

She waved her arms. "I'm an open book. I have a simple life. I do my legal work. I work on policy initiatives. But I'm not a CIA agent. I don't even know how the men who attacked me could assume such a thing."

"Maybe it's because in your job you have a lot of foreign contacts."

"Perhaps, but there are a lot of people with foreign contacts who aren't spies. I would be the worst CIA agent ever. I'm far too transparent to keep up an act like that."

"The people who want to hurt you don't know the real you, though, do they?"

"Right." She deflated. "I know the truth, but that doesn't help me convince those who want to hurt me that I'm not who they think I am."

He seemed to believe what she was saying, but she also knew she was staring into the eyes of a highly trained operative. So nothing really gave her comfort at the moment.

She let out a planned yawn to help wind down the night. "Sorry. It's been a long two days."

He placed his hand on top of hers, and she had to fight the urge to move.

"I know. I'll leave so you can get some rest, but I'll call you tomorrow to check on you."

"Thanks, Mark. You've become a true friend to me." She smiled.

He gave her a quick kiss on the cheek. "You keep the leftovers. If you don't eat them, then your muscle out there surely will."

She didn't like how he talked about Jacob, but she couldn't seem too offended. "Thanks." She walked him to the door, and he left without much fanfare. Jacob waited a minute before coming back inside.

Before she could open her mouth, he kissed her deeply, catching her off guard. She didn't complain, even in her confusion, but when he pulled back, he placed his finger over her lips.

Then she realized what he was doing. That wasn't a happy-to-see-you-again kiss. That was a shut-up kiss.

He went to the guest bedroom and came back with some type of device that she presumed scanned for bugs—other than the ones they had put in.

After a complete sweep, Jacob turned to her. "We can talk now."

She let out a breath. "That was really intense."

"You did great. I couldn't see either of you, but it seemed by the tone of his voice and what he was saying that he was completely buying everything you were selling."

She flopped down on the couch, suddenly exhausted. "I was afraid he would see right through me, but honestly, I don't think he did. Layla was right. The closer you can keep things to the truth, the better. But with each word out of my mouth, I worried he was going to call me out. When he didn't, I just kept going. It was surreal."

"You did great, Viv. The Agency is going to examine the audio, and then they'll let you know the next move. There's nothing else you can do tonight."

"No safe house, right? I'm staying here?"

"For now. We think it's the easiest approach to manage the Mark situation, but I will need to stay in the guest room or on the couch. We can't leave you unattended."

How was she going to handle being so close to him after what had happened? For her own safety, she knew there was no other option. "Of course. Make yourself at home. Whatever you need, just let me know."

He took a seat next to her. "We do need to revisit our conversation from earlier."

She didn't like the sound of that. "And that is?" She was going to make him work for it. There was no way she was just going to concede.

"We need to keep things strictly platonic between us. There's no room for error here."

Annoyance grew inside her. "What, you just make that pronouncement and I'm expected to follow it?"

"Last time I checked, it took two to tango."

Her anger simmered. She was frustrated not just with him but also at the entire situation. "You're trying to annoy me. Trying to push me away. You know what, Jacob? This whole experience has reminded me just how precious life is and that not one additional moment is guaranteed."

"I'm not arguing that point." He hung his head. "I'm just not the man you need to be with."

She refused to give in, and she lifted his chin so they made direct eye contact. "The whole 'it's not you, it's me' thing is so tiresome. I just wish you would be honest. With me and with yourself. Those kisses earlier meant something. You can't look me in the eyes and say otherwise."

He didn't break eye contact. "I'm not denying there's an attraction here. A very strong attraction."

"Attraction? It goes deeper than physical attraction, and you know it." She took a breath and tried to keep her fragile emotions in check. "If you need time to come around to my way of thinking, then I'll give that to you. But I'm not going to give up on us. On what we could have. Together." She stood and walked toward her room before turning and looking over her shoulder. "Good night, Jacob."

◆

Viv's words rang through his head. *I'm not going to give up on us. On what we could have. Together.*

He'd taken several catnaps during the night, but now it was almost six o'clock, and he decided it was time to start the day.

Viv just didn't understand him. Of course he would love to be with her. To have the perfect romance. But guys like him didn't end up with women like her.

He knew everyone had baggage, but what he had wasn't baggage. It was a freaking two-ton weight on his back. Everything he'd experienced in the field as a SEAL. His career-ending injury. And while Viv knew about that stuff on the surface, there was so much more she didn't know about. Like his completely screwed-up family and how messed up he was from all of that.

After taking a hot shower, he walked into the kitchen. Viv was still in her room, so he decided to make coffee. How was he going to make her understand that the two of them would never work? He'd quickly learned that she was a stubborn and persistent woman. She wasn't going to let this go unless he set some really strong boundary lines and enforced them. But that would be on him. He'd just have to do it no matter how difficult it was. In the end, he was doing this because he cared about her and she needed things he couldn't give.

His phone rang, and he saw it was Director Phillips.

"Director. Good morning."

"How'd Vivian do last night?"

He was going to tell the truth even if it meant they would keep pushing Viv further into this. "Great. You never would've known that she had no experience."

"Good. I got the impression she was a tough one. We have eyes on the target. If he makes physical contact with his friends, we'll know it."

"What's next?"

The director sighed. "There's a debate at the Agency about whether we need to get surveillance inside Mark's condo."

Jacob clenched his fist. "Wait a minute. You aren't suggesting that Viv be the one to do it?"

"That's the rub. I don't doubt she could do it, but if he finds them, then her cover could be blown. I think they're going to see how next contact goes and then make that call."

It was just as Jacob feared. Viv was in quicksand. "This is getting more dangerous for her by the moment. We can't use her like a pawn. I hope you understand that."

"I do. And at the risk of poking my nose in where it doesn't belong, you seem to care about Vivian. I would hope, given the stakes here, that you would keep the relationship between the two of you strictly professional."

See, everyone but Viv understood this was for the best. "Absolutely, sir. You have no pushback on my end on that."

"What about hers?"

What could he even say?

"Never mind. Don't answer that. Just do your job, son. Keep her safe. These guys aren't random street criminals. They're high-value terrorists intent on wreaking havoc to further their ideological goals."

"Roger that."

The conversation ended, and he turned and saw Viv standing in the doorway with her arms crossed.

"Who was that?" She walked into the kitchen.

"The FBI director. He was checking in. They've got Mark under surveillance."

"What if he realizes that?"

"He won't. The FBI team knows what they're doing."

"I hope so," she muttered. "What now?"

"As far as Mark goes, hang tight until we get further direction on next steps."

"I'd still like to keep reviewing the files we have on Ambassador Zidan. I want to make sure we haven't missed anything."

"That's fine. I'm going to check in with Delaney and see if they need anything from us while we're waiting."

Viv grabbed a coffee cup. "I think it's going to be a long day."

He felt the exact same way.

CHAPTER
SEVENTEEN

The connection of a US ambassador to a potential Russian spy set off warning bells throughout multiple agencies, but they were yet to find more concrete evidence that went beyond a romantic connection between the two.

Delaney and Weston were in the war room, and she had just finished yet another cup of average State Department coffee.

Weston looked up. "Here's the latest I have from the CIA and Interpol." He displayed some photos on the screen. "These are pictures of the ambassador and Popov together. Most of these are connected to diplomatic events, but there is one candid in downtown Brussels where they look pretty cozy. He has his arm around her."

Delaney studied the pictures. Popov was definitely a handsome man—tall, nicely built, blond. But what she noticed even more was the way he was looking at the ambassador. "Does that look like two friendly diplomats to you?"

Weston grinned. "No. He is totally into her."

"Exactly what I thought, although the ambassador looks a bit more guarded. What level of comfort do the intel agencies have pegging this guy as GRU?" She wanted firmer answers.

Weston leaned in. "That's the tricky part. No one is willing to commit. The way our CIA contact described it to me is that there's a strong suspicion that he's a Russian agent, but he isn't on the confirmed list. That also explains why they have some counter intel on him but not as much as the known spies."

"And where are we on tracing the source of the funds that went into the ambassador's account?" They really needed a break on that.

"I'm told our best FBI financial analysts are on it, but no definitive answers yet."

She stood and walked up to the whiteboard. "Here's what we have." She started writing. "We have the ambassador's chief of staff saying that he thinks she was romantically involved with Popov, and he witnessed them kissing. We have pictures indicating that they were at the very least close, so my money's on that the two were, in fact, romantically involved."

Weston nodded. "Jeff says that he knew Popov but didn't suspect anything."

"I think Jeff's in denial." She wrote *denial* in big print on the board. "But we also have to consider that Jeff did know and that he's still a viable suspect."

Weston crossed his arms. "I don't know, Delaney. The poor guy's been through the wringer. Do you really think he could be that good of an actor?"

She bit the inside of her cheek. "I've seen even better, but we can put Jeff to the side for the moment and talk through the Russian." She jotted on the white board. "If we start with the premise that the ambassador was having an affair with Popov, then why kill her?" She drew a question mark.

Weston moved closer to her. "You're going to think I've read too many spy novels, but hear me out."

"There are no bad ideas here, Weston." She didn't want him to filter his thoughts. He was one of the brightest people she knew, and she wanted to use that to their advantage.

He turned to face her. "What if these two were more serious than a casual affair, and the Russian government was afraid the ambassador could turn Popov?"

She thought about it. "For that theory to work, Popov would have to be a major player. The Russians are bold, but I don't think they're going to put out a hit on a sitting US ambassador over a midlevel spy. If the Russian government was behind the drugging, it could be viewed by our government as an act of war."

Weston sighed. "Yeah, seems kind of extreme, doesn't it?"

"Extreme, yes, but given the current geopolitical environment, every scenario should be on the table." She wrote on the board again. "Let's also play it out the other way. What if the ambassador was passing secrets along to the Russians and getting paid for it? Maybe there were some lines she couldn't or wouldn't cross, and they took her out to try to clean up."

Weston's eyes lit up. "I just had another thought that might be more plausible, given the implications you just outlined."

"Shoot."

He started pacing around the room. "What if the drugging wasn't sanctioned by the Russian government but was purely personal? What if Popov wanted the ambassador to leave her husband? When she refused, he killed her in a jealous rage."

"Also possible, but where does the money fit in to that theory?"

"Oh, I'm still saying she's on the take from the Russians, but they never intended to kill her. They might even be mad at Popov for doing it because now they've lost an asset. Everything we've heard about the ambassador is that she was highly connected, smart, savvy, and a power player. If she and Popov were lovers and he was indeed a spy, the chances of her not knowing are almost zero."

"Good point." So many ideas swirled in her mind. "The problem is that we have these great theories, but given the nature of this investigation, our hard evidence is limited." She sighed.

"I wonder if Nan knows about Popov." Weston stood, arms crossed.

"It can't hurt to ask." Delaney set down the whiteboard marker. "Why don't we pay her a visit?"

"Sounds good to me."

It didn't take them long to make the quick drive from Foggy Bottom to Arlington. Delaney hoped that Nan would be at home, since they'd decided to make a surprise visit instead of calling ahead.

They approached the house and rang the doorbell. It wasn't long before Nan appeared. "Agents, please come in."

"Thank you, Ms. Kennedy. We're very sorry for your loss."

Nan's blue eyes teared up. "Thank you. It's been awful."

Delaney looked at her. "I'm sorry that we have to ask more questions, but hopefully you understand that we're trying to get justice for the ambassador."

"Come have a seat. Can I offer you anything?" Nan was still in perfect hostess form, even given the loss she had suffered.

"No. We're good," Delaney said.

"What can I help you with?" Nan looked at Weston and then back at her.

Delaney figured it was best to get to the point, given Nan was clearly hurting. "Last time we spoke, you talked to us about the issues in the ambassador's marriage. You indicated that you thought things had gotten better once Jeff moved to Brussels. Do you remember that?"

Nan clasped her hands in her lap and nodded. "Yes, I do."

Delaney took a breath. "I need you to tell me what you know about Sergei Popov."

Nan averted her eyes. "I'm not sure what you mean."

Weston leaned toward her. "Ms. Kennedy, your best friend is dead. Trying to protect her secrets now won't do anyone any good. Okay?"

Nan's eyes filled with tears again. "Yes, I know about the Russian." She paused. "Penelope was in love with him."

Love? Delaney hadn't been expecting that. She could have chided Nan for keeping this from them, but there was no point. They needed more information. "The ambassador told you that?"

Nan twisted a strand of hair nervously around her finger. "Yes. With men, Penelope always had the upper hand. Most of them were nothing more than distractions for her. Almost like a game. But Sergei was different. She truly enjoyed spending time with him. They went to all the same diplomatic functions. She felt like they were truly equals in every way. Penelope told me that he was smart, funny, caring." Her cheeks reddened. "And a lot of other details I'd prefer not to get into."

Delaney got that message loud and clear. "Do you know how long they had been seeing each other?"

"About a year," Nan said.

"Do you think Jeff knew?" Weston asked.

Nan shook her head. "Probably not. Penelope was pretty smart about these things."

Delaney had to ask. "Did the ambassador talk much about Sergei's job?"

"Not a lot. I knew he was a diplomat who worked at the Russian embassy in Brussels, and because of that, they had many opportunities to see each other. It's how they met, and the relationship grew from friendship into something much more intense."

"Are you sure that's all she told you?" Delaney asked.

"Yes. Why, is there something else?"

They were going to keep the spying aspect to themselves. "We're just trying to be thorough."

"You don't think that Sergei could've hurt Penelope, do you? I never got the impression that he was a threat to her—just the opposite. She might have considered leaving Jeff for him if it wasn't for the fact that she couldn't have kept her job."

"Why not?" Weston asked.

"There was no way our government would approve of her continuing her work as an ambassador if she married a high-ranking Russian diplomat." Nan sighed. "Penelope didn't love easily—rarely at all. But I think she actually did love Sergei. Deeply so."

And love could make you do crazy things. Even become a traitor to your country.

◆

Viv sat at the coffee shop, waiting for Layla to arrive. Jacob was a few tables over, seated with the perfect vantage point.

He'd been on high alert since they'd left her condo, although she really couldn't blame him.

Her phone rang, and she saw it was her sister. She'd given the number of her latest burner phone to Willow because she refused to be cut off from her only family, and Jacob had reluctantly agreed, since she was no longer at the safe house. "Willow, how are you?"

"I'm good. More important, how are you?"

"I'm doing better. A lot better, actually." It hurt that she couldn't tell her sister the new danger she was facing, but that was an impossibility.

"Viv, you're my twin. I can tell you're holding back on me."

"There's just a lot going on here." She took a breath. "But you know I love you, right?"

"Yes, and I love you too. But now you're scaring me even more."

That was the last thing she wanted to do. "I'm sorry. I guess I'm just a little emotional these days."

"You can tell me if something is bothering you or if you're in some type of trouble."

Viv needed to divert quickly. "Well, about that SEAL . . ."

"Oh! So this is what has you tied up in knots. I knew something was going on between you two."

"There wasn't. Well, I guess there isn't. He doesn't want there to be."

"But you do."

She sighed. "Yes. He's hardheaded."

"You'll have him convinced in no time. What's gone on between you two?"

"We kissed."

Willow let out a little shriek. "You really like this guy. I can't believe it."

201

"I do, but he's pushing me away."

"Give him time. Guys have to convince themselves that it was their idea." Willow laughed.

Viv saw Layla walk in and waved her over. "Willow, I'm meeting Layla for coffee. Can I call you back later?"

"Sure. And I'll be wanting updates on the SEAL."

Viv laughed, said good-bye, and hung up. Layla smiled widely and took a seat across from Viv.

"I got you your usual." Viv pushed a latte toward her friend.

Layla grabbed it and took a sip. "Mmm. So good. Thank you." Her eyes drifted over to where Jacob was sitting. "I see your bodyguard is in full effect."

Viv had to tell her best friend what was going on. "I need to talk to you about that."

Layla's eyes narrowed. "Is everything okay?"

Viv leaned forward. "We kissed. Multiple times."

Excitement lit Layla's expression. "Get out of here. Are you serious?"

Viv tried to contain her giddiness, but this was her best friend she was talking to. Layla had been with her through everything, so there was no need to hold anything back. "Yes. One minute we were working out in the gym at my condo, and I was hitting a punching bag, worried about what was about to happen with Mark, and the next minute . . ." Viv lifted her hands.

Layla arched an eyebrow. "Did it end there?"

Viv nodded. "Yes, definitely. And Jacob has made it clear that he thinks those kisses should be the end of everything."

"And you don't," her friend countered.

"Layla, you know it's unusual for me to really like someone like this. And I'm not going to let it just slip through my hands." She paused. "And before you start lecturing me on why there are a million reasons that this is a bad idea, I'm going to tell you that I'm pretty set in my feelings on this."

Layla glanced at Jacob. "I wasn't going to tell you it was a bad idea. Just to be careful. I don't want you to get hurt. And if he is sending up warning flags, sometimes you need to listen to them, even if it hurts."

"That's the thing. None of his reasons really make sense. He's acting out of fear. Yes, he has a lot of issues, and he's still working through them, but that's no reason to be alone. Especially when you find something special. He's trying to take the high road and claim that he doesn't want me to be hurt. He's giving me the whole he's-not-the-type-of-guy-I-need line."

Layla smiled. "And you're not having any of it. I don't blame you, but I do think you're going to need to be patient. Sounds like he has a lot of things he has to work through in addition to his feelings for you. Not to mention that he's been assigned to keep you safe. His number-one priority is protecting you from these threats. That's his job."

Viv knew that. "I just wanted to share with you what was going on. I knew you would understand."

Layla squeezed her hand. "And I'm glad you did. We've been through so much, and you know you can tell me anything. I would like nothing more than for you to find happiness, and if it's with Jacob, that's great. If not, there will be someone else."

Viv wasn't going to argue. She had her mind made up.

Layla lifted her cup. "So, shifting topics, how do you think it went with Mark? I've read the transcript and listened to the audio, but I want to hear your perspective."

It was strange that so many people had listened to their

pizza night and were probably judging every word that came out of her mouth. Viv hoped she had done okay. "It was scary, but I tried to take in all the advice you gave me. He seemed very receptive. But for all I know, he saw right through me."

Layla shook her head. "I don't think he saw through you at all. Just the opposite. We've been keeping an eye on him, and there's nothing to suggest that he found you out. And from what I heard on the audio, you really outdid yourself. I'm confident you can see this through to the end."

"And what, exactly, will that entail?" Viv wasn't sure what the Agency was going to ask of her.

"That's still being discussed at the Agency and with the FBI, but they're going to want you to meet him again. In a perfect world, I would like him to reach out to you. If he doesn't within a day or two, then you can."

It was good she had Layla to confide in. Her best friend was not only someone she trusted completely but also someone who understood her in ways no one else really could. "It was just so weird. I was trying to stick to the truth, like you said, but there were moments when I was looking in his eyes and he was presenting as one thing, but I knew deep down he was something else." A chill shot through her. "It was downright frightening. It makes you realize that you cannot know someone if they don't want you to. It definitely made me think about some things differently."

"That's completely natural. I have to warn you, though— you did so well, it's possible my friends might be knocking on your door after all this is over to recruit you." Layla laughed.

Viv wasn't laughing. "That will never happen. I enjoy being a lawyer. Just getting ready last night, I thought I might break down."

Layla nodded knowingly. "Remember who you're talking

to. I just wanted to be an analyst, and we all see how that turned out."

"But you're actually amazing at all of it. I know my limitations."

"You're way too hard on yourself, Viv. Give yourself more credit. But I'm going to caution you again, because you do have to be careful. You rocked it the first time out. But each time is going to get more difficult, not easier. The webs will get more intricate, and he's going to start to push for more and more information. We all need to be on the same page about what you're going to share and when."

Viv nodded. "I don't plan to go rogue. I'm going to follow exactly what you all tell me to do. I'm just the vessel here. I'm not the operational brain trust, and I'm not going to pretend like I am."

Layla took a sip of her latte before responding. "But you are. You're going to know Mark better than any of us. You're going to be the one spending time with him, looking into his eyes, reading his expressions. Those things are invaluable. We will need as much of your feedback as possible."

Those words shook Viv. There was too much of this operation riding on her shoulders. "If I didn't know what I do, there's no way I would believe it about him. He is so convincing. Kind, funny, smart. I didn't feel threatened by him at all. Besides the fact that I know who he actually is. Does that make sense?"

"It does. The more information you can feed him, the longer we have to find these guys. Mark is being very careful. It's all about buying time and hoping that he inadvertently says something that helps us."

"I don't know, Layla. I don't think Mark is going to slip up. He's too smart for that. But I'm willing to do anything I can to see if I can make it happen."

"There's something else I need to tell you. Something is being debated between the CIA and FBI that goes directly to your last point about him not slipping up."

Viv's heart sank. She figured this couldn't be good. "What?"

Layla tucked a strand of dark hair behind her ear. "There's some discussion about whether you should invite yourself over to his place so you can install surveillance equipment."

Viv felt her mouth drop open. "You want me to bug Mark's house? While he's there? Have you lost your mind?"

"This isn't my idea. I'm just sharing with you what I'm hearing. There are some who believe the intel we might get from that is extremely valuable, but if he does any standard security sweeps and finds them, then your cover could be blown. For my part, I'm not pushing that strategy. I think we see how else we can play this with him first. And it obviously buys you more time if they think they're playing you."

"Can't they do like what they do in the movies? Where the guy leaves the house, and a cable van or repair truck comes up, and then they go into his place and bug it?"

Layla chuckled. "Something like that, but we believe Mark's place is probably on lockdown. That would make getting in that way very difficult. And if others have him under surveillance on his own side, they would notice right away and warn him. You being able to get in his house at his own invitation is our best shot at planting a bug undetected."

"I'm really not comfortable with that, but what am I comfortable with at this point?" She was slowly starting to feel any control she had over the situation slip away. It was clear the Agency was just going to decide what she needed to do, and she would have to follow orders like a good soldier. Even if it meant putting her life at further risk. An all-too-familiar feeling started to form in the pit of her stomach.

"Don't let that worry you just yet. It's being talked about, but nothing has been decided. Keep your head in the game."

At that moment, it hit her. "Layla, are you, like, my handler or something?"

Layla smiled. "I don't think there is an exact term for anything we're doing right now. We're making up this playbook as we go. Shifting people around into different roles they never thought they would be in, but doing it all for the greater good. Catching these guys is a top priority for the US government."

"I still don't know how they managed to get away in the first place." That was bothering Viv.

Layla frowned. "That's being investigated by the inspector general. They're keeping it all pretty hush-hush. If I had to guess, someone is going to lose their job and probably be arrested."

"Why is there so much evil in this world?" She knew Layla didn't have all the answers, but just talking it through helped her.

"That's where our faith has to come in. It's one of the only things that has gotten me through the dark times—knowing that our God is greater than all of these dark things we're dealing with. It's a source of comfort and strength for me."

And for Viv too. "Yes, I'm finding myself needing to rely on the Lord much more each day." Maybe that was part of it all. This awful experience did have some silver linings. Growing in her faith was one of those, and she would gladly accept it.

"I've got to get to the office. Is there anything else you need from me?" Layla asked.

"No. Thank you for everything."

Layla stood, and Viv hugged her. She held on an extra

second, thankful for her friend. Once Layla left, she just sat there, thinking. After a couple of minutes, Jacob joined her.

"Everything okay?" he asked.

"Yes, just taking a moment."

"Take all the time you need. Do you want me to move back to the other table?"

No way. "Please stay. I want to talk to you."

His signature scowl returned. "Okay."

"I felt like you opened up to me a little bit, and then after we kissed, you shut everything down."

"All for the best."

"I know you keep saying that, but is keeping all your feelings bottled up inside really for the best? You said you felt better when you talked things through with me. I'm just making that offer again. You want to talk about anything? No strings attached. I'm here for you."

Jacob sat in silence for a moment. "I don't have words to describe you, Vivian Steele."

She laughed. "I don't think that was a compliment."

"You're just unlike anyone else I've ever known. I try to push you away, and you come back with kindness. I'm not used to that."

She reached out and took his hand. He flinched but didn't remove it. "I know you're hurting. There are issues you still need to deal with. There are probably things I don't even know about. A lot of them. But I live my life honestly. That sometimes means getting hurt. It often means being misunderstood. But I want you to know where I stand. And I want to see something good in this otherwise nightmarish situation."

"You like trying to find the good in bad things, don't you?"

"It's the only way I've gotten through life at this point.

After my parents died so suddenly, my world was shaken. But each day that followed, I committed myself to finding one thing to be thankful for. It wasn't always easy. But I made it through with God's help. I could've never done it alone." She paused. "I told you about my family, but I don't know anything about yours."

He looked down.

"Another painful topic?" She realized she was still holding his hand, and she gave it a squeeze. "You don't have to tell me if you don't want to, but I'd love to know more about you and where you came from."

He blew out a breath. "Where do I even start?"

Maybe she was making progress getting through to him after all. "Wherever you want."

◆

Jacob had figured it was only a matter of time before this topic came up, given how much they talked about her family. He struggled for a moment with whether he should just shut it down and say they needed to go, but in a strange way, telling her his family issues might make her feel better by giving her something else to focus on, at least for a few minutes. He decided to start talking.

"I was born in south Florida. I never knew my dad. And unfortunately, my mother battled a lot of demons and had very bad taste in men. My grandmother raised me until she passed away when I was eleven, and that's when things got really jacked up."

"What happened?"

How did he even explain it? "My mom was having a really rough time after her mom passed away, and the dude she was with got her into some heavy drugs. She decided one day that she'd had enough. And then she was gone." He felt his eyes become wet with tears. Something that almost never happened. But then again, he never spoke about his mother's death to anyone.

Viv bit her bottom lip. "I'm so sorry. I know that words aren't adequate for situations like this."

"Yeah. It was rough."

"What happened to you after she died?"

"I got put into the system, and it wasn't pretty. It did make me very tough. That's one of the reasons I went into the military. I needed that structure and discipline badly."

"Do you even know who your father is?"

He nodded. "My grandmother told me before she passed away, but he got mixed up with some bad people who killed him when I was six."

Viv paled.

That reaction was exactly why he didn't talk about his family. "I'm sorry. I told you my family history was a complete mess. I probably shouldn't have laid it on you like that."

She shook her head and took his other hand in hers so that now she held both. "I asked for you to open up, and that's exactly what you're doing. I can't begin to imagine how difficult that was for you. But as someone who also lost her parents, I can empathize somewhat. At least I had my sister. It sounds like you didn't have anyone, right?"

"Right. It was just me. When I was little, I wished I had a brother. That's what the military ended up giving me. A whole host of them."

"And when you couldn't be a SEAL anymore, that was taken away from you too." Viv looked down before meeting his eyes. "Jacob, you've sustained more hurt than most people ever will. I really do think it would be helpful if you talked to a professional about this. I'm always here to lend an ear, but having someone who knows what they're doing to help you work through all this . . . it could be really good for you. Whether you want to believe it or not, all of this pain is still very present with you. I can see it in every breath you take."

Her words shook him because he knew she was telling the truth. Maybe she had a point. Maybe it was time for him to put aside his ego and get some help. He'd had to see the Navy psychiatrist a few times because he was ordered to, but to say that was unproductive would have been an understatement. He'd been so blocked off then that he wasn't willing to talk about anything. But there was something about being around Viv that softened him up. He wasn't quite sure yet whether that was good or bad.

"Just tell me you'll think about it," she said. "There's no need to make commitments. It's just a thought. And like I said, you've got my ear, and you're kind of stuck with me. Just like free therapy."

That made him laugh. "I needed that."

"How did you end up in DSS? That's one thing I've been wondering."

"A connection from the SEAL teams. He made some phone calls and helped get me on the fast track. At that point, I knew just having the opportunity to be in security and work in law enforcement was huge. Even though I wasn't sure what all the job entailed, I knew I'd be stupid not to jump at the chance."

"It's a good fit for you, and you're very good at your job."

"It doesn't look good to have the deaths of two ambassadors on my watch at the diplomatic dinner."

"Everyone knows that's not on you, or they never would've put you on the task force."

CHAPTER
EIGHTEEN

The next morning, Delaney and Weston sat in the living room of the Kings' apartment, ready to talk to Jeff again. They'd talked it out and gotten approval from the CIA to share the information about Popov with him.

"Do you have updates?" Jeff asked.

"We do," Delaney said.

Jeff let out a big sigh. "It's about time. I was really hoping that's why we're meeting today."

Delaney kept her expression neutral. "Unfortunately, you won't like what we have to tell you."

Jeff looked down. "Just say it."

She'd already given him the news about the affair, so hopefully this wouldn't send him into a complete tailspin. "We talked last time about your wife's relationship with Sergei Popov."

"You don't have to remind me, Agent O'Sullivan. Believe me, it's fresh in my mind."

"And I'm sorry to talk about it further, but after our last meeting, new information came to light about Popov."

"What information?"

"Our government believes there is a good chance that Sergei Popov actually works for Russian intelligence and his diplomatic post is his cover."

"So not only was my wife having an affair, she was having an affair with a Russian spy?" His voice cracked.

Delaney glanced at Weston, and he jumped in. "I know this is tough to process, but the reason we're telling you is because we're trying to determine if there's any way that Popov or the Russians could have had a hand in drugging your wife."

Jeff's eyes grew large. "You think the Russians killed her?"

Delaney didn't want him to get too far ahead of himself. "We just don't know. We're not even one hundred percent sure that Popov is Russian intelligence, but he is suspected to be. It's possible that your wife's romantic relationship with Popov could've crossed into business."

"Just when I think this can't get any worse." Jeff groaned. "Does this have to come out right now? The funeral is tomorrow. I'd hate for her reputation to be tarnished at a time like this."

Weston shook his head. "Oh no. We don't have any intention of this getting out. Ever, if we can help it."

"Good."

"The ambassador has been murdered. We will bring those responsible to justice, but the last thing we want is to drag her through the mud in the process," Delaney said. "It will be a balancing act, but you have my word that nothing will come out about this anytime soon. We're still digging through a lot of different channels to make sure we have the full story."

Jeff sighed. "I really appreciate that. Things are tough enough as it is. Especially on Penelope's family."

Weston nodded. "We understand. We're trying to turn over every stone. Have you thought of anything else since the last time we talked?"

Jeff looked at Delaney. "I keep going back through all the times I saw Sergei and Penelope together. I didn't want to say anything, but now that you brought up this spy thing, I guess I have to."

Delaney's pulse started to ramp up. "Please tell us anything you can remember."

"I once saw Penelope give Sergei something. I think it was a jump drive, but honestly I can't say for sure. At the time, I didn't think much of it. I just thought it had something to do with work, and I definitely didn't think it had anything to do with spying." His voice cracked again as he stared out the window. "I just can't believe that Penelope would spy for the Russians." He let out a strained laugh. "But then again, I didn't think she was still cheating on me either. I'm beginning to think maybe I didn't know her at all."

Delaney didn't want Jeff to spiral. "We don't know exactly what was going on. We will get to the bottom of it, but please don't assume the worst. There could be innocent explanations."

"Not for the affair," he snapped.

His response startled her, but she figured he had the right to be angry and hurt after all he had gone through.

Weston leaned in. "We're not trying to pour salt in the wound. We're just looking for the truth and to get justice for your wife."

Jeff ran his hand through his hair. "I really thought that once I moved to Brussels things would change. And I thought they had. I guess I was wrong." He hung his head. His cell phone rang, and he looked at it. "I'm sorry. This is the funeral home. I need to take this."

"We'll see ourselves out."

Once they were back in the car, she turned to Weston. "We need to get a meeting with Cody and someone from the Agency. It's time we push the CIA for more answers."

"I'll set it up."

◆

Viv was sitting in her condo with Jacob and Layla. She was still trying to wrap her head around what was being asked of her.

Layla looked at her. "Mark invited you over, Viv. If you turn him down, that will make him suspicious."

"I told him I'd have to bring Jacob, and he didn't put up a fight on that."

Jacob started pacing around the living room. "I don't like this at all. Yes, I'll be there, but I'll be outside. I won't have any visibility into what's going on inside the house. I think it's far too risky."

Layla blew out a breath. "That's not the riskiest part. The Agency wants Viv to plant listening devices. She may not get another chance to go inside Mark's place. This might be our best and only chance."

Jacob turned to her. "Viv, tell me you're not considering doing this."

"What choice do I have, really? If I say no, he'll wonder why I'm putting him off. Getting closer to him still buys me time and has the chance of leading to the escaped detainees." It wasn't even her decision to make, so she was trying to face it as strongly as she could.

"Your life will be on the line the moment you step inside that man's home. Do you realize that?" Jacob asked.

Her frustration level was rising. "You're not being helpful. I have to do this, so let's move on from whether I'm doing it to how to best keep me safe in the process."

He muttered something under his breath. She'd never seen him this agitated, and she wondered if this was one of the reasons he hadn't wanted to get involved. Because his emotions were definitely coming into play. There was no doubt in her mind that if she were anyone else, he would have been all systems go.

Jacob lifted his hands. "I get it. I don't like it, but I get it. Layla, did you bring the equipment?"

Layla opened up her purse and pulled out a small bag. "These are super tiny." She pulled out a small disc about the size of a dime.

"How many are there?"

"We gave you ten, but you won't use them all. It's just in case there are any issues. Ideally, you'd spread them out in as many rooms as you can get into."

Viv's pulse thumped. "That's not going to be easy."

"Some rooms will be. Others won't. All we ask is that you do the best you can."

Layla explained a few other technical things about the equipment before giving her a hug and leaving her alone with Jacob.

He ran his hand through his hair. "I know you're upset with me."

She shook her head. "It's just that I don't have any options here, so I need your support in helping me complete this operation instead of worrying about the fact that I actually have to do it."

"I have faith in you, Viv. I do. I just can't help but worry."

She walked over to him and took his hand. "I'm glad you care."

"I probably care way too much, and that's an issue," he said softly.

She didn't wait for him to keep making his point. Instead, she stood on tiptoe and kissed him. He didn't stop her at first, but after a minute, he pulled back.

"Viv, we can't keep doing this."

"Why not?"

He groaned. "You know why. This is getting way too complicated. Your entire focus should be this operation. Kissing me should be the last thing on your mind."

"But it's not," she shot back.

He ran his hand through his hair again. "You are infuriating, do you know that?"

She smiled. "You've mentioned something like that before."

"Besides my first point, which is the most important, you and I would never work. Just look at how different we are. How we bicker all the time."

"We don't bicker about foundational issues though, do we? I know we are both dedicated to our work. We both love our country. We share the same faith commitment. Those things matter a lot more than arguing about silly stuff. We've moved far beyond the point of you being annoyed by lawyers, so let's just be real here."

"I told you before. I don't want to hurt you, and I know I will. I've hurt every woman I've ever had a relationship with."

"And why is that?"

"Don't you think I'd like to know?"

"I think I do know," she shot back.

"Psychoanalyzing again?"

"I don't think you believe you deserve true happiness and someone who loves you unconditionally. From what little you've told me about your childhood, it doesn't take a professional psychologist to figure that out."

"So now you've diagnosed me. What are you going to do about it?" he asked, scowling.

"I'm going to be by your side as you work through this stuff. As you face it head on and then move on so you can be in a real, healthy relationship." She paused. "With me." She was putting it all out there, so why not keep going? "I get that you're afraid of facing the past and dealing with real feelings, but you know what? I'm afraid too." Her voice started to shake. "I'm scared that I'm going to walk into Mark's house tonight and never come out again and that I won't get the chance to build something with you. Because, Jacob, you mean something to me." She stared into his eyes as she finished baring her heart.

He closed the space between them and wrapped his arms around her. "I'm going to do everything in my power to make sure that you are safe tonight."

"I want more than safe, Jacob. I want you." She looked up at him.

"I'm not sure I can give you what you need."

"I'm willing to take that risk if you're willing to try." She held her breath, waiting for his response.

Her cell rang loudly, and it couldn't have been worse timing. She walked over and picked up her phone from the coffee table. "It's Mark."

"You should answer and put it on speaker."

She knew she had to. "Hey, Mark."

"Hey there. Just wanted to make sure we're still on for tonight?"

"Yeah. Six o'clock? Should I bring anything?"

"No. I told you I was going to cook for us, and I meant it."

"Sounds good. I'm looking forward to it." She turned to Jacob and shrugged. She wasn't sure how eager she should be.

"See you then."

A thought hit her after she ended the call. "You don't think he'd poison my food, do you?"

Jacob frowned. "He still thinks he can get some information out of you. As long as he believes you could be useful, you'll be okay."

"Are you just saying that to make me feel better?"

He shook his head. "I wouldn't do that. You can count on me to tell it to you straight when it comes to any operation."

"What about the personal stuff?"

He looked away. "Can we just shelve that for now?"

She'd pushed him enough for one day, but she still needed him. "Yes." She walked over and wrapped her arms around him. At first he didn't move, but then he pulled her in for a hug.

"You're going to be okay, Viv," he whispered in her ear.

She hoped he was right, and that she would survive the night.

CHAPTER
NINETEEN

Delaney huddled up with Weston and Cody at the State Department. Lydia Major sat across from them. The petite, middle-aged CIA officer clearly didn't want to be there, but given the circumstances, she had no choice.

"Thanks for coming in, Lydia." Delaney hoped to soften her up. Agency types were notoriously tight-lipped, especially with the FBI.

"Let's get right to it," Lydia said. "As I told Weston on the phone, we really don't have that much to offer."

Delaney refused to accept that. "Initially, you acted like you had nothing. Then we got some pictures from you. What else are you holding back?"

Lydia sighed. "The truth is that we just don't have much on Popov. Some of his behavior is indicative of intelligence activity, but we have no hard evidence to say he is, like we do with other Russian diplomats using that as their cover."

"Do you have any reason to believe that any sensitive,

classified information the ambassador was privy to has gotten into the hands of the Russians?"

Lydia frowned. "So far there's nothing, but I'd caution you that we don't always know these things, and especially not quickly."

"But you have no reason to think the ambassador was passing along information to the Russians?"

Lydia shook her head. "Absolutely not. I admit I don't like the optics of a romance between the two of them, and I'm not saying that the relationship couldn't lead to something developing on the operational side, but I don't have anything yet to support that." She straightened her shoulders. "The US's relationship with Russia has always been complicated, and it's even more so now. I think it's a pretty farfetched theory to think the government would've ordered a hit on our ambassador—particularly in such a public fashion."

Weston huffed. "Well, someone drugged her."

Lydia lifted her hands. "I'm just giving you my opinion from the counterintelligence side of things."

"We're just frustrated at the lack of answers." Delaney tried to smooth things over. "If you have any ideas, we're all ears."

Lydia pushed her glasses up on her nose. "I've been immersed in US-Russian relations for my entire career, which has spanned decades. All I can tell you is that I don't think this was a sanctioned government hit. Beyond that, I'm afraid you're on your own." She stood. "I should be getting back to Langley."

Delaney also rose from her seat. "Please contact us if anything changes on your end."

"Will do."

Lydia exited without any fanfare, and Delaney sat back down with the guys.

"She was tough," Weston said.

"Get used to it. That's usually how it goes when we deal with the CIA."

Cody leaned in. "I had a long talk with a few members of the Russian team from State early this morning. They agreed with Lydia and thought a Russian hit was basically out of the question."

"Why is everyone so sure of that?" Weston asked. "I get that it would be highly unusual, but everything about this investigation is."

Delaney understood Weston's frustration. "I hear you, but I think they're right, and if that's the case, we have two viable suspects on the table."

Cody shifted in his seat. "Popov and the husband."

"Bingo. We've got to follow up with the financial group and see if they finished their analysis on the money trail. That could be the only direction we get here that goes beyond innuendo and suspicion."

"While you guys are working on that, I've got one more person internally to talk to." Cody grabbed his stuff and left the room.

"Well, well," Weston said.

"What?"

Weston smiled broadly. "Cody likes you."

"You're crazy." She felt the creep of a blush starting at her neck and moving toward her face.

Weston's eyes widened. "And you like him too." He slapped the table. "This is too good."

"I don't know what you're talking about."

"Then why is your face ten shades of red? This is a great thing. Are you going to make the first move?"

She tried to steady herself. "Weston, what did I tell you about playing matchmaker?"

He lifted his hands. "I'm not playing anything. I'm telling you what I'm seeing unfold right before me. Cody couldn't stop looking at you. Even when Lydia or I were talking, he was focused on you."

"He was probably just thinking."

Weston laughed. "I'm a dude. I can tell when another dude likes a woman, and you can, too, or else you wouldn't look like a tomato. Your face matches your hair."

"Enough. We need to get back to work. Put in another call to the financial group and tell them we need something ASAP."

"Fine. But remember that I called this one."

"There's nothing to call." She opened the folder on her desk and tried to refocus.

But she couldn't help wondering if there was any truth to Weston's words. Did she have a crush on Cody Rico?

◆

"Remember, I'll be right out here in the car."

Viv looked at Jacob and took a deep breath. They were parked directly in front of Mark's ranch-style home in Alexandria. She thought she might be sick, but she was putting on a brave face for Jacob.

It was one thing to have Mark in her place with Jacob right outside the door, but this was different. Jacob wouldn't be able to hear a thing. Yes, he was just in the car, but she was really on her own. *Lord, please help me.*

"I have to ask you one last time. Are you sure you want to do this?" Jacob asked.

"No. But I need to." She took his hand and squeezed.

"Remember, there's Agency backup only a few blocks away too. We have you covered."

"I know." She was beginning to think he was trying to reassure himself as much as her. "I need to go now."

They looked into each other's eyes for a moment. She knew he felt something for her, and it was that hope for a future for them that was keeping her going.

She put her purse on her shoulder, got out of the SUV, and walked up the driveway and then to the front porch. She rang the doorbell and once again took a deep, steadying breath.

The door opened a few moments later. Mark greeted her with a big smile and a quick kiss on the cheek. "Welcome to my home."

She walked into the house and tried to focus on the mission. She could do this.

"I hope you like chicken kebabs on the grill with mixed veggies."

She wondered if he was trying to play her, but as she looked up at him, he seemed totally chill. "I do." Her eyes landed on the hummus and veggie plate sitting out. "I also love hummus."

Mark smiled. "Perfect. Dig into the hummus and veggies. Then we can go out on the porch and grill the kebabs."

So far, so good. "You said you wanted to talk. Is everything okay?" She figured she had to eat, and she said another prayer before taking her first bite of carrot dipped in hummus.

When he also dipped a piece of cucumber in the hummus and ate it, she held back a sigh of relief. "I've been thinking about your situation."

"I know it's messed up."

"It is. You're basically living under a lockdown, and it's not fair."

She didn't know where he was going. "But I have to. My life is in danger. People have died."

Mark touched her forearm. "Oh, I'm not denying that at all. I'm just saying that you need to be more assertive in figuring out what is happening to you."

"Like how?" The more she let him talk, the better.

"I told you about my PI friend. I talked to him about you. Don't worry, I kept it all very high-level, but he thinks he could help."

Who was this friend, actually? She wasn't sure how she should play this. "I don't want to do anything that conflicts with the actual investigation."

"But are they really investigating what's happening to you? Or are they focused on the attacks on the ambassadors?"

She bit her bottom lip. "Obviously, the ambassadors are top priority, but my friend Samir was murdered too, remember?" Now was the time when she needed to plant false seeds. "I know I can trust you."

He took her hand and squeezed before letting go. "Yes. You can tell me anything. I just want you to be safe and for you to be able to put this ordeal behind you. I told you that I'd be here to listen and help however I could."

"I shouldn't tell you this," she whispered, hoping to increase the drama.

"I know this is extremely difficult for you."

She nodded. "It is. I just want to do the right thing." She paused. "The task force believes that people inside the Egyptian government might be behind all of this."

His eyes narrowed. "Really? Why?"

"Those who are more radical don't like the Egyptian president's progressive moves. Both Ambassador Zidan and Samir were aligned with the president."

Mark frowned. "But where do you fit into that?"

"I visited Samir at the embassy before I was attacked. They

think that could've put a target on my back." She sighed. "I could get into big trouble for telling you this."

He placed his hand on his chest. "I gave you my word, Viv. Your secret is safe with me."

"Now you understand why I can't go to a private investigator."

Mark nodded. "I do. I assume you're working closely with the Egyptian government on all of this?"

"Absolutely."

He took a sip of his tea before continuing. "Let me ask you this. What if they're wrong?"

"About what?" She picked up another carrot.

"Is there any other reason that you and your friend Samir could be targeted?"

Yikes. This was getting uncomfortable. At least she'd bought herself a moment to finish chewing the carrot. "I don't think so."

"How did you know Samir?"

"Oh, he and I worked together on a project about a year or so ago."

"What was that?"

The CIA had talked to her about this extensively, and if asked, she was going to tell him, because he would know she was lying otherwise, and it would affect everything they were trying to do. "Once again, it's really sensitive."

"I know. All of this is."

This was getting more difficult by the moment. She didn't think she could put him off much longer. "I worked with him on a prisoner transfer. I provided legal advice about the transfer."

"Like international law stuff?"

"Exactly. I wanted to make sure that we were abiding by all

applicable laws and that the prisoners were treated humanely. That was really important to me."

"And were they?" He raised an eyebrow.

She nodded. "When I was with them, they certainly were."

He thought a moment. "Did they give you details about why the transfer was happening?"

She shook her head. "It was very need-to-know, they said. My job was singularly to oversee from a legal perspective. I didn't know what the underlying purpose was, and I got the sense I wasn't supposed to ask. Do you understand what I mean?"

"Yeah. I get it."

"Honestly, I was probably in over my head, but I didn't get a say-so in whether I took the assignment."

"Don't be so hard on yourself."

She fidgeted with a carrot stick and gave him a pleading look. "Can we talk about something else for a bit? This is stressing me out."

He patted her shoulder. "Yeah. Why don't we go out back?"

This would at least provide some opportunity for her to do her job. They went outside to the back patio, and he started the grill. They made small talk for a few minutes, and then she decided it was time.

"I'm just going to run to the restroom," she said.

"Go through the living room, and it's down the hall on the right. You can't miss it."

"Thanks." She smiled, then walked back inside and grabbed her purse. He wouldn't think anything of a woman taking her purse into the restroom with her.

Glancing outside, she saw he was turned away, and she quickly placed one of the listening devices under the coffee table in the living room. Then she placed another in the dining room and headed to the bathroom. She couldn't imagine there'd be much talk in the bathroom, but since she had the privacy, she opened the cabinet below the sink and placed one up inside.

She finished quickly and then washed her hands. The big question was whether she made an attempt to go to his bedroom. It seemed too risky, but she'd already come this far, right?

Taking another breath, she exited the bathroom. She kept walking down the hall and saw what had to be the master bedroom. Not wasting any time, she placed a device under the dresser.

She'd done it. Now was time to get out of there. She took a deep breath and let it out.

Then she turned around and almost ran into Mark.

"Hey," he said.

"Sorry. I was just being nosy, looking around your place."

He raised an eyebrow. "My bedroom?"'

Uh-oh. What now? She'd really overplayed her hand. "You have a nice house. I like it." She tried to brush it off and walked toward the door, but he grabbed her arm and turned her around.

"Are you sure you were just back here checking out my place?"

"Yeah. I'm sorry. I didn't mean to be rude."

He moved closer. "If you're having second thoughts about us just being friends, you can say so."

Oh no. On one hand, she was relieved that he wasn't on to her, but on the other, she was petrified. The way he was looking at her scared her for entirely different reasons. He moved in and pressed her up against the wall, his body far too close to hers, and kissed her. It took everything she had not to slap him away, but could she really do that? Then what would he think?

She withstood it as long as she could but then broke the kiss and stepped away from him. "I'm sorry, Mark. I'm just not ready for that right now." She felt herself holding her breath. Hoping he would let it go.

He smiled and grabbed her hand. "Let's go eat."

◆

It took everything Jacob had not to burst out of the car and save Viv from that maniac. He knew exactly when she started planting the listening devices because he'd heard the conversation in the bedroom. She had played it like a real pro, but he also understood what was happening, and he hoped Mark hadn't touched her.

Once they went outside to the porch, he had to wait in silence as the minutes ticked by in excruciating fashion. His thoughts went back to Viv's words.

Yeah, he had a lot of underlying issues, but who didn't? Was that really the reason he could never hold down a real, healthy relationship? He'd never thought about it that exact way before. He'd just figured he wasn't the relationship type. It was easier to go it alone. What did he bring to the table?

But as those questions floated through his mind, he could see that maybe even they were informed by his past. The bigger question was what he did about it.

When Viv had told him that her biggest fear was not coming out of tonight alive and missing out on the chance of a relationship with him, he didn't even know how to respond. Her brutal honesty and openness were so refreshing. So many of the women in his life were all about games.

Starting with his own mother, God rest her soul. His grandmother was the only woman he had ever loved and trusted. There hadn't been any truly special women in his adult life. He'd dated and had short-term relationships, but he hadn't even been a tenth of the way in. With Viv, she'd demand one hundred percent. In a way that thrilled him, but it also scared him to death.

He really did care about her, and the last thing he wanted was to break her heart. But he had a hard time seeing a happy ending to this. Viv was a romantic. He could see it in her eyes and feel it in her actions. His life read more like a tragedy than a romance. One thing he did think, based on everything, was that he probably should talk to a professional. He'd been so hardheaded about it for a long time, but if this experience had shown him anything, it was that he did need some help so he could move forward in a better place.

When Viv opened the car door, he was broken out of his thoughts. "You're done?"

"Yeah."

He looked at the time and saw it was almost nine. He'd allowed himself to wallow in his thoughts for quite a while.

"Are you okay?" He turned toward her and saw tears rolling down her cheeks. "Did he hurt you?"

She shook her head.

"Talk to me. What happened?"

"Let's drive. I'll be okay."

She sure didn't sound or look okay, but he pushed the gas and got out of there. She didn't seem to want to talk, so they rode in silence.

But once they got safely back in her condo, he couldn't stay quiet. "Viv, please talk to me. Don't shut me out."

"I don't know if I can keep doing this." Her voice shook.

He didn't even think. He just pulled her close to him in a tight hug. "I've got you now. No one can hurt you."

When she started shaking in his arms, he thought he might lose it. What had that guy done to her? He would pay. Jacob would see to that.

"I thought the attacks were the scariest things I'd ever have to go through, but after tonight, I don't think that's the case."

Still holding her, he asked, "What happened in there?"

"Could you hear us talking in the bedroom?"

"Yeah."

"What you didn't hear was him cornering me up against the wall and kissing me."

Jacob saw fire. He prayed it had ended there. "Did you stop him?"

"Yes, but I was afraid that if I reacted too strongly, he'd be suspicious. It completely threw me off, and then I had to pretend the rest of the night like we were friends and everything was okay. And keep my head in the game about what I should and shouldn't say."

"We'll figure out another way. You shouldn't have to subject yourself to that again."

"I gave him the info I was supposed to."

He listened intently as she gave him a play-by-play of the evening, but his blood was still boiling about Mark kissing her like that.

Viv looked down. "I'm not cut out for this, Jacob. I thought I could handle it, but I was wrong."

"You've done everything asked of you and more. Don't be hard on yourself. You succeeded tonight. You got multiple listening devices inside his place. That's a huge win."

"I know, but I don't feel like a winner," she said softly.

"I've got you." He squeezed her shoulder.

"Don't leave me," she whispered. "I'm afraid he's going to come for me. He's going to figure out that I planted those bugs, and he will come."

"I'm not going anywhere." And against his better judgment, he leaned down and kissed her.

CHAPTER
TWENTY

Late Wednesday, Delaney walked into the war room and saw Cody working on his laptop. When he looked up and smiled at her, she couldn't help but smile back. "Where's Weston?"

"He just called and said he was working on a lead and that we should get started without him."

"Oh, really?" Was this some setup move by Weston, or was it legitimate? Regardless, she had work to do. "Let's get going, then."

Cody turned to her. "I've been calling in a lot of favors in Brussels."

Her heartbeat sped up. "Do you have something?"

"More of the same. Multiple sources have confirmed that they saw the ambassador and Popov together acting extremely friendly."

"I think we're at the point where we can say about as conclusively as possible that there was a romance involved." She bit her bottom lip as she thought. "But once Jeff moved there, wouldn't he have noticed that she was out a lot with another man?"

"You would think, but I'm sure she used her job as cover as much as possible. There are a lot of diplomatic events. Jeff wouldn't have attended every single one with her. The spouses tend to go to the bigger functions but not always the routine ones. She could put in a quick appearance and then bail to conduct her own personal business."

"So she's having what seems to be more than just a passing affair with this man. Her best friend thinks she had fallen in love with him." She tapped her fingers on the desk.

"What're you thinking?" Cody asked.

"Maybe we are looking at this too globally. Maybe it is just personal. If we rule out the husband, then we can focus our energy on Popov. But if he's guilty, that will be a beast to prove and even harder to hold him accountable because of diplomatic immunity."

"Why not focus on Jeff King for now, and then at least you'll have it narrowed down regardless of the answer."

She sighed. "My first instinct was that it was Jeff, but then everything started pointing in other directions."

Cody's eyes softened. "I know firsthand what it's like to be cheated on, so I get the pain and frustration. But murder is a completely different level."

Delaney's thoughts were still on what Cody had said about his past. "I'm sorry about what you went through."

He shrugged. "It's made me a bit skittish as I've tried to move forward. Unsuccessfully," he said with a laugh.

She patted his arm. "Don't be so hard on yourself." As she looked into his dark eyes, she made the decision to open up. She wasn't sure why she felt comfortable having this conversation, but it just felt right. "I'm not sure if you know this or not, but my husband was killed in the line of duty a couple of years ago."

His eyes widened. "I had no idea. I'm really sorry, Delaney. I can't even imagine."

"Yeah. So while it's a totally different sort of pain, it's still pain, and I understand where you're coming from."

He shifted in his seat. "Can I ask you something?"

"Sure."

"Have you been able to move on at all?"

She looked down and then back up. "Truthfully, not yet. But my first priority was grieving and getting myself back together. I feel like I've finally accomplished that, although it took a long time. Weston has tried to set me up with his friends, but I've been a bit wary. I would like someone closer to my age."

"Which is twenty-five, right?" He grinned.

"Smart man." But she didn't mind revealing her age at all. "I'm forty-one."

Cody took a breath. "What do you think about you and me maybe grabbing dinner sometime?"

She didn't respond, just let his words sink in.

He lifted his hand. "I'm sorry. It looks like I overstepped. Please forget I said anything."

She couldn't see him suffer, so she caught his hand. "Dinner would be perfect."

His eyes lit up. "Great."

"But while we're at work, let's just keep it professional."

"Of course."

She laughed. "I'm the one who took your hand, so maybe I should tell that to myself." She gave his hand a squeeze before letting go.

The door opened and Weston walked in. "What did I miss?"

"Nothing," they both said in unison.

Weston looked at her but didn't push it. "I think we've caught our break." He set his laptop down and plugged it into the projector. "Our financial group just sent these over."

She glanced at Cody before turning her attention to the screen. She couldn't believe she'd just said yes to a date. Much to her surprise, she felt good about it. What an unexpected turn of events.

"Take a look," Weston said. "It took a lot of digging, but our analysts were able to track the deposits into the ambassador's account to this account."

She stared at the account number on the screen. "And who owns that account?"

Weston smiled. "A shell corporation, but after much tracing, they were able to tie it back to funds from Jeff King's personal savings account."

Her stomach dropped. "Are they sure?"

Weston nodded. "Yup. So, Delaney, looks like your initial gut instinct about Jeff was right."

She sighed. "Why would he go through so much trouble to put money into his wife's offshore bank account? Could this just be a case of tax evasion or something?"

Cody cleared his throat. "Maybe I'm just cynical, but what if it's a setup?"

Weston snapped his fingers. "Jealous husband finds out his wife has cheated on him yet again, even after he moved to Brussels, and he decides he'll get even."

"So he makes it look like she's getting paid off. Jeff knows we'll make the connection to Popov because of their relationship." She played the story out. "But does that mean Jeff actually was the one to drug her?"

Weston shrugged. "Not sure. How are we going to approach this?"

"We come at him hard. See if we can get him to crack."

"I know I'm not an FBI agent, but if this guy went through this whole setup to frame his wife, do you really think he'd confess?" Cody asked.

Cody's instincts were spot on. "That's why we show him the hard financial evidence and see what excuse he can come up with," Delaney explained.

Cody raised his eyebrows. "Ah."

Weston laughed. "Delaney looks harmless, but she has brought grown men to tears."

"Thanks for the vote of confidence, partner."

"Is there anything you two need from me?" Cody asked.

"Not right now. We'll make a run at Jeff," Delaney said.

"Keep me posted." Cody stood and glanced over his shoulder at her before leaving.

"Good work, Weston," she said.

He moved into the seat next to her. "No way. Hold up. Before we get to that, what was happening between the two of you?"

"Nothing," she said quickly.

Weston put his hand on his chest. "Delaney, c'mon. This is me you're talking to."

"Exactly. I think you have an overactive imagination."

Weston grinned. "The fact that you're pushing back so hard tells me everything I need to know. I'll just ask Cody."

She grabbed his arm. "Please don't do that."

"Then 'fess up."

She let out an exasperated sigh. "He asked me to dinner. Are you satisfied?"

Weston chuckled. "Actually, I am. I think the two of you are a great fit."

"Please don't talk about it, though. I want to keep things professional in the office."

"My lips are sealed." He ran his fingers across his mouth.

"I'm serious, Weston."

"I'm just giving you a hard time. I promise I won't say a word. It's taken you a long time to get to this point, and I'm not going to do anything to mess it up. Promise."

"Thank you."

"But if you need any advice, I have a pretty good track record with the ladies."

She laughed loudly. "I'll pass." She stood. "With this new evidence implicating Jeff, I'm going to call Agent Miller in Narcotics. He was Ryan's partner, and I know he'll help us out. I want to talk to him about how hard it is to get your hands on street fentanyl. Maybe we can track some leads that way. If Jeff is guilty, he had to purchase the fentanyl from someone."

"That sounds like a great idea. I feel like the case is starting to come together."

"It is. I'm getting out of here. I'll see you tomorrow morning, okay?"

"Watch your six," Weston said.

"Always."

Delaney was relieved to get out of Weston's inquisition and have a little space to process what had happened with Cody. She hoped she hadn't made a mistake, but she was going to have to start taking risks again at some point, and based on what she knew about Cody, he was a good guy. Were they going to have some amazing romantic connection? She had no clue, but she was proud of taking that first step—it was a huge one for her.

By the time she walked into her place and threw down her keys, she was deciding what she wanted for dinner after having skipped lunch. Her stomach was growling as she walked toward the kitchen to survey the possibilities.

She opened the refrigerator, humming a tune and thinking about Cody's warm brown eyes. Then strong hands wrapped around her, one over her mouth and the other around her waist. She started fighting, using all of her training. She felt like an idiot for not taking her stalker threat more seriously. But there was no time for self-recrimination. She needed to face this danger head on.

"Calm down," a male voice said in her ear. "I'm not going to hurt you, but I need to talk to you." He had an accent, but she couldn't immediately place it because she was too busy trying to buck him off.

She also didn't believe him, because his grip was too tight to be friendly. She slammed her head backward, trying to headbutt him, but she didn't get a direct hit.

Stomping down hard on his foot and dropping low, she finally wrestled out of his arms and drew her gun.

The man lifted his hands, and she finally got a good look at him. Tall, blond . . . Russian accent.

"Sergei Popov," she whispered.

He smiled. "I figured you'd recognize me."

She didn't put down her gun. He was still in her home uninvited and had attacked her. "What are you doing here?"

"I need to talk to you." His blue eyes locked on to hers.

Then another thought came to her mind. "Are you the one who's been following me?"

He nodded. "Yes."

"Why?"

"You can put down the gun," Popov said.

"Answer my question." He might be a respected Russian diplomat, but he might also be a member of the GRU.

He kept his hands up. "It's about Penelope. I know you've been investigating and asking a lot of questions about me."

"How would you know that?"

He smiled. "I've got friends and contacts everywhere in Europe."

"Why are you in the United States?" She had so many questions.

"I came over immediately when I heard what happened at the dinner." He looked down. "Penelope and I were in love."

As she looked into his light blue eyes, she could feel his pain. It appeared he was being truthful. "What do you want me to know?"

He took a step back. "I had absolutely nothing to do with this. I never would have hurt her."

"Was she working with you?"

He laughed. "No. Although I hoped with time a lot of things would change between us—namely her leaving her job and her husband. But no, she definitely wasn't passing information to me, if that's what you're getting at. I also know that you think I'm GRU. I'm not."

She wasn't sure whether she believed him on that point. "What do you have for me, then?"

He slowly lowered his arms. "Jeff King is the man who killed her. I know he's playing the grieving husband, but you can't believe it."

"Do you have any evidence?" *Please say yes.*

Popov looked down. "I have some of my contacts working on it."

"Sit. Hands where I can see them." She motioned for him to take a seat at the kitchen table.

Popov did as he was told. "I told you. If I wanted to hurt you, that would have happened long before now. You were oblivious on the jogging trail the first two times. For an FBI agent, you need to be more careful."

She grimaced. That wasn't good, but she didn't want to focus on it. "Did you meet Jeff in person?" She wanted to know if his answer matched up to Jeff's.

Popov nodded. "Multiple times."

"Why do you think it's him?"

He blew out a breath. "Because Penelope told me she was afraid Jeff had figured out she was seeing another man. That was another reason I wanted her to leave Jeff, even if she couldn't openly see me because of her work. If I'd pushed her harder, maybe she'd still be alive. That's something I have to live with."

Popov fell silent. Delaney waited for him to continue, still holding her gun on him.

"I just wanted Penelope to leave him for me, but obviously it's a little difficult for a top American diplomat to publicly have a relationship with a man like me." He paused again. "I took a great risk by coming here, but I did my research on you, Agent O'Sullivan. I believe you are trying to do the right thing by Penelope. I can't have Jeff King walk. If you can't bring him to justice, then I will. This is a courtesy call."

That couldn't happen. Not on her watch. He sounded more like a GRU agent now than a diplomat. "You know I can't support that."

"Which is why I need *you* to do your job, Agent O'Sullivan." He stood. "And you should keep this conversation to yourself. I was never here. Understand?"

"Now you're threatening me?" She couldn't believe this guy.

He shook his head. "No. I'm just stating the obvious. It's not good for either of us to have met like this." He took a step.

"Easy now."

He lifted his hands. "I've done my part, but I'm not a patient man. Either you get Jeff King, or I will."

◆

The next day, Viv sat in a conference room at the CIA with Jacob by her side. They were waiting for Layla and both the CIA and FBI directors to join them.

"Something has to have happened," she said.

Jacob looked at her. "Yeah. I doubt they'd bring us all together for a routine update. Maybe they got something from the surveillance you planted."

"I hope so," she whispered. She hadn't been herself since the encounter with Mark—or whoever he really was. He'd frightened her. She had felt so completely helpless in that moment. Looking back, she might have overreacted, but she couldn't help how she had felt when he cornered her against the wall. It was definitely a power play, and one she didn't like. The gentleman who had saved her was long gone in that moment.

Another chill shot down her back just thinking about it.

"Are you cold?" Jacob asked.

"No. I'm all right. I hope they don't keep us waiting much longer."

He grabbed her hand. "I'm still right here with you, and I'm not going anywhere."

When he squeezed her hand, it gave her some level of reassurance. She wasn't afraid when he was by her side. But being alone in that house with Mark had been too much. She was not cut out to be any type of CIA operative.

The door opened, and Layla walked in first, followed by Director Phillips and Director Mince.

Viv realized she was holding her breath. She let it out as they all sat down.

"What happened?" Jacob didn't waste any time jumping in.

"There's good news and bad news," Lang said.

Viv sat up straight. "Why don't we try the good news first? I could use some."

"We were able to pick up something from the surveillance you set up, Viv," Layla said. "The first big news is that we have Mark talking about ordering the hit on Ambassador Zidan. It's definitive evidence tying this all together."

"Wow," Viv said.

Layla nodded. "There's more. Based on what we heard from Mark, we were able to track down one of the escaped detainees. Ali Abboud has been taken in."

"That's great news. So he's in custody?" Viv asked.

"Yes. Ali isn't saying much," Director Mince said, "but we have been able to determine that during his time in Egyptian custody, he became aligned with the opposition forces in the country. We already knew he was an active member of Al-Nidal, but that time in Egypt pushed him into supporting the radical opposition. Ali wanted Zidan dead and activated his resources in the Al-Nidal network to make it happen."

"Why don't you let me take a run at him?" Jacob said. "Maybe I can get even more out of him."

"No way," Lang responded. "The CIA has the situation under control. Unfortunately, there was some fallout from the takedown."

"What?" Viv feared to ask.

Director Phillips looked at her. "When Ali didn't check in, Omar got rattled and reached out to Mark. We have that conversation on tape, but that is the last one we have.

We believe that after Mark talked to Omar, he discovered the equipment, and we have to go on the assumption that you've been made."

"What do I do now?" Viv asked.

"We're moving you to a new safe house," Layla said. "We can't let you have any contact with Mark again. The risk is too great."

She sighed in relief. "I'm actually glad to hear that."

Director Mince cleared his throat. "But Mark will most definitely want to see you. He will reach out again."

"And what do I do?"

"Nothing," Jacob piped in. "You can't expect her even to talk to this guy, given the turn of events."

"It's up to you, Viv," Director Phillips said. "It's possible that through another conversation something else could be revealed, but if you prefer to cut all ties, we can live with that. You've already risked a lot, and we all recognize that."

Talk to Mark again? She wasn't sure about that. She was relieved she wouldn't have to see him, but if he knew what she had done, what was to gain by having any conversation? "Why talk to him? He knows what I did."

"There's still a small chance he doesn't know it was you who planted the devices."

"This is too much." Jacob leaned in. "Viv's been through enough. Everyone's energy should be focused on finding Omar."

Director Phillips nodded. "It's all hands on deck for Omar. And we've still got eyes on Mark. An FBI team is monitoring him twenty-four seven, even though we lost the internal audio."

"Just think about it, Viv," Director Mince said. "No need to answer this second."

Was it always going to be another request from them? She looked at Layla, who didn't give her any assurance.

"Is that it?" Jacob asked.

"Yes. We'll have a team take you to the new safe house and get what you need from your condo," Director Mince said.

"Thank you." What Viv really wanted to ask was when this was ever going to be over.

CHAPTER
TWENTY-ONE

Viv had been taken to a new safe house in McLean, Virginia. It appeared the CIA wanted to keep close tabs on her. The two-story Cape Cod in a cul-de-sac of a seemingly quiet neighborhood was the perfect hiding place—or so she hoped.

Jacob had been in a foul mood since they'd left Langley. He clearly didn't want her talking to Mark anymore, and after all she had confided in him, she couldn't blame him.

She did feel pretty good about the security at the safe house. Besides Jacob, who wasn't going anywhere, they'd assigned her a four-man team.

She and Jacob had eaten some Thai takeout and were now sitting on the couch with the news playing in the background. She was barely listening to it, but her phone ringing got her attention.

She picked it up and let out a sigh of relief. "It's my sister," she told Jacob. "Willow, I'm so glad you called."

"Hello, Viv. I guess you weren't expecting to hear from me," a male voice answered.

"Mark? What are you doing? How do you have Willow's phone?" Her heart dropped as she thought about the answers to her own questions. Willow wasn't even in the United States, was she?

Jacob was frantically motioning for her to put the call on speaker, and she did.

"I'm glad you recognized my voice, Viv. You know, you almost had me. You played your role to a T. All that stuff about just being a lawyer and not working for the CIA."

Her temper started to flare. "I *am* just a lawyer, and I do not work for the CIA."

"You know what did it for me? You looked so scared of me when we were in my bedroom after I kissed you. There's no way you should've had that reaction unless you really knew who I was. You came so close, but then you blew it."

She had to get to the real heart of the matter—and fast. "I don't care about any of that. Where's Willow?"

"Here's the thing, Viv. We picked up Willow thinking she was you. After some rather intense questioning, we figured out she was your twin. I'm hurt you never told me about your sister. She looks just like you. Turns out she left her humanitarian job abroad to come check on you. Bad timing for her. Great timing for me, though."

Her heart sank, thinking about what they had done to her sister, but that feeling was quickly replaced. Anger built in her like a mighty volcano. "If you hurt my sister, I will kill you."

Mark laughed. "You're not in a position to be making demands."

It was like the world was closing in on her. First her parents. And now her twin sister? "How do I even know she's alive? That you haven't killed her?"

"Here. Say hello to your sister, Willow."

"Viv." Her sister's voice cracked.

"Are you okay? Did he hurt you?"

"I'm okay," Willow whispered. "But please do what they tell you to do. I don't think they're bluffing."

"Where are you?"

"Enough!" Mark got back on the phone. "Here's how this is going to go. If you want your sister to live, you're going to turn over Ali. Midnight tomorrow. I'll email you the place to meet right before. Do you understand?"

"Yes."

"And there's one more piece to this trade."

"What?"

"You're coming with Ali."

Viv sucked in a breath. "What do you want from me?"

He hung up. She looked at Jacob and felt hysteria start to take over. They had Willow. She gripped her chest, unable to catch her breath.

Jacob was talking, but she couldn't comprehend what he was saying. Her whole body shook as visions of worst-case scenarios danced through her head. The only family she had left was being threatened by a murderer.

"Viv, can you hear me?"

Finally, Jacob's words broke through. She nodded.

"We've got to call this in. We'll figure out a plan to rescue your sister."

Jacob may have been speaking the words, but when she looked into his eyes, she knew he lacked confidence in what he was saying. As she pictured what Mark could be doing to Willow and the fear of losing her set in, it was all too much.

Her world went black.

◆

When Viv fainted, Jacob felt entirely helpless. But it was even worse when she came to because then they had to deal with the reality at hand. He had told her they would rescue her sister, but based on his experience, the likelihood of Willow coming out of this alive was extremely low. That was the last thing he was going to tell Viv, given how upset she was, but at some point, he'd have to level with her. She needed to be prepared for the harsh reality. Terrorists had kidnapped her sister, and they were out for revenge.

He'd called the FBI director and told him that they needed to move Viv to another safe house ASAP, given Mark could try to track her burner phone, and that the directors needed to come to her. She was in no condition to go to Langley. So now they were seated around a large kitchen table in the new safe house with both directors and Layla.

Jacob recounted the phone conversation to the group so Viv wouldn't have to. She was still in a state of shock, but he'd also never seen her so angry. Her love for her twin was apparent, and she was willing to do anything to save her.

"We have to find my sister," Viv said.

"I understand your frustration," Director Phillips said.

She looked at him, her hazel eyes ablaze. "I don't think you do. My twin sister is being held by terrorists because they thought she was *me*. She didn't deserve to be brought into this, and her life is being threatened. I don't care what you think is right or wrong, because I know what I need to do. I will turn myself over to save her."

Jacob was about to jump in, but Layla beat him to it.

"Viv, I know how much you love your sister, but sacrificing

250

yourself isn't the answer either. We need to be smart about this." She laid a hand on Viv's arm.

Viv pulled away. "You too? I expected this response from the directors, but not from my best friend. I cannot—I *will* not—sacrifice Willow to those monsters. I will do whatever I have to do to save her, with or without your help."

Layla's dark eyes softened. "Viv, I wasn't insinuating that we shouldn't try to rescue Willow. My only point is that we shouldn't give you up in the process. There are other ways."

"Like what?"

"That's why we need to come up with a plan. A smart, well-thought-out plan," Layla responded.

Jacob feared this was going south quickly. "Viv, what Layla's trying to get at is that once you turn yourself over, we have no leverage. There's no guarantee of your sister's safety."

"Then we're wasting time by sitting here instead of coming up with a rescue plan. They could kill her right now."

Jacob leaned forward. "Yes, they could, but they want you and Ali. I suspect they want Ali much more than you. These guys know you'd do anything to get your sister back, and they're taking advantage of that. They're banking on the fact that you'll find a way to make the trade."

Director Mince cleared his throat. "I hate to be the one to say this, but it has to be said. Under absolutely no circumstances are we turning over Ali Abboud. It's completely off the table."

"But—" Viv started.

Director Mince lifted his hand. "But we could use a decoy as part of the plan to secure your sister and bring them all in. That's assuming, of course, that Omar will be in the same place as Mark. Regardless, whoever is at the meet, we will apprehend them."

"They're going to be ready for that," Jacob said.

"Yes, they are, but it's the best play we have," Director Mince said.

"Will there be a decoy for Viv too?" Layla asked.

"No," Viv interjected. "I need to see this through. They'll know right off if it's not me."

"That's far too dangerous," Layla said. "Then you *and* your sister could both end up dead."

Viv stood. "No one was *that* concerned about the danger when all of you sent me off on this ill-conceived mission to begin with. My sister would be safe if I hadn't gone down this path. A path you pretty much made me go down. Yeah, you said there was a choice, but there really wasn't."

Layla walked over to her. "Viv, can I talk to you for a minute?"

"Yes," Viv said reluctantly.

The two women walked upstairs. Jacob hoped Layla knew what she was doing.

He turned his attention back to the directors. "You know Viv's right. You got her into this mess. She deserves your full support to help get her out."

Director Phillips nodded. "But she's not thinking rationally right now. She's willing to be reckless to try to save her sister, and we can't afford that. There is a bigger picture here."

"There's always a bigger picture, but there's also an innocent woman's life on the line. That should count for something." Jacob wasn't holding his tongue.

Director Mince lifted his hand. "We need to figure this out. We can't let Viv go down some path that's going to get her and others killed."

"Agreed," Director Phillips said. "Jacob, can you help

coordinate an FBI assault team? We know they're going to have reinforcements."

"Of course, sir."

Lang frowned. "I want your honest assessment with Vivian out of the room. You're a SEAL. I know you've dealt with a lot of dangerous operations before. What is the likelihood of Willow Steele getting out of this alive?"

Jacob sighed. "I'd say less than ten percent. You agree, Mince?"

Mince nodded. "Which is another reason we can't just sacrifice Vivian in the process. It's not worth it."

"It is to her, though," Jacob said. "And that's the problem. We're going to have to keep her on complete lockdown, or she might try to do this on her own."

The thought of that frightened him to the core, and he realized how much he'd come to care about her.

Viv turned to her best friend, ready to lash out, but Layla pulled her into a deep hug and whispered in her ear.

"I'm going to help you save Willow. I promise."

Viv moved back. "What do you mean?"

"That was an act back there for the directors. They're always going to prioritize the detainee over your sister. Always."

Finally, someone was speaking the truth directly to her. "I know they are, but what do we do about it? I feel a bit helpless."

"We're going to need assistance from Jacob. We can't do this alone, but we have to make sure we can trust him one hundred percent."

"He's loyal to me. I know that."

Layla raised an eyebrow. "I figured things had only gotten more serious between the two of you."

Viv nodded. "It's been pretty intense."

"We can't control the fact that the directors will never let us trade Ali, but we could still conduct a rescue mission for Willow. Here's the thing. To make this work, we have to keep that to ourselves when Mark emails you the location. We can't tell the directors."

"Won't you get in trouble?"

Layla shrugged. "Let me worry about that. I've built up some political capital that I plan to use."

Viv's mind raced. "I can't lose Willow."

"I know." Layla squeezed her hand. "That's why I knew we had to act."

"I should've never doubted you." Layla had never let her down.

"I needed to make it look convincing."

"You did a good job. What do I do now?"

"We're going to go back in there, and I'm going to say that we talked and we're on the same page. That you realize you not being directly involved is the best solution."

Viv groaned. "I hope I can pull that off."

"You played a role for Mark. You can do it again."

Viv blew out a breath. "Not well enough. He made me."

"It took him some time, though, and we got valuable intel in the process. You did exactly what you needed to do and then some. You're the MVP here, and don't you ever think otherwise."

Viv gave Layla another hug. "Thanks for being by my side no matter what."

"Always."

CHAPTER TWENTY-TWO

Delaney had given a lot of thought to her encounter with Sergei Popov, and she decided to tell Weston. He was her partner, and one of the things she had preached to him from day one was that partners couldn't keep secrets from each other. Secrets could get you killed. She'd given Weston the full rundown of what had happened with Popov, and they had agreed on next steps.

They had contacted Jeff that evening and asked him to meet them at the FBI headquarters in the morning. He was clearly under the impression that they had big news to share with him. Some major break in the case. He had no idea he was about to be interrogated because of what the FBI financial analysts had found.

Delaney was working against the clock more than ever. Popov would be breathing down her neck if she couldn't put this together, and while she wanted Jeff to face justice, she didn't want it to be at the hands of a vigilante. The system was in place for a reason, and that was why she needed to succeed in this interrogation.

She'd stayed up late preparing for the interview, and this morning she wore her favorite black pantsuit and a red blouse.

"You look game ready," Weston said.

"We can't afford to mess this up."

"As always, I'll just follow your lead."

They'd had a long call last night, too, going over her notes to make sure Weston was on board and supported her strategy. They only had one chance to make the big financial reveal to Jeff, and they had to make it count.

Weston looked down at his watch. "Jeff's late."

Delaney hoped he wasn't going to bail on them.

"While we're waiting . . ." Weston smiled. "Have you talked to Cody?"

"Yes, but not the way you're insinuating. It was all about work."

Her phone pinged with a text from the agent escorting Jeff to the interrogation room. "He's almost here."

Weston patted her on the back. "You've got this, Delaney."

She appreciated that Weston believed in her. She'd worked tirelessly as an FBI agent to be the best she could be, and now was the time to put all her hard work to the test.

Jeff walked into the room. He looked particularly disheveled today—his hair was unruly, and his plaid shirt was wrinkled. "What's going on?" he asked.

"Please have a seat," Weston said.

Jeff looked around the room. "Why are we in here?"

"So we can talk," Delaney said. "We have a lot of things to discuss with you."

Jeff's eyes lit up. "Are you ready to make an arrest?"

She scooted her chair forward. "We're getting very close, which is why we needed to talk to you."

He settled into his seat. "Whatever you need. I've always said that. We need justice for Penelope. Her funeral was one of the hardest days of my life. I can't believe she's actually gone."

Delaney readied herself to pounce. "But she is gone. Murdered."

Jeff rubbed his eyes. "Please tell me you've caught the guy."

She cocked her head to the side. "Jeff, can I be open with you about something?"

"Sure."

"When we first met, I actually believed you were responsible."

He nodded. "I got that vibe loud and clear. It's always the husband, right?"

"Right," Weston answered.

Delaney took a breath. "I've been an agent for almost twenty years, can you believe that?"

"You don't look old enough," Jeff responded.

He was trying to flatter her. That had zero chance of success. "And one thing I've learned is that my first instincts are almost always correct."

Jeff frowned.

"I thought it was you to begin with, and sitting here today, I'm right back at that spot. The only difference is that I now have hard evidence to support my gut." She leaned forward. "What do you think about that?"

"This is crazy." Jeff turned to Weston. "Talk some sense into your partner, man. I know you want to solve this case and get it closed, but you can't just point the finger at me because you don't have answers and I'm the easy target. Not after all I've gone through. I just buried my wife!"

She wasn't going to let up, because she needed to read his reaction. If she ended up being wrong about this, she'd pay the consequences. "The evidence doesn't lie, Jeff."

"You're wrong." He looked down. "I think I need a lawyer."

She wasn't going to let him off that easy. "Are you sure about that? You lawyer up, and any incentives for us to push the DA to cut you a deal go out the window."

Jeff bit his bottom lip. "There will be no deal, because I'm innocent. I know my rights. I want a lawyer. Now."

"Of course."

Delaney had planned for this. Jeff wasn't stupid. As soon as he realized she was targeting him, she knew he would lawyer up, but she still had to try to convince him otherwise. Knowing that was now a failing battle, she would move on to the next phase of her plan.

They weren't letting him go, so after about an hour of him stewing alone in the interrogation room, his fancy, high-priced attorney arrived, and they all made introductions.

Gerard Newton unbuttoned his navy designer suit jacket and sat down beside his client. "What's this all about, Agents?"

She was interested to see what the lawyer's strategy was going to be. "I'm sure your client already told you over the phone, but he is our prime suspect in the murder of Penelope King."

Gerard laughed. "The FBI is so off base with this one. I have to tell you that after all the heartache and trauma my client has been through, I will file a lawsuit against the FBI for this outrageous harassment. This is really beyond the pale."

"Save your theatrics." Delaney wasn't going to give an inch. "Do you know, Mr. King, that lying to a federal agent is a felony?"

Jeff shrugged. "I guess I was aware of that, but I haven't lied to you."

So that was how he was going to play this. Pure denial. "Oh, I believe you have. Let's start with the fact that you told us you had no idea how those cash deposits ended up in your wife's offshore account."

"Don't say anything to that," Gerard instructed his client. "I didn't hear a question there, Agent O'Sullivan."

"I'm just getting started." She pulled a large stack of folders out of her bag and placed them in front of her. "Mr. King, it must have really hurt when you found out your wife was still cheating on you, didn't it?"

No answer.

"You'd forgiven her countless times. More than most men ever would. Then you uproot your life and move to Brussels, and she's having a salacious relationship with a Russian diplomat, one who might even be a spy." She opened the first folder and slid the pictures of Penelope and Popov getting cozy across the table. Jeff looked at them but didn't say anything.

Gerard sighed loudly. "Agent O'Sullivan, these pictures don't prove anything."

"*Prove* may be a strong word, but I do believe they establish a clear motive."

Gerard picked up one of the pictures. "You don't even know from these pictures that anything illicit is going on between the ambassador and this man. I don't see anything remotely problematic here, much less anything that would provide a motive."

She pointed to the photos. "With these pictures, you're right. But I have more."

Jeff's face started to turn red. Good, she was getting to him.

Delaney opened another folder—this one containing the financial information. "You almost had us fooled, Mr. King, but as you and your attorney can see by reviewing these documents, we've been able to conclusively tie those deposits in your wife's account back to you and your personal accounts."

Gerard didn't miss a beat. "My client has the right to remain silent."

"True, but he's spoken very clearly on these issues before and lied to us. Wasting our time. It's the perfect revenge move, except for the fact that Mr. King didn't completely cover his tracks."

"Enough!" Jeff pounded his fist on the table.

Gerard placed his hand on Jeff's arm. "Agent O'Sullivan, I'm going to end this interview right now if you don't stop harassing my client."

She shook her head. "You have no power to stop this interrogation. It's far from an interview, so let's keep going."

"Are you charging my client?" Gerard's blue eyes flashed with anger.

He was calling her bluff. She leaned forward. "Do you really want me to answer that question?"

"Just get on with it, then." He let out an overly dramatic sigh.

Gerard was no amateur lawyer. He understood that where there was smoke, there was fire. He also had a strategic interest in the questioning continuing so he could get an understanding of what the FBI had on his client.

"Unless you start talking and provide an alternate explanation for these money transfers, the only real question is whether there's any appetite from the DA regarding a deal, and frankly, I'm inclined to tell her that the FBI is not pro-deal at this point. It's ultimately her call, but it doesn't look good for you. All you've done from day one is lie to us. You were so hurt and angry over the repeated infidelity. The pain and humiliation you felt caused you to concoct this elaborate scheme. To make your wife look like a drug addict who was betraying her country. This is your last chance to give me any reason to change my recommendation to the DA."

"I need a moment alone with my client," Gerard said.

Delaney held back a smile. She and Weston exited the room, and she let out a breath.

Weston patted her on the shoulder. "That was a masterclass you just put on."

"I don't know if it will be enough. If I were his lawyer, I'd probably advise him to hold out. We don't have direct evidence tying him to the drugging yet."

"True. But the chance of getting a deal might be too good to pass up."

"I guess we'll have to wait and see."

She could only hope she'd done enough.

◆

Jacob watched as Viv took a seat on the sofa beside him at the safe house. Her security detail was still stationed by the doors and on the street.

"I need to talk to you," she said.

"I know you're still upset about how the meeting went yesterday."

"I am, but it's more than that."

"What?" he asked.

"I'm going to make a big request."

He was worried he knew what was coming next. "All right."

"When Mark contacts me, I need us to handle this on our own with Layla's help. We can't bring in the FBI team or whatever plan the directors are trying to concoct."

Exactly as he feared. "I warned them you might try to go rogue."

"You've gotten to know me well."

He had to talk some sense into her. "I don't like it, Viv. We have the best chance with the most resources."

She leaned her head back on the couch. "I don't think they really intend to mount a true rescue effort."

"Why not?"

Turning to him, she grabbed his arm. "They're just trying to appease me. That whole thing about decoys and plans. Once I give them Mark's location, I'm out of it. They'll do whatever they must in order to apprehend the men they want. My sister is secondary, if important at all. Collateral damage."

"Don't say that."

"You know it's true. Tell me it isn't."

And that was the thing. He couldn't. "I can't make promises that I have no control over keeping." He could only control his actions. Definitely not those of the CIA.

"Which is why I need to save my sister. I know it's asking a lot of you, but I don't think we have any chance of succeeding without you." Her eyes pleaded with him.

He was torn. The FBI and, more important, the CIA had a different goal for this mission. Viv's only thought was of her twin sister, and he couldn't fault her for that. But his main concern was Viv and her safety. There were too many competing interests.

He hated that he had to say this, but now was the time. "I get that you're willing to risk it all for your sister, but I have to be brutally honest with you. Any mission, whether it's run by the FBI, CIA, or us, has very little chance of bringing Willow back alive. I don't want you under any illusions about that. It's really hard to hear, but Viv, the men holding her don't play by any rules."

She bit her lip, and tears welled up in her eyes.

"I don't want to hurt you, but you must know what we're up against."

She nodded. "I get it. Which is even more reason to try to get Willow out ourselves and not rely on any other agency to do it for us."

Jacob realized that what he was about to tell her would probably end any relationship between them before it even started—and maybe that was for the best. "I want to help you. I really do. But I can't engage in a mission that I know will most likely end with you and your sister dying."

Viv's bottom lip quivered. "You're refusing to help me."

This hurt, but she wasn't thinking clearly. "Viv, there's no way that you, Layla, and I can take on this task by ourselves. It's just not possible. It's like walking a death march, and I care too much about you to sanction this. I realize you may hate me, but I have no other choice. We should work with the FBI and CIA and use their resources to try to get your sister back. That's the best shot we have. It's our only shot, actually. I promise. It's not a rogue mission. I've got a tactical assault plan mapped out with the FBI team. We're ready for multiple contingencies."

"But you basically already admitted that Willow's not their priority."

There was no arguing that point. "True, but she's our priority, and we'll need their support if there is any chance of saving her."

She looked down. "I need some time to think."

He would give her space, but he was also going to let the security detail know that there was no way they should let her out of the safe house without him.

◆

Delaney's frustration level was off the charts. After Jeff had spoken to his lawyer, he'd called her bluff. She didn't have enough yet to charge him, which meant she had to cut him loose. She'd told the FBI surveillance team to keep very close tabs on him.

Sitting alone in the dark on her couch, she tried to take some steadying breaths. She needed more evidence against Jeff. Which meant she must stop her pity party and get back to work.

She stood, walked over to her small desk, and fired up her laptop. There had to be a way to take this guy down, and she would find it.

Scrolling through her notes, she studied everything again. Where was his weak point? Where could he have messed up and left evidence?

Who had actually killed Penelope? Had Jeff hired a hit-man? Or had he killed her himself? He was at the dinner and had the opportunity to place the fentanyl in her drink. She'd been keeping close tabs with Agent Miller in Narcotics to see if they had any leads on dealers for fentanyl who could have sold to Jeff, but so far they couldn't get anyone to talk.

Her cell rang. Nothing good could be happening this late on a Friday night.

"O'Sullivan," she answered.

"Agent O'Sullivan, this is Agent Price. I'm on Jeff King's surveillance team."

Her stomach dropped.

"There was an attempt on his life outside of his apartment. We were able to get to him in time, and he's being transported to the ER. Gunshot wound to the shoulder. Unfortunately, given our small surveillance team, we weren't able to pursue the shooter because we had to administer aid to Mr. King."

"But he's not critical?"

"Thankfully, no, but you had some really good instincts to warn us. I assume we're going to need to provide a more robust security detail now?" Price asked.

"Yes. I'll meet you at the hospital. I want to talk to Jeff in person."

"See you soon."

She jumped up and grabbed her stuff. She didn't know whether Popov was firing a warning shot or whether Jeff got lucky, but either way, maybe this brush with death would make Jeff talk.

CHAPTER
TWENTY-THREE

Viv checked her watch again for the millionth time. It was almost eleven, and still no word from Mark.

The FBI was all over her email, monitoring it every second. She was dependent on them for updates, as they'd taken away her laptop. So much for any attempt to hide anything from them.

Was her sister already dead? She didn't know what to do, and she had spent the evening locked in her room, crying out to God for protection. Was she already alone in the world? She really thought she'd know if her twin sister was dead, but now she was second-guessing herself.

A million questions swirled in her head. She was upset with Jacob, but deep down she knew he was right about them not having any chance of rescuing Willow without serious backup. There was still a great fear inside her about whether anyone really cared about Willow. It was all about getting the prisoners back because the CIA had screwed up, and her sister was going to pay the price.

But at the end of the day, it was her fault that her sister was in grave danger. And it looked like that was another burden she would have to live with.

Finally, she decided to go downstairs and find out if there were any updates.

The house was eerily quiet. She didn't see Jacob, but another member of the security detail was sitting at the kitchen table, drinking a cup of coffee and working on his laptop.

"Where's Jacob?" she asked.

He looked up at her. "He's not here."

"What do you mean? Where is he?"

Her security detail looked down and away from her. And it hit her.

"He left without me, didn't he? Mark has already emailed?"

The man stood. "I'm sorry, ma'am. I'm just following orders."

"Which were?"

"To keep you safe and inside."

"What's your name?"

"I'm Agent Pete Marino."

She held her tongue. The poor guy was just doing his job, but she could have strangled Jacob for leaving her. "Do you know where they were going?"

Pete shook his head. "I'm sorry, ma'am, I don't. They got the communication they were looking for and all left very quickly."

Viv started pacing around the kitchen. She wondered if Layla had been in on this too. And now she was completely helpless. All she could do was wait.

◆

Sweat rolled down Jacob's back as he led the assault team toward the warehouse that Mark had emailed to Viv. He feared the worst, but he was going to give it his all for Viv's sake. If they did make it out of this alive, then Viv might be the one to kill him, but sneaking out was the only way he could protect her, and he would risk everything for her.

Of course, they didn't have Ali with them because the CIA would never trade. There were two objectives for this mission: rescue and capture.

Jacob moved swiftly with the assault team past the perimeter and approached the front entrance. Another team was covering the back.

He lifted his hand, signaling the rest of the guys around him. The man on his right was getting ready to breach the door. Jacob gave the final signal, and the door blew open.

He ran inside with his gun drawn and a team of agents around him. The warehouse was dark and dank. He pulled on night-vision goggles and moved quickly through the space.

"Clear!" someone yelled.

"Clear!" another voice said.

He didn't see or hear anything. What was going on? "Sit rep," he yelled.

"Over here!" an agent called out.

He ran over to where the agent stood. "We need a medic!"

Jacob squatted down, and someone shone a bright light over a body lying in a pool of blood. There was no doubt in his mind that this was Willow Steele.

He checked for a pulse and found one—albeit weak. Her throat had been cut, but she was still alive. It was a very fresh wound, which meant Mark, or whoever had done this, was still close.

"Make sure a team goes after him. He couldn't have gotten far." Jacob barked a few more orders while one of the agents tried to stop the bleeding and the medics ran in.

Lord, please don't let Willow die.

◆

Viv was still doing laps around the first floor of the house. Agent Marino knew better than to comment on her pacing even though she was sure it was annoying him. What else was she supposed to do?

Agent Marino's phone rang, and she ran over, hoping for an update. The expression on his face made her stomach drop. This couldn't be good news.

He ended the call and moved toward her, grabbing her arm. "We've gotta move. Now."

"What happened?" She feared the answer.

"I'll explain everything in the car."

She started to take a step, but two gunshots shattered the silence. Agent Marino collapsed in a heap on the floor, and she shrieked. He'd been shot in the head. Before she could do anything else, strong arms grabbed her, fingers digging into her skin.

Struggling, she turned to see her attacker. Mark.

"Where's my sister?" She continued to fight against him.

He tightened his grip on her as he dragged her across the living room. "I slit her throat."

Viv gasped. Was he bluffing or serious? She dug her heels into the carpet. "You didn't."

He stopped and looked down at her. "I did. Just in time for your friends to find her bleeding out. I'm sure she's dead by now."

Pure rage overtook her, and she fought with everything she

had. She broke his grip and started to run the other direction, but he tackled her to the carpet.

She kicked and screamed, but he was stronger than her. And he had a gun. But he hadn't killed her yet, which meant he thought he needed her alive.

A burst of adrenaline coursed through her body, and she kneed him hard in the groin. He groaned, and she broke away. She scampered through the kitchen and grabbed a knife from the drawer. But he was right on top of her. She lashed out, thrashing around with the knife, and sliced his arm.

Mark let out a curse as blood started to flow down his arm, but the cut wasn't deep enough to stop him. He quickly gripped her wrist and squeezed, forcing her to drop the knife to the kitchen floor.

He grabbed her tightly around the waist and dragged her toward the hallway leading to the door. "Maybe the CIA wouldn't play ball with your sister, but with one of their own officers, I think they will."

She shook her head. "You have it all wrong, Mark. I am not CIA. I never have been."

He pulled her close to him so they were face-to-face. "You can cut the act, Viv. I know you are, and you're my ticket to releasing Ali and the others."

She needed to buy time. Had he killed her other detail outside? She feared the answer had to be yes. "I'm not going with you."

He laughed and looked her right in the eyes. "You have no choice. We can do this the hard way or the easy way. It's your choice."

"Did you kill my other security detail?"

"Don't look so appalled, Viv. The naïve act is getting old. I know what you do for a living."

He shifted his grip, and his fingers dug into her arms, but she refused to give him the satisfaction of crying out. "You're going to be the one who figures out the hard way that I'm not CIA—they don't care about me or my sister."

"You're not expendable. Or else they wouldn't be going through so much trouble to protect you—although they failed. Your personal security guard is nowhere to be found, is he? Oh, that's right. He's chasing his tail while I'm here with you."

"How did you find me?" *Keep him talking. Stall, stall, stall.*

"Everyone has a price."

She sucked in a breath. The leak had to be at the Agency. And now she was most likely going to die and join her sister. And her parents. "You targeted me that night, didn't you? You set up the attack on me. Why go through all of that?"

His eyes narrowed. "You were never part of the plan until you walked into the Egyptian embassy. When we identified who you were, and that you were the CIA agent at the prisoner exchange, we saw a valuable opportunity to expand our operation, and it looks like my gamble paid off big time, because you're going to get my men back."

"Why are you doing this? Why do you kill innocent people?" This she actually did want to know.

He grabbed her throat. "You're not innocent. Look at all the harm the CIA has done. The drone strikes that kill innocents. The wars your country fights that kill innocents. You can't claim the moral high ground here."

"I agree that we've made mistakes as a country, but the way to right wrongs is not to do more wrong. You can stop this." She tried to think of something else to say, but before she could speak, loud voices filled the safe house.

Mark spun her around and pulled her up against him, holding the gun to her head.

She screamed, and all of a sudden the room was full of FBI agents. But in front of them all was Jacob with his gun drawn.

Jacob took a step toward them. "Time's up, Joubert. Let her go, and you'll live."

Mark's grip tightened even further. "No way. You're going to let us walk out of here unscathed. Then, if you ever want to see her again, you're going to have the CIA turn over the rest of the detainees. Not just Ali, but all of them you took from Egypt."

She could barely breathe. His grip was so tight. Jacob had said he was an expert marksman. He could do this. She had no doubt.

Saying a quick prayer, she mouthed, *Shoot him*. She held her breath and stayed as still as possible, knowing any move on her part could lead to her being shot.

After a couple of seconds, she thought Jacob wasn't going to do it, but then the gunshot rang out. She let out a breath, wondering if she was still alive, but once Mark's grip fell away, she looked down and saw him on the floor. Dead. Jacob's shot to the head had been amazingly accurate.

Jacob ran over to her. "Are you okay?"

"Thanks to you, I am." She tried not to hyperventilate. "My sister. Willow?" She grabbed his arms and prayed Mark had been bluffing.

Jacob frowned. "She's at the hospital."

"So she's alive?" she whispered.

"Barely."

"I need to see her. Please. We have to go." She looked up at him.

He nodded and wrapped his arm around her. "Let's go."

◆

"Talk to me." Jacob's eyes were on the road, but he needed to know Viv was okay. They had an FBI escort in the car behind them on the way to the hospital.

"No, you first. What happened? You just left me!"

He'd known this was going to be a huge deal for her. "You have every right to be mad. Everyone thought this was the best way to keep you safe, and I didn't argue with them."

She sighed loudly. "Layla was on board too?"

"Not at first. She was the last holdout, but even if she hadn't agreed, she would've been trumped by the directors. The important thing is that you're still alive. I know you're angry, but it was the best call we could make at the time." He paused. "I supported the decision because I didn't want you to die. I couldn't lose you. Not after losing everyone else I've ever cared about." He realized his voice was starting to shake.

"Oh, Jacob," she said softly. "I'm all right, thanks to you."

"We barely made it back to you in time."

But they had. "Tell me more about Willow and what happened."

He took a breath, deciding how best to describe it.

She spoke first. "Mark told me he slit her throat."

"He did. But we got there quickly enough to stop her from bleeding out. I don't think Mark knew exactly what he was doing, and that might end up saving your sister's life. I have to warn you, though, she still lost a lot of blood. I don't know her exact status."

"Which is why I need to get to the hospital." She touched his arm. "I'm so thankful you were there to help her. I can't allow myself to think about life without my sister."

"And I'm glad I was able to get to her and to you. What did Mark tell you?"

"He thought the CIA would trade the detainees for me. That's why he didn't kill me on the spot. He was truly convinced that I'm CIA."

Jacob let out a low whistle. "He's dead. He can't hurt you or Willow anymore."

"But what about Omar?" she asked.

"He was outside the safe house, standing watch for Mark, and has been taken into custody, so you can breathe a little easier on that front. Don't dwell on that right now. Let everyone else deal with that so you can focus on Willow."

"I know," she said. "I just pray she makes it. I can't lose her." Her voice cracked.

He kept one hand on the wheel and used the other to squeeze hers. "We've made it this far, Viv. Keep the faith."

"You're right. I should also thank you for saving my life. I'm not even sure what I said after it happened."

"You were in shock. Rightfully so."

"Thanks for taking the risk and making the shot."

"Were you afraid I wouldn't do it?"

"No. I could see the confidence in your eyes. You're a SEAL. You told me early on that you were an expert marksman, and that stuck with me. I knew you'd get him. I was just worried about staying still." She sighed. "This nightmare is unlike anything I could ever imagine. I still don't think it's sunk in that Mark is dead."

"He is, and at least that's one burden off your shoulders. I know you're worried about Willow, but we'll tackle this one thing at a time, okay?"

She looked over at him. "I've been a bit of a bear to deal

with. I'm sorry about that. I realize that all you've done, you've done to protect me."

"That's absolutely the case. When I ran into the safe house and saw you in that monster's arms, I can't tell you the amount of fear that streaked through my body." He was probably being too open with her, but he wanted her to understand.

"You seemed cool as a cucumber."

"That was the training taking over. But I was seeing red. I knew he was hurting you, and I had to stop him. I wanted to wrap my arms around you and protect you from the dangers coming from all sides. Things you definitely don't deserve. You've sacrificed so much."

"As long as Willow is alive, I feel like I can keep fighting."

"We're almost at the hospital." He prayed that Willow would still be alive when they arrived.

CHAPTER
TWENTY-FOUR

Delaney hadn't exactly received a warm welcome from Jeff King, but she wasn't going anywhere. She'd also called Weston, and he was with her in Jeff's hospital room at the ER.

"Who is trying to kill me?" Jeff asked her.

"My best guess is that it's Sergei Popov," she responded.

Jeff shook his head. "No way. He's stationed in Brussels."

It was time to really squeeze him. "We have information that he is in the States."

Jeff's eyes widened. "Are you serious?"

"Deadly." She paused. "I know you said earlier that you didn't have anything else to say to us, but I hoped you would reconsider."

"But I don't understand the connection between the two," Jeff said.

"You don't think Popov tried to kill you because you murdered the woman he loved?"

Jeff frowned. "That's preposterous."

"Is it?" Weston jumped in.

She needed to press this point home. "Popov didn't succeed, but I bet he will be back."

"What? Are you just going to let me die?" Jeff's voice cracked.

"Of course not," Delaney said. "We're providing you with around-the-clock FBI protection, and I expect you to tell us the truth."

He scowled. "I don't want to talk to you without my lawyer present."

Delaney stood. "Of course. Your protective detail isn't going anywhere. You know how to reach us if you want to talk." She started to walk to the door.

"You're certain the detail isn't going to leave me?" Jeff asked.

"Yes. We're going to do everything in our power to keep you safe, regardless of whether you do the right thing or not."

◆

Viv rushed into her sister's room at the hospital, and Jacob waited in the hall with the security detail they'd placed at the hospital. Viv was relieved to see Willow's doctor standing next to her sister's bed.

The doctor did a double take when she came into the room. "I guess I know who you are." He gave her a weak smile.

"How's Willow doing?" She looked at her sister, who lay in the hospital bed, connected to a lot of machines.

"She's very fortunate to be alive. Even one more minute without treatment, and she probably wouldn't be here."

Viv sucked in a breath as the full reality of the situation hit her head on.

"She's not out of the woods yet, but thankfully the cut, while still causing her to lose a lot of blood, didn't damage anything critical, since her assailant missed the carotid artery."

"When will she wake up?"

"It could be anytime, but I would like to keep her sedated as much as possible this first twenty-four hours."

"Can I talk to her?"

"Sure. She probably won't respond, and if she does wake up, then don't keep her talking long. Ring for a nurse, all right?"

She nodded. She understood that Willow needed rest, but she also wanted to have a moment alone with her sister. The doctor left, and she sat down beside the bed and took her sister's hand.

"Willow, it's me. I'm so sorry that this happened to you, and it's all my fault. I love you more than anything in this world, and I will make sure you are safe. You have my word on that." Tears were streaming down her face as she studied her twin and the thick gauze wrapped around her neck.

"We'll get through this together, little sister." While Viv was only a few minutes older, she still felt like she had to take care of Willow. There was no one else but them, and she was going to help her sister, no matter what it took. "I love you, Willow."

Her sister's eyes fluttered open for a second, and then fear filled them and she started to move.

Viv pushed the nurse's button and tried to calm Willow down. "Willow, it's me. You're safe now. You're in the hospital. You're going to be okay. Do you understand?"

Willow's hazel eyes grew large, but she nodded.

Viv held tightly to Willow's hand. "They're going to give you something else to help you rest. Your neck was cut, and you lost blood. You're going to be in pain, so we're going to keep giving you something for that until the pain is under control."

"Scared," Willow whispered.

Viv shook her head. "No one can hurt you now. I promise. The man who did this to you is dead. We've got a security detail outside the door." *And they'd have to get through me.* "Don't try to talk anymore. Just close your eyes."

"Hurts," she whispered again.

"The nurse will be here soon with more meds."

On cue, the nurse walked into the room. "Ah, you're awake, Ms. Steele."

"Yes, but she's hurting," Viv said. "And it seems like she can only whisper."

"She had a lot of neck trauma. That will get better with time." The nurse administered some more medicine through the IV.

Her sister's eyes closed again, and Viv let out a breath.

"I think your sister's going to pull through this," the nurse said. "I've been with her from the moment she came in. She has a fighting spirit."

Viv couldn't help but cry, and the nurse gave her a hug. "Can I stay with her?"

"Yes, but now that you've talked to her once, please don't try to rouse her. If she wakes, you can see how she's feeling and call the nurse on duty, but what her body needs more than anything is rest."

"Thank you so much." Viv appreciated the woman's kindness. Knowing that Willow was probably going to be okay was almost too much for her to handle. She settled in the chair beside her sister and wept.

◆

The next afternoon, Delaney got the big break they so desperately needed in the investigation. Agent Miller finally had a lead on a supplier of the specific street version of fentanyl that had killed the ambassador. If the dealer could positively identify Jeff King as having purchased the fentanyl, then she could make an arrest.

She and Weston were waiting in one of the FBI conference rooms for Agent Miller to bring in the dealer.

After a few minutes, Agent Miller entered the room with a short Caucasian male who was probably in his thirties. They made quick introductions, including finding out the supplier was named Lenny O'Shea.

Lenny took a seat. "Before I say anything, I want to make sure it's clear that I will not be held responsible for any of this. That's what Agent Miller told me, but I want it in writing."

They'd been prepared for this contingency and had already gotten the DA's assurance on immunity with regard to the murder of the ambassador. Delaney slid a piece of paper outlining an immunity deal from the DA. "You can take a moment to read it."

After a few minutes of staring at the paper, Lenny looked up at her. "Okay. I'll talk. I conduct my side business out of my body shop. I need to make sure none of my employees are brought into this."

She didn't care anything about those guys. "Agreed. This is just about you and what you saw." She didn't want to waste a moment and opened a folder with several pictures of Jeff King. She slid the pictures in front of Lenny. "Do you recognize this man?"

Lenny didn't speak for a moment, staring at the pictures.

She didn't want to push him. For this to work, she needed him to react without her interference.

He looked up at her. "Yeah. I remember him."

"Did he tell you his name?" she asked.

Lenny laughed. "We don't trade info in my line of work. People want to be anonymous."

"But he was one of your customers?"

Lenny nodded. "Yup."

"How did he pay?"

"Cash. Just like everyone else."

Delaney took a breath. "I assume he didn't tell you what he was going to do with the fentanyl he purchased from you."

Lenny leaned forward. "Nope. And I didn't ask. Never do. It's bad for business."

She wasn't in the position to make judgments about the drug dealer. Her primary target was Jeff King. "When did this happen?"

Lenny drummed his scrawny fingers on the desk. "Within the last month or so. But I saw him twice."

"What?" Weston piped up.

Lenny shifted in his seat. "Yeah. I didn't have any powdered fentanyl on the day he visited me. I was out of stock, so to speak. I had to resupply quickly. I told him to give me two days. He came back, and I had procured what he was looking for, so he paid me a premium for the quick turnaround."

"Would you be able to testify under oath that this man in the picture was the man you're describing?"

Lenny nodded. "Assuming my immunity deal stays in place, yeah, I would."

She wasn't thrilled about the prospect of putting a drug dealer on the stand, but they had to work with the evidence they had in front of them. And maybe, just maybe, this would be enough to elicit a confession from Jeff that he had murdered his wife.

CHAPTER
TWENTY-FIVE

The past two days had gone by in a blur for Viv. It was Monday afternoon, and she was still by her sister's side in the hospital. But the news was entirely hopeful. Willow had gotten past the worst of it, and the doctor was even starting to talk about releasing her later in the week.

"Willow, why were you even in the US?" Viv asked.

Willow sighed. "I knew something was wrong, and you weren't telling me. I got worried that you really were in danger. And it looks like I was right."

"I'm so sorry you got brought into this." She didn't know how to forgive herself.

Willow shook her head. "No you don't, sis. Do not place any guilt on yourself over this. The ones to blame are the men who did this, not you."

Viv hung her head. "I wish it were that simple, but I can't help but feel responsible."

"I know you do, and that's why I'm telling you to let it go. Do it for me, because I don't want that on me either. I worry about you. You've been through so much over the past few weeks. I can't even comprehend how you did it. You're so strong and fierce. I'm really proud of you. You stepped up in a major way when you didn't have to."

Viv had shared a lot of what had happened with her sister in bits and pieces over the past day.

"You need to give yourself some grace," Willow said. "Look at how strong you are. The men who did this are either dead or in custody. Take a breath."

Viv appreciated her sister's keen insights. No one knew her like Willow did. "Thanks for understanding me."

"That's my job." Willow smiled. "I still want to talk to Jacob. I know he's the one who saved my life."

"He'll be here soon. I told him you needed to talk to him."

Willow raised an eyebrow. "You've got it bad for him, don't you?"

Viv sighed. "I do, but it's not that straightforward."

Willow held tightly to her hand. "Take it from me. I've stared down death, and it only solidifies what we both already knew. We aren't guaranteed another day. We have to live life to its fullest and not be afraid of taking a chance on love. I don't want all of this to have taken that out of you, because you've always been the romantic in the family. Don't let fear stop you."

Her sister's words hit home. "I don't know how he'll feel about all of this."

"Why don't you ask him?"

"We'll talk once everything settles."

Willow shook her head. "Don't make excuses—especially not on my account."

At a knock on the hospital room door, Viv turned to see Jacob.

He walked into the room and addressed Willow. "How're you feeling?"

"I'm doing okay, and thanks to you, I'm alive. They tell me the pain will only be temporary. I can't thank you enough."

"I'm glad you're feeling better," Jacob said.

"I do have one more request of you," Willow said.

"Name it," Jacob replied without hesitation.

"Please get my sister out of here. She hasn't left since she got here late Friday night."

"I'm not leaving you, Willow," Viv protested.

"Yes, you are. You need a break. I'll be fine. I promise. Please go home, get some rest, food, a shower." She arched an eyebrow. "You need it."

Viv laughed at her sister's final comment. "I get the message."

Jacob placed his hand on Viv's shoulder. "I can take you."

She relented, knowing that she did desperately need a couple hours of sleep and a hot shower.

She told her sister good-bye and walked out of the room with Jacob. They didn't talk much on the way to her condo.

"I know this is silly, but will you check my place out before you leave?" she asked.

"I'm not leaving."

"What do you mean?"

"You shouldn't be alone right now. I want you to rest without worrying."

Her heartbeat sped up. "But I thought you said the threat was neutralized."

"It absolutely is, but I still know that you'll be worried regardless, and that's completely natural."

"Thank you." She wasn't going to reject the help. Not now.

After sleeping for about four hours and taking a long, hot

shower, she finally felt more human again. She opened her bedroom door and found Jacob on the couch. He was also napping. He looked so peaceful lying there, but she knew he was a warrior. A warrior who had saved both her life and the life of her sister. Her warrior.

She knew Jacob wasn't perfect, but she couldn't help how she felt about him. It went far beyond his being her protector.

"I can feel you watching me." Jacob's eyes opened and met hers.

"Sorry, I didn't mean to bother you."

"You're not bothering me. I was just taking a catnap. How did you sleep?"

"Good, actually. It's amazing what sleep and a hot shower can do for you."

"But you also need to eat," he insisted.

"Can we talk first?"

He walked over to her. "Sure. What's on your mind?"

"Us." She lifted her hand. "And before you start rattling off the eight million reasons you think we shouldn't be together, can I say something?"

He smiled. "I'm listening."

"I know you're still battling demons, and after all that's happened to me, I'm sure I'm going to feel the effects of this for years to come. But here's the thing. I want to work through all of that with you. To be the one to walk by your side and help lift you up—and for you to do the same for me. Yes, I'm sure we'll bicker and not agree on everything, but I firmly believe that the foundation of our relationship is strong. That we are ultimately looking for the same things and have the same core values."

"Are you done yet?" He took her hands.

She smiled. "That depends on what your reaction is."

"I won't lie to you. Before Friday night, I'd come up with lots of speeches in my head that I planned to give you. How I was going to convince you that we weren't right for each other. But after almost losing you, that's no longer the case. Even though I might not want to admit it, Viv, you're really good for me. I still worry that I'm not good enough for you and can't give you everything you need, but I realize that I have to trust you and what you say you want."

Her eyes started to fill with tears. "You're what I want, Jacob. I'm looking forward to exploring what our life could be like together outside of all this."

Jacob leaned down. "I want that too. I don't want to go back to a world in which I don't know you, Viv. You're the light to my darkness. I'm falling for you. I know it's really soon to say that, but I don't want to hold back. Not when I know how easily it can all be gone. I need you to know how much you've come to mean to me."

Her heart felt like it was about to explode. She pulled his head down to hers, and he kissed her. For the first time in a long time, she had hope that love wasn't just something out of fairy tales but something she could have with Jacob.

◆

The next morning, Delaney's pulse thumped wildly as she paced back and forth, waiting for Jeff King to arrive with his lawyer at FBI headquarters. Her adrenaline was off the charts. When they got word that Jeff and Gerard were settled in the interrogation room, she knew it was time to bring this one home.

She and Weston walked into the room. This time she had highly damaging evidence in her possession. The big question was how much hardball these guys would play. She couldn't wait to see Jeff's reaction when confronted with the cold truth.

Before she could say anything, Gerard jumped in.

"Agent O'Sullivan, I won't let you continue to badger my client. We're here purely as a courtesy. I need to make that clear at the outset. We will walk if you start again with the outlandish and unfounded allegations."

"I think you will soon agree that nothing I'm about to show you is outlandish or unfounded." Now that she actually had hard evidence connecting Jeff to the murder, there was no need for games.

Gerard's eyes narrowed. "What do you mean by that?"

Her nerves kicked in, and she squeezed her left hand into a fist under the table to settle herself down. "We have some new evidence to discuss with your client."

"What kind of new evidence?" Gerard asked.

She opened the folder in front of her. "This is a sworn affidavit from Lenny O'Shea."

Gerard put on his glasses and looked at the affidavit. "Who is Lenny O'Shea, and what does he have to do with my client?"

She glanced at Jeff, who didn't break his poker face. His arm was in a sling, and she could see the bandages on his shoulder peeking above his collar. She hoped Popov would back down once she had Jeff in custody.

"You can take a moment to review it, but in short, Mr. O'Shea is prepared to testify that your client purchased street fentanyl from him. The same street fentanyl that was found in the tox screen of your client's wife. The same street fentanyl that killed her."

Gerard cleared his throat. "You're relying on the word of a drug dealer versus my upstanding client—who, of course, denies these radical allegations."

"I wouldn't be so fast to disregard Mr. O'Shea's statement. If you'll read closely, you'll see that your client visited him not once but twice. And this morning, I found out that Mr. O'Shea has surveillance video of his body shop where the meetings took place. I bet if we look at that video, we'll see your client. There's no point in engaging in this charade any longer."

Gerard looked at Jeff. "I think I need a few minutes alone with my client."

She stood. "Sure. We'll give you some time alone."

She walked out of the room and looked at Weston as he joined her. "We've got him."

Weston gave her a high five. "It's over. He's going to cave. I can feel it."

Finally, justice for Penelope King.

The director walked out of the connecting room, and she realized he'd been watching the interrogation. "Delaney, can I have a word in my office?" he asked.

"Sure." She looked at Weston, who shrugged. She guessed he didn't know what was going on either.

She followed the director up to his office and wondered what this could be about. Normally, they just talked wherever they were, but formal office visits like this were rare. She hoped she hadn't done something wrong in the interrogation room.

"Please have a seat."

She sat in the large chair across from his desk.

"Your work on this case has been outstanding," Lang said.

At least that was a promising start. "Thank you, sir. I couldn't have done it without Weston and Cody. It was a real team effort."

"Spoken like a true leader." He leaned forward. "I'm going

288

to get right to the point. I'm promoting you to assistant director of the Criminal Investigative Division. As you know, there's been an interim director, but he's moving into a different division. You'll be in charge of CID."

That was not what she expected. It hadn't even been on her radar. "Thank you, sir, but frankly, I'm shocked. I didn't realize I was even in the mix."

"Honestly, you weren't on the short list before this case, but you were on the long list. I've watched this case unfold, and I think you earned it and then some."

"Thank you, sir." Her mind raced. She had been completely taken off guard.

Lang smiled. "You deserve this, Delaney. I know you're concerned about Weston, as I can tell you have a soft spot for him. You can pick who you reassign him to. Does that work for you?"

She nodded. "Yes, sir, and I won't let you down."

"I know you won't, or I wouldn't have made this decision." He stood.

"Thank you." She bolted out of his office and went back down to meet Weston.

"What was that all about?" Weston asked.

"I'll tell you after we talk to Jeff King again." She started walking toward the interrogation room, but Weston pulled her to a stop.

"No way. What gives?"

She looked up at him. "You're not going to believe this."

"Is everything okay?"

She didn't want him to worry. "More than okay. I was just promoted to assistant director."

His eyes widened before he caught her in a big bear hug and swung her around. "I'm so happy for you, Delaney. No one deserves this more than you." He set her down. "I know that wasn't that professional, but you're like family to me."

"Thank you, Weston. I feel the same way about you."

He gave her another quick hug.

"I appreciate you caring so much, but we can't get distracted. We have a killer to take down."

He nodded. "Okay, but we're going to celebrate after this is all wrapped up."

"I like the sound of that." Delaney wanted nothing more than to enjoy the good news, but her work was far from finished.

Epilogue

Viv's life seemed boring now compared to the way it had been four months ago, but she would gladly take it. The task force had received many accolades for their work. Their mission to solve the murders of the two ambassadors was accomplished, and thankfully, she was back at her regular job as an attorney for the State Department. Her CIA days were over, and she planned to keep it that way.

Penelope King had been murdered by her husband, Jeff, who, in exchange for a plea deal, provided a full confession that revealed he had placed fentanyl in one of his wife's drinks at the diplomatic dinner. Jeff had drugged his wife with an amount of fentanyl that he believed would kill her on the spot, but she had been strong enough to fight for her life. Although, in the end, nothing could save her.

Jeff had come clean that he found out about Penelope's affair with Popov and had cooked up an elaborate plan to make it look like she was working with the Russians. He had overheard a conversation Penelope had with Popov that had given him the impression Popov was Russian intelligence. It was still unclear to the CIA whether Popov actually was a spy and if Penelope had been compromised. Because of that, they were taking additional security measures related to any classified information she had accessed. What was clear was that the Russians hadn't been paying Penelope anything. Jeff had told Penelope he was moving funds into her account at the advice of their financial planner, and she hadn't questioned him.

He'd taken a deal for life in prison with no chance of parole so he wouldn't face the death penalty. The case seemed to have skyrocketed Delaney's career at the FBI, and in Viv's mind it was much deserved. Viv was thankful that Jeff was being punished through the justice system. He wouldn't see the outside again, and that seemed like a fitting punishment.

As for Ambassador Zidan's death, after many hours of interrogation, Omar had corroborated the fact that Mark had ordered the hit. Al-Nidal was supporting the radical forces in Egypt and thought taking out Zidan would be a big win. Through a handshake at the dinner, the hit man had given Zidan the drug that made his heart stop. That assassin was also now in custody and had confirmed he had been hired by Mark for the job.

The Egyptians were still facing some internal unrest politically, but the president was trying to form a circle of those he could trust around him again. The CIA had also identified and apprehended the rogue CIA agent who had helped the detainees escape and provided Viv's safe house location to Mark. The traitor had been charged and was currently in federal prison.

"What're you thinking?" Jacob asked.

"I'm just glad we're here tonight." She smiled up at him. They were in Layla and Hunter's backyard for a dinner party, and the fall weather couldn't have been better. Her friends had all accepted Jacob with open arms, and she couldn't be happier.

"Viv, come here." Layla waved at her. Viv walked over to her friend, and Jacob got pulled away by Hunter. "We're going to take a girls' picture since it's been so long since we've all been able to get together."

Viv looked at the group of girlfriends—which had started out as three but had now expanded.

Izzy was a busy bee at law school but was thriving and at the top of her class. She and Aiden were still going strong, and it made Viv so happy after all Izzy had gone through.

Lexi had rekindled her relationship with Derek, who was also here tonight, hanging out with the guys. She was re-settled in DC and back working at JAG headquarters.

Marco was building a new house and had confided in Viv and Layla that he was planning to propose to Bailey within the next few weeks.

Willow had decided to stay in the US for a bit and work at a nonprofit in DC. It was wonderful having her sister so close again instead of halfway around the world.

The biggest news of the night was that Viv had learned Layla was pregnant. She hadn't told anyone but Viv and Bailey, but she was planning to share with the larger group once she got further along.

The group of women took multiple pictures, with the guys serving as photographers. Laughter filled the air, and Viv's heart couldn't have been more full.

Music was playing, and Jacob walked up to her. "Let's dance."

She laughed. "You're not much of a dancer."

He grinned. "This is slow dancing. It doesn't require much special skill." He pulled her a few yards away from the others and then into his arms.

"Are you having a good time?" she asked.

"Definitely. I enjoy hanging out with these guys." He paused. "Hunter's been trying to convince me to become a PI, but I told him I wasn't quite done with government work yet. Maybe one day, though."

She looked up at him. "It's good to have options." Jacob pulled her close, and she rested her head on his chest. "I love you."

"I love you too. This has been a great night," Jacob said.

They'd been going to counseling separately and together. It had been good for both of them, and they were building something special.

"I have to admit that I keep waiting for something bad to happen," she said. "It's hard for me to realize that we're finally free of the past."

"We are. There is no threat to you anymore. I'm certain of it."

"I know," she sighed. "Having you by my side makes me feel safe, and I know we can get through anything together."

He looked down at her. "Viv, I know we're not ready to take any big next steps."

She wasn't sure where this was going.

"But I do want you to know that I want to be with you. That's where I want this to go. Do you understand?"

"Yes." She smiled. They both still needed more time to work through their issues and to grow in their relationship, but she knew she loved him more than anything in the world. The timing would be right when they were both ready. "I'm not going anywhere."

Jacob pulled her closer. "Not without me."

She knew this moment would last forever.

Acknowledgments

It's hard to believe that this is the end of the Capital Intrigue series! I hope you enjoyed getting to know these characters as much as I did. I thank the Lord for giving me the ability to create these stories. I am truly blessed in so many ways, and I thank God for all He has done for me.

I'd like to thank everyone at Bethany House, especially Jessica Sharpe and Dave Long for their tremendous editing and helping to make all of my books the absolute best they could be.

I appreciate all the love and support I receive from my readers, especially the members of Rachel's Justice League!

Alison, it's hard to think that our friendship started on Twitter back in 2012! What a crazy writing journey it has been for the both of us, and I can't wait to see what happens next.

Lee and Dana, I love you both. You make this writing journey so much more fun. Thanks for being there in the good times and the bad times.

Aaron, thank you for pushing me to be the best I can be. I love you.

To all my family, thank you for sharing about my books!

Special shout out to Tog and Shane for your constant promotion. Love y'all.

Mama, I love you! You taught me from a very young age that I could do whatever I put my mind to, and that I should chase my dreams. Thank you for always encouraging me to dream big.

Rachel Dylan is an award-winning and bestselling author of legal thrillers and romantic suspense. She has practiced law for over a decade, including being a litigator at one of the nation's top law firms. Books from her Atlanta Justice series, which feature strong female attorneys, have won the Holt Medallion, the Maggie Award, and the FHL Reader's Choice Award. Rachel lives in Michigan with her husband and five furkids—two dogs and three cats. She loves to connect with readers. You can find her at www.racheldylan.com.

Sign Up for Rachel's Newsletter

Keep up to date with Rachel's news on book releases and events by signing up for her email list at racheldylan.com.

More from Rachel Dylan

When elite members of the military are murdered on the streets of Washington, DC, FBI Special Agent Bailey Ryan and NCIS Special Agent Marco Agostini must work together to bring the perpetrator to justice. As the stakes rise in a twisted conspiracy and allies turn to enemies, the biggest secret yet to be uncovered could be the end of them all.

End Game
CAPITAL INTRIGUE #1

You May Also Like . . .

After one of her team members is murdered and the CIA opens an internal investigation on her, Layla Karam reluctantly turns to her ex-boyfriend and private investigator Hunter McCoy to help clear her name and uncover the real killer. With threats on all sides, Layla must put her trust in the man who broke her heart and hope they both come out alive.

Backlash by Rachel Dylan
Capital Intrigue #2
racheldylan.com

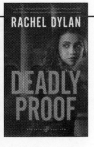

In the biggest case of her career, attorney Kate Sullivan has been appointed lead counsel to take on Mason Pharmaceutical in a claim involving an allegedly dangerous new drug. She hires a handsome private investigator to do some digging, but when a whistleblower is found dead, it's clear the stakes are higher than ever. Will this case prove deadly for Kate?

Deadly Proof by Rachel Dylan
Atlanta Justice #1
racheldylan.com

When authorities contact the FBI about bodies found on freight trains—all killed the same way—Alex Donovan is forced to confront her troubled past when she recognizes the graffiti messages the killer is leaving behind. In a race against time, Alex must decide how far she will go—and what she is willing to risk—to put a stop to the Train Man.

Night Fall by Nancy Mehl
The Quantico Files #1
nancymehl.com

BethanyHouse

More from Bethany House

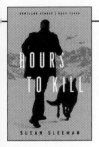

Attacked and left in a coma, FBI Special Agent Addison Leigh has no memory of the incident or her estranged husband when she wakes. Full of regret over letting his military trauma ruin their marriage, Deputy U.S. Marshal Mack Jordan promises to hunt down the man who attacked her, and soon it becomes clear that the killer won't rest until Addison is dead.

Hours to Kill by Susan Sleeman
HOMELAND HEROES #3
susansleeman.com

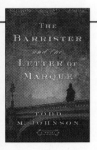

As a barrister in 1819 London, William Snopes defends the poor against the powerful—but that changes when a struggling heiress arrives at his door with a mystery surrounding a missing letter from the king's regent and a merchant's brig. As he digs deeper, he learns that the forces arrayed against them are even more powerful than he'd imagined.

The Barrister and the Letter of Marque by Todd M. Johnson
authortoddjohnson.com

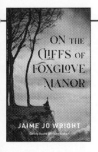

In search of her father's lost goods, Adria encounters an eccentric old woman who has filled Foxglove Manor with dangerous secrets that may cost Adria her life. Centuries later, when the senior residents of Foxglove under her care start sharing chilling stories of the past, Kailey will have to risk it all to banish the past's demons, including her own.

On the Cliffs of Foxglove Manor by Jaime Jo Wright
jaimewrightbooks.com

BETHANYHOUSE

Printed in the United States
by Baker & Taylor Publisher Services